Craing Dominion

By

Mark Wayne McGinnis

Chapter 1

The Marquess of Silionne, Zackary Rama, stood before the Jhardon ruler, King Caparri. In his early sixties, the king was tall and broad shouldered. Like all Jhardanians, he had their typical violet skin and long eyelashes. Tradition and ceremony played a significant role among the people of Jhardon and he still wore the same embroidered, long white robe his father had worn when he was king, some twenty-five years earlier.

"Your Eminence, six planets are directly in the path of the approaching Craing."

"How many ships are there?"

The Marquess's expression turned to one of regret, or perhaps one of sadness. "Fifteen hundred in total, Your Eminence. But there's a breakaway group of six massive, distinctly different, black warships approaching."

The king looked out through the curved, floor-to-ceiling observation window that encircled the upper crest of Broadspire Station. Built as a beacon to those entering Jhardon space, the massive space station was more than a military fortress. It was also an artistic symbol of an advanced and cultured society. Bright white, with fluid, arcing lines that converged into a rising spire above a broad, barrel-shaped inner construct, the structure had become one of the most recognizable symbols throughout the Alliance. The king's gaze fell from the star-filled distant space above him to the glowing, emerald green planet below. Just looking down at her filled his heart with emotion. With the exception of his queen, Lonna, and his daughter, Dira ... nothing in life was more precious than Jhardon.

"What's the status on getting Alliance support?" King Caparri asked; the irritation showing on his face was equally evident in his voice. The king knew the Alliance had more ships, more war power, than at any time in the past. But their forces were scattered, the majority stationed on Earth and her moon.

"Without an Allied vessel in the vicinity to provide us an *interchange* wormhole, we're relegated to standard, slow, interstellar communications. It will be too late for us to reach Admiral Reynolds and the Allied forces," Marquess Rama said.

"So that's it? We simply stand by and watch as six fringe planets, including our own, are decimated?"

Marquess Rama was about to answer when he realized the question was most likely rhetorical. Both stood in silence, staring out to space, for several long moments. The king contemplated the fate of over a billion people. Perhaps some could be rescued— evacuated off the planet.

The king turned to Rama and said: "Evacuate as many as you can without creating mass hysteria. Ensure that Parliament, and the House of Jhardon members, are moved away from this sector of space. Ready Broadspire Station for battle. Relay to all on board that the survival of their world below hinges on their brave actions here today."

Jhardon was a peace-loving world. Weapons of any kind were forbidden and only here, miles above the surface, was there a small military contingent. The king wanted to stay—to fight and direct the battle himself. But there were clear-cut directives that made that action impossible. His place would be leading his people, as few or as many who'd survive, after today.

Both, suddenly startled, looked toward the stars. A distant planet, normally no larger looking than a tiny yellow moon, exploded outward in a resounding ball of fire. The heavens flashed white momentarily and, just as quickly, there was nothing left of it in space.

"Oh my God. Beautiful Lapoine ... She's gone." Both stared upward for an indeterminate length of time before the king said, "Have the queen meet me on the royal clipper."

* * *

Commodore Ot-Mul showed no emotion as the small yellow planet, and those that inhabited her, ceased to exist. He inhaled as the heavens momentarily flashed white—as if, in that brief microsecond, he could fill his lungs, his total being, and consume the life force of those he had vanquished. The briefest smile crossed his lips—then just as quickly was gone.

Slowly, Ot-Mul looked to his left and then right. With the exception of one officer, this bridge crew was the finest he had served with in over ten years commanding the Craing Empire's elite Vanguard fleet. His six black dreadnaught warships were feared across all Craing space. There were only a few details Ot-Mul delegated to others when it came to enlisting potential crewmen. Each and every crewmember was intensely vetted—academic excellence most certainly was necessary ... but it was the purity of an applicant's bloodline that was truly the key requisite; the familial Craing heritage of each candidate was paramount. Perhaps that was why the Vanguard's Craing personnel looked so different from Craing crews on board other vessels—destroyers, light and heavy cruisers, and dreadnaughts. Consequently, the Vanguard's crew had come to represent the physical ideal: fearsome, taller than the typical three-foot-tall Craing, they were four or more feet tall, had small tufts of black hair on top of their heads, and rutty, pitted, complexions. These features alone distinguished the elite Vanguard fleet personnel.

The commodore brought his attention to the next planet. His orders were simple: spend no more than one day in Allied space—the six targeted planets, for the most part, were undefended and would easily be removed from the Allied territories; then, move with haste and rendezvous with the rest of the Craing fleet on the outer end of the Orion arm.

Ot-Mul ground his teeth, irritated by the acting emperor's orders. It made no sense. Why not move toward the rest of the Allied planets immediately? Reconnaissance reports showed little fleet activity in recent days—a perfect time to strike. He approached the center of the bridge and a pool table-sized horizontal display. Three bridge crew officers moved to either side while he leaned his forearms on the padded edging. The five remaining planets were spaced far enough apart that he had little time to dilly-dally. None of them posed a particular threat; their military defenses would not be a problem—in fact, he considered these planets ill-prepared, their defenses pathetic.

But destroying any planet was no small feat. It took all six of his Vanguard dreadnaught warships, firing their oversized plasma cannons simultaneously, close to an hour. Typically, the end results were spectacular—thrilling, really. But some planets were nearly impossible to destruct within that time frame—those with higher H2O contents—primarily, those worlds with large oceans. It had something to do with their atmosphere's refractive properties. Looking down at the display, he saw none of the telltale blue of an oceanic world on any of the remaining four planets.

The commodore cleared his throat, something that had become a habit in recent months. "These four worlds ... disintegrate them. This one here, the green one—"

"Yes, that is Jhardon, Commodore," his second-in-command said, sounding bored and disinterested.

"Jhardon. I like the sound of that word. Jhardon," he repeated aloud. "I want to replenish our food stores. Capture no less than one thousand indigenous people for our cages. Tonight we feast at the caldrons."

Together, in unison, the bridge crew bellowed, "Consume our conquered!"

Chapter 2

It felt good to be back on The Lilly. Jason entered her bridge, finding his father in the command chair. The admiral, seemingly lost in thought, noticed Jason and hesitated before standing and shaking his son's hand.

"Good work down there. What you accomplished is—"

Jason smiled and nodded. "Yeah ... It definitely was something."

"You look like shit," the admiral said, scanning Jason's face.

"Battling one too many time realms on Earth, I guess."

"You need some R and R; you all do."

"Uh huh, I wanted to talk to you about that."

"Why don't we grab some grub—catch up," the admiral said, already heading off the bridge.

They walked together in silence down the corridor, through the DeckPort, down Deck 2's corridor, and into the deserted mess. Plimpton was behind the counter with a rag, cleaning metal surfaces.

"Good evening, sirs."

"Evening, Plimpton," Jason replied. "We catching you at a bad time?"

"No, sir. I have some lamb stew in the slow cooker for tomorrow. Or make anything else you want to eat from the replicator."

"I could go for some of that stew," Jason said.

The admiral held up two fingers. "Sounds good." He scratched at the stubble on his chin. "You talk to Boomer yet?"

"No, not yet. Delicate subject."

"The longer you wait—"

"I know. I'll talk to her. We'll take a shuttle down to Earth later today."

Jason took the oversized steaming bowl and placed it on a tray. Large chunks of lamb, potatoes, and carrots, smothered in thick brown gravy, made him realize just how famished he was. They sat across from each other, both buttering their biscuits at the same time.

"What's coming will not be easy," said the admiral. "Not only for the military, but also for every man, woman and child on Earth. I'm talking about a war like none other, Jason."

Jason looked at his father as he took a bite of stew. Burning his tongue, he cursed out loud. "Seems there's a lot going on. Things I'm not up to speed on," he remarked a bit huffily.

The admiral looked up sharply. "It's not my job to inform you of every one of my decisions, Captain."

Jason kept his face free of emotion. "What's going on with you, Dad? That's a bullshit answer and you know it."

The admiral continued to eat in silence. Jason felt unsure if his question had been heard or if he was simply being ignored. Then the admiral leaned back and stared at him until Jason raised his eyebrows.

"What?" asked the admiral.

"Tell me," Jason said.

"They're coming, Jason. And it won't be a fleet of fifteen hundred ships or twice that many or even twice that. They're coming to make an example of us."

"Coming where?"

"Earth, the Alliance, damn it! The Craing ... They're

11

assembling a massive contingent with only one intention: to turn every planet within the Alliance to nothing more than space dust."

Jason listened and realized things were so much worse than he had thought even minutes earlier. "We knew they'd be coming. Just not this soon. So how do you know the details? Where are you getting your intel?"

"Multiple confirmed sources: space traders, outer fringe planetary systems sympathetic to the Alliance, and others. They've seen them ... thousands of Craing warships recalled from deep space—all moving toward the Craing worlds."

Jason rubbed his forehead, Plimpton's stew now churning in his stomach. "We've beat them before, we'll beat—"

The admiral cut him off. "As you know, the Minian's been spotted in Craing space. Our friend Granger is obviously making some kind of deal with the Craing. Can you imagine the Craing having phase-shift technology? Or worse, access to the interchange? Right now we have an advantage; we can call up a wormhole and pretty much move about the universe at will. Give that same capability to the Craing and it's game over." The admiral tossed his spoon into his empty bowl and sat back, looking defeated.

Jason said, "Then we'll get her back. Let's talk about Her Majesty. How close are we to getting that bucket of bolts space worthy?"

"Close. Brian wants to show us the ship, go over the plan one more time."

"And what about the Alliance? What are we doing to ready ourselves for a possible, probable, attack?" Jason asked.

"Two things that need to happen quickly: First, the day after tomorrow, our presence has been requested at the Pentagon."

"Why? What do they want?" Jason asked.

"I want them to have a greater influence within the Alliance."

"That's new. Where's that coming from?" Jason asked.

"Well, I'm thinking it's a good thing. Aside from the problems we had with Admiral Malinda Cramer and her fanatic Montana militia, now may be the right time to get the U.S. government and our own people more involved."

Jason gave his father a wary look and shook his head.

The admiral sat up taller and said, "Come on ... Who are the most innovative people in the history of our planet?"

Jason shrugged, "The Americans."

"When Pearl Harbor was attacked, sending thousands of our boys to the bottom of the sea, who fought back with a vengeance? Who entered World War II, kicked ass, and turned the tide?"

"The Americans," Jason replied.

"When Hitler's German army invaded much of Europe and sent countless Jews and others off to the camps, who brought their military might to their allies, who made the difference?"

"The Americans."

"So, let me ask you: who would you most want on your side when fighting an unbeatable foe?"

Jason stared back at his father, then also sat up straighter ... "The Americans."

"Damn right! The Americans," the admiral said. "It's time we get the kind of support necessary to win this war."

Jason didn't say anything, simply looked back at his father.

"Listen, we've tried diplomacy and working within the political confines of the Alliance. Oh my God! The constant bickering. Trying to motivate all the planetary leaders to fight the Craing has been exhausting, right? As if they're doing us, me, a big favor, when all we're trying to do is save their thankless hides from planetary subjugation, or worse—total annihilation!"

Jason saw where his father was going. "Okay ... So now we

take command, start acting as though our own survival's at stake ... which is certainly true," Jason said.

"Which it abso-fucking-lutely truly is," the admiral said with conviction. "As the military commander of the Allied forces, I've led the Planetary Alliance in a fair and democratic fashion. Always knew that a strong military presence behind us was imperative. But it's never been that way. Like a bunch of squabbling children ... Sixteen years of this bullshit. So, again, what people most possess grit and fortitude? What military machine do we want having our back?"

"Okay, okay, I've got the idea," Jason said. "You think the U.S. government, its military, should take a more active role within the EOUPA and the Alliance."

"What I'm saying is this: Screw the EOUPA. Get rid of it. The American people and the U.S. government will fulfill that role directly."

"Are you serious?"

"Yes! Serious as a heart attack."

"Our allies and enemies alike will see this as more power mongering. All we'll accomplish is adding more enemies to the list—on Earth as well as with the Alliance," Jason said.

The admiral smiled. "I'm miles ahead of you, son. Our allies, the entire world, know what's coming: the Craing. And in a very bad way. It's all everyone's been talking about while you were down on Earth fighting dinosaurs for the last week. No, they're not happy about it, but they're starting to see the logic. We're starting to see good unilateral support on Earth for a stronger U.S. influence within the Alliance."

The admiral continued, "Day after tomorrow we're due at the Pentagon. They've requested you be there, along with me. Not everyone's on board with my idea."

Jason nodded. "What was the second thing?"

"You already said it. You'll be taking The Lilly out to the furthest fringes of Craing space, just beyond what's called the Orange Corridor. There you'll wait for Ricket to gain access to the Minian."

"So this has changed from a simple intelligence-gathering mission to one where we board and abscond away with the most sophisticated vessel in the universe?" Jason asked, looking astonished.

"Something like that. But if you don't get that ship, Jason, we're doomed ... the Planetary Alliance, Earth ... we're all doomed."

Chapter 3

Captain Stalls paced. Up and back, and up and back again, he strode the narrow corridor behind the cockpit of his small shuttlecraft. Flexing his fists, he replayed the events in his head for the hundredth time. Again, he had been humiliated, beaten down. Worse, he'd been beaten down in front of Nan. Anger began to boil over—more than consumed, he was drowning in hatred. Stalls repeatedly hammered a fist down onto the nearest bulkhead—the sound reverberating throughout the small cabin. He would make him pay. If it took him the rest of his life, he would bring Captain Reynolds to his knees, make him beg for mercy. Stalls leaned up against the bulkhead and let his imagination wander ... Oh yes, he would take great pleasure in seeing him grovel. But no. Death would not be granted too quickly. He'd need to prolong his pain. What would cause him the most pain? Stalls took in a long breath and allowed himself a fleeting smile. That damn kid of his, Mollie. Stalls let his imagination conjure up a delightful vision for the near future. Oh, yes, that was it ... he'd make him watch the slow, painful, torturous death of that bratty kid of his.

A proximity alarm sounded in the cockpit, returning Stalls' focus to matters at hand. He moved back into the cockpit and sat at the controls. He surveyed the outside surroundings.

"Huh ... It's amazing what one can find floating in space these days," he said aloud. Stalls kept the shuttle on its current course, at the edge of Earth's solar system, as it approached an accumulation of space debris. He slowed the shuttle until it was barely moving. Obviously, an incredible battle had taken place in the area.

What amazed him the most was that no one had thought to round up the tons of metal and raw material now floating around him. "There's more than a little money to be made here," Stalls exclaimed aloud.

Four Craing heavy cruisers were adrift together in various states of embattled deterioration. In the distance, two smaller light cruisers looked to be in somewhat better shape. But not by much, he thought. Stalls maneuvered forward slowly. Hearing clanging against the shuttle's outside hull, he activated the ship's shield to its lowest setting, not wanting to scuttle into deep space any of the debris around him—his potential future profit-makers. He came to a full stop, tilted his head forward, and smiled. Now we're talking!

Shaped like a bug, it was a Craing light cruiser. The vessel looked to be in relatively good shape, and it had power. At both tips of its stubby wings, placed starboard, were a series of blinking amber lights. Stalls hummed quietly to himself as he brought the shuttle around the stern of the cruiser. Both drives look to be okay ...

Coming around the far side of the vessel, he saw the damage: a scorched opening, more than twice the size of his shuttle. Strange. The jagged metal edges were protruding outward. An explosion from the inside out. He stopped and idled there ... Deciding. He massaged his bruised cheekbone and continued to stare at the pitch black gap. Why not?

He throttled the shuttle's small engines just enough to coax the little craft into the ragged hole. He flipped on the running lights, as well as the shuttle's primary forward-placed, directional spotlight.

He estimated he was in the engineering part of the ship—

specifically, its environmental systems area. He began to get a rough idea of what had occurred here. But what happened to the warship's crew? he wondered. Perhaps it was more of a fluke, than anything else? Stalls positioned the shuttle's spotlight to illuminate the dark, cavernous inner confines of the vessel.

Then he spotted it in the distance. The missile was metallic— long and lethal-looking. It had failed to detonate, cutting through three bulkheads and coming to rest where it now sat, held suspended, half in and half out of a very large electro-mechanical device. Apparently, it had caused a massive burst of pressure to vent out the way it had entered. He could clearly see that the missile had also taken out row upon row of oxygen transfer filters. The crew, those who weren't vented into space, must have slowly asphyxiated. But why hadn't the AI sent out warnings? It should have alerted them they needed to get their asses into environmental suits—like immediately! "Their loss— my gain," he chortled.

Maneuvering the shuttle around in the confined area was becoming problematic. He'd have to leave the shuttle and investigate further in an environment suit. But at least from the look of things, there didn't seem to be any other substantial damage.

Another alarm sounded and he felt his anger rise again. The shuttle's remaining oxygen levels were dropping fast. He needed to find a viable air supply within the next hour or he, too, would be floating lifeless among the rest of the space debris.

"What the hell?"

Stalls tapped at the console and sat forward in his seat ... looking at the display for several moments. "Not possible," he said aloud. The shuttle's sensors were showing multiple life signs. Not in this vessel but in the next ship over. Where there's life, there's oxygen.

Stalls maneuvered his vessel back out the way he'd come in—into open space. The other light cruiser, no more than ten miles off his starboard, was in far worse looking shape. Half its hull seemed to be missing, blown away in what must have been a catastrophic explosion. Stalls approached warily, bringing up the shuttle's shields to their maximum level. He didn't want to take any chances. Too many times he'd witnessed the devastation a warship like that could reap. Damaged vessel or not, he wasn't taking any chances. He maneuvered around to the cruiser's away side and stopped all forward movement. This area of the ship was in better shape. Three flight deck hangar entryways sat open to space. A small drone fighter awkwardly hung halfway out of the center opening—one of its landing struts caught beneath deck plating. Soft light emanated from inside the flight deck.

Stalls glanced at his flashing low-oxygen warning indicator. He goosed the throttle some and entered the light cruiser's flight deck. He heard his engines rev up, compensating for the added gravity within the compartment. He slowly skirted the perimeter of the deck and decided to set down close to one of the ship's primary bulkheads, at the forward section of the compartment. He shut down the engines and sat there, listening to the clicks and ticks as the engines cooled. All life sign icons were behind the bulkhead, less than thirty feet from the nose of his shuttle. He counted twenty-five of them. There was no way to tell if there were armed beings there or not—the little shuttle had nowhere near that level of technology.

Stalls rose and made his way to the locker where he'd stored his environment suit and weapons. He looked the suit over, inspecting it for wear ... for any tears or holes. It had seen better days, but it looked to be in once piece. Certainly fine enough for the thirty-foot trek across the flight deck to the hatchway situated there.

With the environment suit now on and his helmet secured, new warning lights flashed on the suit's primitive HUD. Terrific. He had about a ten-minute supply of oxygen left, if he didn't exert himself too much. Grabbing up a plasma rifle, and clipping on five power cartridges to his belt, Stalls also checked the plasma pistol at his side and saw that it had nearly a full charge. He used the small, two-man airlock and climbed down to the cruiser's flight deck. As he approached the smaller Craing-sized metal hatchway, Stalls wondered if he'd be able to open it. For certain, they'd have locked this place up tighter than a drum.

Ten feet from the hatchway, Stalls stopped and listened. Something was happening. There was a series of metallic clangs and the hatchway began to open. Stalls looked left and right: nowhere to take cover—nowhere to hide. He brought his weapon up and was poised to fire. Three Craing appeared, wearing environmental suits. They stood there, staring up at Stalls for several moments, until one of them gestured with a hand: come in.

Stalls didn't move. He looked back at his shuttle and realized he had no choice. Suffocation was a really bad way to go. He moved forward, following the three Craing. The hatch closed and secured behind him. He was in a large airlock. The Craing began removing their environmental suits while talking among themselves. He removed his helmet but kept his suit on. He knew enough of the Terplin language to understand the gist of what they were saying. Then it made sense: they'd wanted to be rescued, preferably by the Craing, but anyone would do at this point. They'd been marooned here for the past year and Stalls was their lifeline out.

Chapter 4

Jason wanted to talk to Chief Petty Officer Woodrow in private, before Mollie arrived for her morning class. Billy had worked with Woodrow on and off over the last few years and had earlier provided Jason with an overview of what the man was like. Apparently Woodrow's reputation was twofold. As a trained wartime sniper/killer, his capabilities were most impressive. Ruthless and determined, it was a given his skills with handheld weapons also went unmatched. But he was also characterized as obstinate and self-absorbed, and thought, by some, to be a borderline psychopath. Was he the type of person Jason wanted influencing his daughter, whose life had been so ripped apart by the brutal attack on herself and her mother?

Mollie was different now. He'd seen it, the moment he'd returned, in her standoffish manner. She dressed in dark clothes and wore her hair pulled back in a severe ponytail. Everything about her screamed she'd been hurt and she wanted to hurt back. Her present life revolved around intense training with this Navy SEAL combatant, who had spent the majority of his life perfecting the art of killing.

Jason had been very explicit with his father, and with the rest of the crew: Mollie was not to be told her mother was alive back on Earth—that there were now two Mollies: herself, and a second Mollie, who was living at the scrapyard with their mother. How the hell do you tell a young girl, barely coping with reality, that her world would be shaken up again?

Woodrow looked up as Jason made his way across the gym

mats. The man stood at attention and gave a proper salute.

"As you were, Chief Petty Officer."

Woodrow relaxed and nodded toward Jason. "Good morning, Captain."

"You know what I'm here to talk to you about, Woodrow?"

"Aye, sir."

"Let's start with the why."

Woodrow hesitated, then continued to speak. "I could say that I was simply following the orders of the admiral, sir. But soon after meeting your daughter, seeing the condition she was in, I decided to do what I could to help her."

"You're not a trained psychologist, are you, Woodrow? Have some kind of child counseling capabilities I'm unaware of?"

"No, sir, nothing like that."

"Then what gave you the special insight to know what's best for my daughter?" Jason asked, his voice sounding stern and measured.

"She asked me a simple question at the onset of her training: could I help her to not feel so much like a victim. She wanted to have some sense of control over her life again. No, sir, I'm not the one for her to turn to for emotional coddling. But I can help her get her confidence back. I can relieve her of some of her fear."

Jason listened to what Woodrow was saying, but more than his words, he was surprised by what he saw in the man's eyes: kindness. Understanding. He truly cared about Mollie.

"But at what cost, Woodrow?" Jason asked. "Come on ... she's a little nine-year-old girl, who's already hardened ... even cynical."

"And how would you have me handle that? Teach her how to slit a man's throat, while encouraging her to feel really bad about doing so? No offense, sir, but isn't that your job?"

Jason didn't answer. Didn't know how to answer.

Woodrow withdrew a solid-looking metal pipe from the top

shelf of a cabinet. He gripped it and slapped it into his open palm several times. "We're the end result of the events that occur in our lives, Captain. Made up of an accumulation of stuff ... good stuff, bad stuff. My job, as I see it, is to keep more of the bad stuff from happening to her. If you want me to stop coaching her, no problem. There are others on this ship wanting my expertise. And I have my other duties."

Mollie and Teardrop entered the gym. Her expression quickly turned to one of alarm.

"Dad! What are you doing here?"

"Hello to you too, little one."

"I don't like it when you call me that," she said, glancing over to Woodrow as if a secret part of her had been revealed. A part she did not want her teacher to know about. "Can't you just call me Boomer, like everyone else does?"

Jason felt stung, reprimanded by the most important person in his life. He smiled and nodded, "I can do that, Boomer."

"Thank you. And you'll have to leave now. This is a closed training."

"I'm leaving. Come right back to the cabin when you're done. I need to talk to you. Do you understand?"

She shrugged but didn't say anything. Stretching, she looked at her father and then at the exit.

"I'm going, I'm going."

* * *

When she arrived back at the cabin, she was eating an ice cream cone.

"You stopped off at the mess?"

Mollie shrugged. "What was your first clue?"

"Knock off the smart mouth. Throw it away and sit down

23

next to me."

She hesitated, took several large licks, and did what she was told. She sat down at the far end of the couch while continuing to stare down at the floor, looking bored.

"Is this how you want it to be? You want to push me away, make me angry? What?"

She shrugged, as though indifferent, and started to rapidly tap her foot against the leg of the couch.

"There's not one person alive more important to me than you. There's nobody I love more, or want to spend more time with. I would die for you a thousand times, Mollie. I am, and always will be, your biggest fan. So tell me why you are so hell-bent on hurting me right now?"

Her eyes filled with tears and the tough, hard-seeming little girl transformed back into the Mollie he knew.

"Why are you always leaving me? Where have you been for the last week?"

"Well ... You might not believe me if I told you."

"Why wouldn't I believe you?"

"Suppose I told you I was fighting dinosaurs in Montana, and cavemen in South Africa."

She stared at him with a sideways look that said stop kidding me.

Jason then proceeded to tell Mollie about his past week and his encounters with different realms of time on Earth. Within two minutes she was sitting at her father's side, listening to every word he spoke—interjecting comments, asking questions, prodding for more detail. By the time he finished she was smiling and exuberant. Eventually, she became quiet and rested her head against his shoulder.

"Do I really have to call you Boomer?" he asked her.

"No. But I do kind of like it."

"Listen. I have something to tell you, Boomer. It'll be the real truth; I'm not kidding or making anything up here. Understand?"

She looked up at him and nodded, her forehead scrunched into little lines of concern.

"You know how I told you about the time realms on Earth? How, at the end of everything, Earth was locked into a time period several weeks in the past?"

Mollie's eyes went wide, her mouth fell open ... "Oh my God ... Oh my God!!! Please tell me she's alive ... please, please, please ..." Tears streamed down her cheeks as she held her hands together, as if praying.

Jason's heart opened and melted. She looked at him impatiently, waiting for him to confirm the most miraculous possibility in the history of the world.

"Yes, your mother's alive."

The shriek that emanated from Mollie's mouth was ear shattering. Tears flowed down her cheeks. She was up on her feet and strutting around the cabin "I don't ... Oh my ... When ... When can I see her? Can we go now? Please?"

Jason laughed and nodded. But now for the tough part. "Very soon ... tomorrow. Sit back down, okay? There's more. Something else."

She sat back down, her expression showing deep concentration. She wanted to figure this out on her own, for some reason—find the last remaining puzzle piece. Her expression turned to something else. Was it concern? Or indignation? Then it changed again to something unexpected ... was that curiosity?

"Wait. If Mom's still alive then there would be two of ... me?"

Jason didn't know which emotion to express to her. Should he be sorry? Sorry she was no longer his only daughter? But apparently there was no need for concern.

"Dad! She'll be like a sister? I have a sister, right?"

Jason nodded light-heartedly, but with guarded optimism—he was in totally uncharted territory. Hell, never had there been a conversation like the one they'd just held.

"I'm the big sister. Since Mom and Mollie are living two weeks in the past, I'm older. Right?"

"That makes sense. You would be the big sister. Are you okay with all this?"

"I'm okay. It's weird, but I'm okay. Now you'll definitely have to call me Boomer. Two Mollies would be confusing. Do you think she'll like me? I hope she'll like me ..."

Chapter 5

Later that day, Jason and the admiral entered *Her Majesty's* bridge at the same time. Seeing the modified luxury liner's helm only confirmed Jason's doubts about the upcoming mission. The admiral turned and surveyed his surroundings, only to be startled by the hopper standing close by to his right.

"Christ almighty! Make some noise or something, will you?" the admiral admonished.

The hopper hissed, clicked and flicked its long black tongue, then brought its attention back to Brian, who was lying on the deck, half-buried under a console. Next to Brian was another pair of legs. No one else could be that skinny. Had to be Bristol, Jason thought.

Brian brought his head out from under the console and looked up at Jason and his father.

"Admiral. Captain. Welcome aboard *Her Majesty*."

The admiral put his hands on his hips and gestured for his son to stand up. Brian disappeared again and in a muffled voice said, "Don't forget, we need to mirror this same modification to each of the other consoles."

Another muffled, higher-pitched voice replied, "You think? It was my idea to do this in the first place."

Brian pulled himself free of the console and stood. "Last minute mods. But let me assure you, she's tiptop. We'll be ready to shove off within the hour."

"Let's talk about this mission," the admiral said. "Jason's been out of the loop, so why don't we spend a few minutes reviewing the mission's key objectives."

"Absolutely. We can talk in my ready room." Brian wiped his hands on a rag and made his way to a hatch on a starboard-side bulkhead. Jason and the admiral followed him into an elaborately decorated compartment. Adorned with dark wood paneling and more of the ship's gold-painted scrollwork, Jason and the admiral spun about, taking it all in.

"I know, pretty cheesy. But you get used to it. Hell, I think I'm even starting to like it," Brian said, taking a seat behind a large leather-topped desk.

Jason and the admiral took the two chairs facing him. "So, taking Bristol with you?" Jason asked.

"He knows this ship. Anything happens with the cloaking device, he'll be needed to get it up and running."

Jason nodded slowly. "Who else?"

Brian and the admiral exchanged a quick glance. "Um, of course, Betty will be here, and an engineering and security force, but I was going to talk to you—we … were going to talk to you," Brian said. "We also need someone in the military who has competent bridge-handling experience. Someone who could jump from navigation to comms to tactical."

Jason was already getting ready to object. There was no way he was giving up Gunny …

"So, I thought of Lieutenant Commander Perkins. Strictly on a one-time loan basis," Brian added.

Jason held his tongue and tried to look as if he was fighting some inner decision-making battle. The truth was, Jason could not have been more relieved.

Jason let out a breath and nodded reluctantly. "So you want my XO?"

Brian nodded and shrugged apologetically.

"As long as it's for this one mission only."

Brian smiled and looked generally pleased. The admiral, who had worked with Perkins even longer than Jason, didn't buy Jason's act and gave him a sideways glance.

"So what's the plan here? You'll take *Her Majesty* into Craing space. What then?" Jason asked.

"We'll act as a base there, maintaining a cloaked presence, ready to assist the on-planet team, as necessary."

The admiral spoke, "We've actually put quite a bit of thought into this mission, Captain. If all goes well, Gaddy and Ricket's presence won't evoke any suspicion. Gaddy has not visited her uncle, or the Emperor's Palace, in some time. Apparently, Gaddy was close to her uncle—his favorite niece. In fact, bringing a boyfriend along may evoke some initial tension, but it should be expected from someone her age."

"Ricket is no spring chicken—what is he, two hundred years old? Two ten? And he's stiff, nothing like I'd imagine a young Craing graduate student would act," Jason said, shaking his head.

This time Brian interjected, "I don't think that's going to be a problem. The last thing we want is an overly suave character showing up with Gaddy. Actually, he's the perfect type: a nerdy, post-grad science guy."

"But his looks? He looks like Emperor Reechet, and before that, Dr. Reechet, the famous Craing scientist," Jason countered.

"Already dealing with that aspect, as we speak. Ricket is currently undergoing physical alteration within a MediPod. It's temporary, lasts about one week before his own natural bone structure returns to normal," the admiral said.

"Sounds like you have it all figured out," Jason mused. "How about him gaining access to the *Minian*? Gaddy's boyfriend or not, they're not going to let Ricket wander around secured areas unescorted."

"Ricket's come up with a few ingenious devices to get him

into those areas unobserved. He'll be wearing a belt that looks no different from any other young Craing's attire, only this belt will be tied into his internal nano-devices and will provide all the same phase-shift capabilities as those worn on our battle suits. He'll also be transmitting live visual and audible feeds via his nano-devices. And when the time comes he can interface with their systems network. He'll have incredible data-accessing resources. He knows the stakes. He knows everything relies on him gaining access to the *Minian* and bringing her home. He's willing to die trying, if necessary."

Jason didn't like it—too many things that could *and probably would* go wrong ... *How is Ricket going to take control of the ship? What if Ricket's cover is blown—is there a backup plan?* All these things would have to be ironed out before they moved forward.

* * *

Jason waited at the side of the MediPod where Ricket's looks were being altered. Dira was in and out of Medical, busy with one thing or another.

"It'll be another few minutes. Want to sit? Can I get you something—a coffee?"

"Coffee would be perfect, thanks."

Dira disappeared for several minutes and returned with a steaming mug.

"Here you go. Black, right?" she asked, looking happier and more radiant than he could remember.

"I contacted home ... my mother."

"And?"

"It seems I've stirred things up."

"How so?"

"She's worried about me. They want me to come home. Still want me to do the princess thing back on Jhardon."

"Are you considering that?" Jason asked.

"I don't know. I do miss them. I miss my home. We didn't talk long, the transmission went dead mid-conversation ... a bit strange."

Dira must have seen Jason's face fall. "Hey, no decision's been made yet," she said. "I might take a leave of absence for a while, or something. But only if that's permissible ... Mr. Captain," she said, moving in closer.

"Pfft ... of course it is!" Jason said nonchalantly. "You've given this ship, this crew, more over the last year than can possibly be repaid."

"No more than anyone else. But I'll think about it. Not ready to make a decision right now. I'll talk to my mother in a day or two. You know that we haven't been on the best of terms for years; it's all a little strange."

Jason watched her talk. Watched her lips move and how the corners of her mouth turned up in an easy smile.

"It's just that she's asking specifics about my friends, my relationships—" Dira's face flushed a brighter shade of violet as the words stumbled out of her mouth.

Jason took a sip of his coffee and placed the cup on a nearby countertop. He decided to let her off the hook. "You've mentioned me?"

Dira nodded. "Uh huh."

"She wanted to know if we were an item or not?"

She pursed her lips and smiled. "Yes, that's a good way to put it ... an item."

She let the words hang a moment as she nervously bit her bottom lip. She quickly busied herself with the MediPod's settings and then checked her virtual notepad. Jason smiled and put a reassuring hand on her arm, bringing her eyes back to his.

"Just let her know, at least from my humble perspective, we

most definitely are an item."

She stopped and looked at Jason—neither moved for several beats. "So we're an item? And you're sure about that?" she asked him, taking another tentative step closer.

He breathed in her light fragrance and the world around him disappeared—the MediPod, Medical, The Lilly. Her eyes mirrored the smile on her lips and sparkled as they welled up with emotion. He pulled her into himself, wrapping his arms around her narrow waist. Her mouth met his and they kissed. She pressed into him—and him into her. Her fingers raked through the hair at the back of his head, then tightly grabbed two fistfuls as their passion grew.

The high, whirling sound of the MediPod's clamshell opening pulled the two of them free from their passionate embrace. Out of breath and caught off guard, they pushed away from each other. Ricket's eyes fluttered open and he sat up.

"How do you feel?" Dira asked, her voice sounding husky as she bent closer to inspect Ricket's face.

"I feel fine," Ricket answered, bringing his hands up to trace the new contours of his cheeks, and the now-hairless top of his head.

"I wouldn't recognize you. It's really pretty amazing," Jason said leaning in, his hand atop the clamshell lid.

Dira helped Ricket out of the MediPod, keeping a guiding hand on his back until she was sure he could maintain his balance.

"Hello, Gaddy," Ricket said, peering around them.

Both Dira and Jason spun around. Gaddy was standing at the entrance to Medical.

Dira nervously asked, "How long have you been—"

"Standing here? A long time. You'd be surprised how long I've been standing here," she replied, scowling first up at Jason and then at Dira. Gaddy moved in closer, pushed the two of them aside, and sidled over to Ricket.

She placed the back of her hand on Ricket's cheek and smiled. "You look so different! I can't believe you're the same person." She stepped back away, looking up at the pair of them again, and scowled.

Dira and Jason exchanged glances and held back chuckles.

Ricket looked confused. "What did I miss?"

"Nothing," Gaddy replied. "You and I have some work to do. If you're going to pass as my boyfriend, you'll need to learn some things about me and my life. You'll need some acting lessons. Get up, time to go to work."

Chapter 6

Stalls could not believe his good fortune. Not only had he discovered one battered but inhabitable Craing warship, but also a second ship that was nearly operational and had, it seemed, a willing and somewhat competent crew to boot. Apparently, they'd lived off replicator rations, but water and other supplies were becoming scarce. A problem he could easily remedy by using his shuttle to transport between their ship and the disabled vessels nearby. Over the past hour he'd been shown what remained of the ship. It wasn't much—some crew quarters; several large cargo holds, such as the one he was standing in now; as well as the bridge. But the vessel was dead in space. Barely inhabitable ... a derelict floating island.

His first order of business would be assembling the crew—see who was usable. Apparently, the only ranking officer still alive was a glum-faced character, named Clig or Drig ... something like that.

"Crig. Assemble the crew. Everyone on board, no exceptions."

"I am Drig."

"Fine, Drig. Whatever."

Drig moved slowly, which annoyed Stalls. There was much needing to be accomplished and there was no time for dilly-dallying. Drig moved off, stopped, and began talking to another uniformed Craing. They were speaking in hushed tones; periodically, they looked over to Stalls.

"I told you to assemble the crew," Stalls said with his hands on his hips—his chin jutted forward, conveying his growing irritation.

Drig turned to face Stalls; the other Craing looked down toward the deck plates. "We do not answer to you. You are not in command of this vessel."

Stalls took that in and let the comment sit for a few beats. Then, as if coming to a decision, he pulled his sidearm and shot the man standing directly to Drig's right. He fell to the floor in a dead heap. Drig's eyes widened as he saw the barrel of the gun now pointed directly at him.

"Address me as Captain, or Captain Stalls. Anyone who disobeys my commands will be shot."

Stalls watched as Drig moved much more quickly now. Within several minutes the cargo hold was filled with little Craing men. All looked nervous and leery of Stalls, not to mention the sight of the lifeless body still lying on the deck plates. Once all were assembled, Stalls did a quick headcount: twenty-four.

"My name is Captain Stalls," he said in his broken Terplin. "I am a pirate by trade and I am commandeering this vessel, as well as others we find adrift that we can make operational. Is there anyone here unwilling to take orders from me? Unable or unwilling to crew for me?"

The Craing looked at one another, then over to Drig. He simply nodded and wore a passive expression.

"Good. Very good. Each of you, tell me what your specialties are on board this vessel. Don't be shy ... who first?"

One by one the Craing crewmembers provided a short accounting of their capabilities. Several were communications technicians, another was a cook, and another was the tactical and weapons junior officer.

Halfway through the Craing crew's accounting, Stalls became impatient. "Who here is an engineer?"

No one spoke for several moments, then two crewmembers

raised their hands.

"Excellent!" Stalls said excitedly. "You'll be in charge of bringing the environmental systems back to life on the other cruiser. This takes precedence over everything else. Everyone will support this effort. Okay, I need a first mate ... a second-in-command."

No one spoke up and all eyes turned toward the floor. "No volunteers, huh? You did hear that I was a pirate, right? The first mate's take of the bounty is significantly more than the rest of the crew. Except for mine, of course."

Stalls saw curiosity in their eyes now. He smiled and paced up and down between the crewmembers. "There's enough bounty in this battlefield to make all of us wealthy. So, who wants to be the richest of the rich?"

Three hands went up. Drig and two others.

"Good. The three of you come here. That's right, come right on over."

The three Craing moved over: Drig, and then one who was stout and heavy-set, and the third, who was lithe—more nimble-looking.

"Everyone circle around. Move it, circle all around us," Stalls said, gesturing at the rest of the crew. "I know Drig, what are your two names?"

The stouter one replied, "NaNang." The nimble-looking one said, "Rup-Lor."

Stalls positioned the three Craing close together at the center of the circle; he then joined the outer circle. "Whoever is still standing in two minutes will be my first mate, and he will have special privileges as my trusted second-in-command."

The three Craing looked first at each other, and then at Stalls. They hadn't noticed it at first, but now saw that the barrel of his sidearm was pointed in their direction. Rup-Lor moved first and was fast. He punched Drig in the face and then kicked NaNang in the genitals. Drig bent over, holding his cheek, but NaNang seemed unaffected by the kick. NaNang took a step toward Rup-Lor, then stopped, smiled, turned, and drove a knee into Drig's downturned face. Drig went down on the floor, holding his smashed nose. Whimpering, he wouldn't be getting up anytime soon.

Now two contenders remained: NaNang and Rup-Lor circled each other, their small fists clenched, held high and tight, like child-sized boxers in the ring. Again, Rup-Lor moved first. He feigned left, then darted to the right, bringing an uppercut to the larger Craing's chin. That punch did some damage. NaNang swung with a wide haymaker and missed the faster Craing by less than an inch. Off balance, NaNang stumbled and fought to stay on his feet. That was all the time Rup-Lor needed to come in from behind and, with his two hands clenched together, bring them down on the back of the bigger Craing's neck. NaNang fell to the deck plates, unconscious.

Stalls walked to the center of the circle applauding—he looked to the others to join in. "Rup, you're my new XO. Your first directive is to assemble a team ... anyone beneficial to our getting the environmental systems on that other ship repaired. We leave in ten minutes."

It took over an hour before the shuttle was fueled and provisioned with fresh oxygen. Stalls piloted the shuttle, with the five selected Craing crewmembers sitting quietly in the rear cabin. As they left one nearly decimated warship behind, Stalls watched as another, nearly perfect, vessel filled the view ahead as they approached it. He started whistling softly to himself.

37

Chapter 7

"So, you ready, Boomer?" Jason asked his daughter.

She nodded without looking up. She looked nervous—chewing on the inside of her mouth.

"Boomer it is, then. I like it."

Boomer shrugged. "Why are we going to the underground base first?"

"Just checking in," Jason replied. "Crewmembers will be staying there sometimes. We've built out the base ... added new barracks and a few officer living quarters."

"I want to see Mom."

"Ten minutes and we'll head up to the scrapyard ... see Mom and Mollie."

She went back to chewing the inside of her mouth.

The truth was Jason himself was more than a little apprehensive about seeing Nan. After thinking she was gone, lost forever, the thought of now seeing her again had him feeling more excited than he could remember.

"Weird, huh?" Jason asked softly.

Two shrugs. Her hair was tied back in what had become her de-facto hairstyle of late. She'd also started wearing dark-gray spacer jumpsuits. He wondered if this was her way of rebelling or, perhaps, of differentiating herself. All he could do was give her space to figure things out.

"Dad?"

"Yeah?"

"Does Mom love Mollie more than me?"

"No. Of course not. She can't wait to see you. That's the honest truth."

"Then why couldn't I see her right away?"

Jason paused before answering. "What you've been through over the last few weeks is more than any little girl should ever have to experience. It's been an emotional roller coaster. One shock after another. You not only learned your mother is alive, not dead, but that there is a second Mollie alive, who's not really your sister, but more like your clone. So before thrusting you into another unsettling, maybe confusing circumstance, we felt you needed a little time to digest it all. Come to terms with everything emotionally. That's why we had you talk to Dr. Brill earlier today. You liked talking to her, didn't you?"

"I guess. She has bad breath and kept asking the same questions over and over again. She asked until I started to cry."

"She wants you to have a chance to connect with your true emotions. However that works best for you."

Boomer finally looked up. "Will I be allowed to stay with Mom or will I have to stay underground with you and Grandpa?"

Jason realized he had done a dismal job conveying the situation to her. Maybe waiting had been a colossal mistake. His heart beat heavy in his chest as he saw the uncertainty in her eyes, the silent pleading.

Jason initiated a phase-shift and the interior of the shuttle flashed white, followed by a resounding shudder as the vessel's struts settled onto the floor of the underground aquifer.

Jason watched Boomer get up and move toward the back of the shuttle. He got to his feet and in two strides was at her side. She quickly wiped at her moist cheeks. She raised her chin— vulnerability replaced by something else. *Was that resolve?*

"Moll—Boomer! Hold up."

Boomer, halfway down the gangway, slowed for a second,

but kept going. Jason felt something brush by him on his right. Teardrop, who had been at the controls, rushed past him to join its human. More protective than ever, the droid was never more than a few steps away from her.

Jason stepped onto the gangway and took in the underground base. There'd been numerous changes since he'd last stepped foot here. Prior to Ricket leaving on his mission to the Craing worlds, Jason had given him a formidable to-do list. Since then, little had been seen of Ricket, who'd spent five consecutive days locked away on *The Lilly*'s sub-deck 4B. Writing code for the most part, he rarely slept, trying to ensure all his projects were as complete as possible.

There was now a small army of droids implementing Jason's conceptualized vision and Ricket's technical programming. Three immense, multi-level, glass-like buildings were newly constructed along the cavern's west wall and seemingly needed only finishing touches. The rocky dirt floor of the cavern had been covered over with deck plating, similar to that on *The Lilly*. Gone was the dark, damp, cave atmosphere, replaced with the 'alive air' of a bustling modern facility. It was a complex that would stay hidden, out of reach from enemies, as well as from possible U.S. government interference.

Jason caught up to his daughter, standing in the middle of the cavernous underground base. Turning to take it all in, she looked astonished.

"Looks a little different, wouldn't you say?" Jason asked, stepping to her side.

"This the same cave under the scrapyard? Doesn't look like a cave anymore."

"No, it doesn't. Come on, I just have to check on one thing."

Jason, Boomer, and Teardrop moved toward the tallest of the three new structures. Glass doors disappeared as they approached, and the AI addressed them as they stepped inside: "Good morning, Captain Reynolds. Good morning, Boomer."

"Good morning," Jason replied.

"Hey," Boomer added unenthusiastically.

They continued down a series of corridors and up a small flight of steps, which ended in a sterile-looking room.

"What's this place?"

"These are my quarters. Just checking to see if I had a place to stay tonight."

She made a face. "It's like one of those clear hamster cages. I can see the toilet over there, Dad."

"Wall opaqueness is programmable. We're not finished setting things up yet. Walls are clear like glass until you program the ones you want to appear solid. Here, watch." Jason walked over to an eye-level panel mounted on one wall's glass surface. He tapped at the display and several walls became translucent, allowing light in the room to be subtly evident, but objects were non-discernible. More tapping and the walls changed to different colored hues—some to light green, others to a shade of blue or red. As the walls changed color, becoming less see-through, the space around them made more sense.

"Huh. I see. It's like an apartment or something." Boomer walked from one area to another, taking it all in. "There's the kitchen ... kinda small. That your room over there?"

"Yep."

"Um, where's my room?" she asked.

"I didn't configure one for you. I could ..."

Her eyes flicked back to Jason. "Why don't I get—"

"Boomer, why on earth would you want to stay here when you can stay in your own room at the house?"

She didn't answer him and continued investigating her father's quarters. "I guess it's okay. But I still think it looks like a

41

hamster cage."

"Yeah, I guess it does, kinda," Jason replied, smiling down at her. "It needs more furniture."

"Maybe that will help," Boomer replied.

Jason turned and put two fingers to his ear, talking to someone else. "Yes ... yes ... Okay, on our way." He turned back toward Boomer and let out a breath. "We're late. We have to go."

"I thought we were going to the new house. I want to see Mom!"

"And she wants to see you, too, and that's exactly where we're going."

"Oh, okay!"

Together they walked in silence out of Jason's quarters, down the stairway and out of the building. Teardrop was waiting there for them.

"You'll be staying here, Teardrop," Jason said.

Boomer looked as if she was going to object, but then asked another question instead. "Dad, did Mom get the house fixed? You do know it was flattened, don't you? Uncle Brian landed a tractor thing on it."

Jason shook his head. "No, that actually didn't happen this time. Remember when I told you about Earth being set back several weeks in time? That's why your mom and Mollie are still alive and well. We were able to stop Captain Stalls from hurting your mother, and also Uncle Brian from landing on the new house. But the house got pretty banged up. I still haven't seen it—your mom wanted to get it back into shape first."

"So are there two Uncle Brians?"

"Well ... No." They continued walking until they came to a large double door. Jason paused a moment while the AI scanned his bio-form. There was an audible click as the door unlocked. Pulling the door open, he gestured for Boomer to go through first.

Boomer smiled. "I know where we're at now!"

"Uh huh, this part is the same as it always was," Jason replied.

Together, they continued walking down the wide rocky tunnel. Spaced every hundred feet or so, lights hung down from long metal cables affixed high above. Jason thought back to a year earlier—the first time he'd run down this same tunnel with Mollie dead in his arms. He had followed close on Ricket's heels to *The Lilly* and into the ship's Medical, where he'd placed her lifeless body into a MediPod. God, so much had happened since then.

They stepped into the metal lift and Jason slid the rickety gate closed. The elevator jerked and started to rise up the vertical shaft. Automobile body parts lined the walls. One stretch was nothing but old hubcaps. Jason thought about hubcaps and how they were a thing of the past, replaced, like so many other things in life.

"Why not? Why aren't there two Brians?" Boomer asked, pulling him away from his thoughts.

"We had to make a quick decision, Mollie, sorry—*Boomer.* The bin lift was going to land on the new house, possibly on Mollie and your mother. Another Brian and Betty were already alive in another location. We fired on the bin lift, hoping to destroy it before it crash-landed on the house a second time. It crashed on top of the old house this time, and I'm sorry to say Brian, Betty and the hopper didn't make it. They died."

"So me and Teardrop are the only extras?" she asked.

"Extras? You think of yourself as *extra*?"

"I don't know. That might not be a good way to say it. But why would Mom need two of us? She already has one Mollie— two seems ridiculous. I'm extra."

The lift came to a stop within the confines of the ancient,

rusted-out bus. Boomer slapped a button and the double doors swung open. They made their way through a tangle of junked cars and heaps of scrap metal before stepping onto the concrete path that led toward the house. Jason noticed Boomer, dragging her feet, was getting more and more nervous the closer they got.

Jason stopped and waited for her. "What are you doing? Why are you walking so slow?"

"I'm not! You have longer legs," she replied irritably. "Why do I even have to be here?"

"Half hour ago you couldn't wait to see your mother again. What's going on with you?"

She shrugged, slowing her pace even more, watching her feet as she walked.

Jason knew there was nothing he could say or do to make her feel any better. They continued on in silence for the ten minutes it took them to reach the back of the new house. He stopped and Boomer, head down, proceeded to walk right into the back of his legs.

"Ow! Warn me when you're going to stop like that, Dad!"

She scowled up at Jason only to see he was smiling at her. Her eyes drilled into him with a mixture of anger and hurt until she noticed something when she looked around him, up ahead. There, ten feet up on the hill, stood the new house she and her mother had seen built. Perfect and beautiful. On the back fence, which ran the width of the back yard, was a hand-painted sign, the biggest she'd ever seen:

WELCOME HOME BOOMER!

As a smile spread across her face, she saw her mother running towards her, screaming her name. Tears welled up and flowed. When Nan engulfed her daughter in her arms she heard what she needed to hear: *Mollie ... Mollie ... Mollie, I love you, Mollie.*

Jason watched his daughter, her eyes squeezed closed, her

mother's arms wrapped tightly around her, as they swayed back and forth to a rhythm only the two of them could hear. Nan stepped back and held her daughter's small face in her hands. More serious now, Nan said, "You know I love you, right? You know that I'm so so so happy you're here with me, right?"

Boomer nodded and Nan wiped at her wet cheeks with her thumbs, then kissed her forehead again.

On the rise, behind the house's backyard iron fence, Mollie stood and watched. Jason smiled up at her and waved. She waved back but never took her eyes off Boomer. This was the moment Jason was most apprehensive about. *How would they react to each other?*

Boomer saw her standing up there, watching them. Nan stepped back and let them both assess each other.

Mollie held out an outstretched arm and pointed, "What's that?"

Boomer, confused, followed the direction of Mollie's finger and looked at her wrist.

"This?" Boomer asked, holding up her arm and pointing to a multicolored braided wristband.

"Yeah, did you make that?"

"Uh huh. I used the garment replicator. It's a few strips of cloth braided together. I can make you one, if you want."

Mollie looked over to Nan. "Mom, do we have a garment replicator in the house?"

Nan nodded. "In the master bedroom. Don't make a mess."

Boomer was off and running and scrambling up the hill. Mollie met her at the metal gate and together they disappeared out of view.

Chapter 8

With zero fanfare, *Her Majesty* moved away from Earth; past a distant Mars; past the orbits, but unseen planets of Jupiter and Saturn; past Uranus and Neptune ... past icy, gaseous Pluto; and then past an area that was strewn with space junk and what was left of a demolished Craing fleet. Brian ordered Bristol to go ahead and connect to the interchange, and he provided the intended end-point coordinates on the other side of the universe. Brian was almost surprised when a wormhole appeared less than a thousand miles before them. *Hell, this might actually work.*

They had initiated the toric-cloaking system before entering the wormhole. To be on the safe side, they emerged several light-years away from the Craing worlds. Even though the entrance to a wormhole was detectable by most vessels' long-range sensors, Bristol assured Brian their vessel was completely invisible and any sudden fluctuation in space's atmosphere would be attributed to just another space anomaly.

"XO, report."

Perkins stood at the far side of the luxury liner's bridge with two fingers to his ear. "Typical space chatter. Wait ... there is mention of a large vessel entering the system. They may have detected us. No, they're talking about a prison barge. Other than that, all's relatively quiet here."

Brian's eyes held steady on the display before him as he scanned Craing space. Hundreds if not thousands of vessels, of all kinds, moved like trails of ants from one planet to another. Other vessels maintained orbits around each of the seven worlds.

The display changed and two Caldurian Crystal City vessels filled the display.

"Captain, these two vessels are in high-orbit around Terplin," Perkins said.

Brian nodded, then took a step closer. "Bring us within three thousand miles. I want to see what's on the other side of the furthest one."

A slight, pasty-looking crewman at the tactical station mumbled something, then spoke up louder: "There's definitely another ship there. Not much showing on sensors, though it could be the *Minian*."

"Helm, get us a better angle on her," Brian commanded.

Her Majesty slowly traversed a sufficient distance for the other vessel to come into view. No one spoke. The image of the *Minian* spoke for itself.

"I still can't believe the Caldurians would want to have anything to do with the Craing," Perkins exclaimed.

Brian shrugged. "Well, it's only these few. For the most part, Caldurians—the progressives—keep to the multiverse these days. No, these are *originals*—renegades—and no doubt Granger is there, on board the *Minian*, as we speak." Brian hailed Ricket.

"Go for Ricket."

"We're well within Craing space," Brian said. "Moving to phase-shift range above Halimar. You and Gaddy ready?"

"Not quite," Ricket replied, sounding distracted. "I need to make another adjustment to my nano-devices."

"You can do that? Without a MediPod on board?"

"Yes. Portable equipment brought along for just that purpose. Now please, Captain, let me complete this task, and I'll be ready to go."

* * *

47

Ricket cut his NanoCom connection to Brian and brought his attention back to the small portable display on his makeshift workbench. His head was encased in a circular construct, not dissimilar to one of the oversized motorcycle helmets he'd seen people wear on Earth. But the similarities stopped there. This device, one he'd nicknamed a CrainyPod, had much of the same technology found within a standard MediPod unit, although this device would only provide its advanced medical capabilities to a patient's head region.

"You look ridiculous in that thing."

Ricket had forgotten Gaddy was on her way to his cabin. "I'm almost finished." He ran the most recent subroutines designed to support the added nano-tech hardware implanted into his brain. He'd borrowed the technology from something he'd seen while on board the Minian several weeks earlier. Testing the changes and additions would have to wait. Ricket removed the CrainyPod and placed it on the workbench.

Gaddy came closer and tilted her head. "I still can't believe you're Ricket. You look so different."

"Well, it is me. I just hope I can pull this off. I'm not so good at this whole play-acting thing ... as you've discovered over the last few days."

"You'll probably be fine. Just don't get nervous. That's when you give yourself away. You need to start acting like Nelmon Lim, postgraduate student at Craing Empire University at Halimar, instead of Ricket. Listen, we're going to have to give the performance of our lives down there. The plan, everything, depends on us getting it right."

Ricket slid from his chair, grabbed his small backpack and headed for the hatch.

"Aren't you forgetting something?" Gaddy asked, catching

him just prior to leaving.

Ricket turned and surveyed the small compartment. "What?"

"What did we talk about? How do two people in love act?"

Ricket's expression softened and he attempted a weak smile. He held out his hand and waited for her to take it, and together they walked out of the cabin and down the corridor.

"You know … I'm just saying … You're not a robot, or a cyborg thing, anymore. You might want to keep that in mind."

Ricket looked more nervous than she'd seen him in the past. His hand was moist and he kept looking down at it, as if inspecting the strange, and overly personal, connection to Gaddy. "I'm trying. This is new to me. I'm not comfortable with …"

"I know. It's all right, Ricket … Nelmon. Try to have some fun with it all. I've been to the Emperor's Palace more times than I can count. Relax, everything will turn out fine. Okay?"

* * *

Gaddy and Ricket phase-shifted onto the planet, into a wooded area approximately one mile from the Craing Empire University at Halimar. Gaddy had ensured him they were wearing the most typical style of clothing worn there, not unlike what students wore at universities back on Earth: jeans, sweatshirts, tennis shoes, and small backpacks. Craing youth were fascinated by anything related to Earth, and the styles of clothing worn there were no exception.

Together, they reached the outer boundary of the university. Here, students and professors alike were hurrying along across campus. A group of five students huddled together up ahead. One was talking excitedly, then abruptly stopped.

"Gaddy?" the student yelled.

Ricket watched the entire group of young adults turn in their direction. Gaddy grabbed his hand and pulled him toward the awaiting group.

"Chala!" Gaddy yelled back excitedly. Gaddy let go of Ricket's hand and ran ahead the last few yards. The two quickly hugged, then stepped away.

"Are you back? I didn't think you were in school this semester," Chala asked, eyes dramatically opening wide.

"Yes, I need to finish ... only have a few more classes."

Chala looked toward Ricket. "And who's this?"

"Oh, sorry. This is Nelmon, Nelmon Lim ... My boyfriend," Gaddy said with pride, looking over to Ricket. "He's a post-grad student working on his doctorate."

That raised eyebrows from the others and Chala looked confused. She looked at Gaddy and then to Ricket as if something about this was askew.

As was customary in Craing society, similar to a human handshake, one or two palms, depending on the formality of the situation, were pressed together and heads were briefly bowed. Chala stepped forward and held out two palms, the more intimate and friendly gesture. "Hello, Nelmon, I am Chala, Gaddy's very best friend here at university."

Ricket felt the eyes of the other young Craing women upon him. He did his best to smile casually and reciprocated her palm gesture. First, Gaddy's insistence on their holding hands, and now this ... Ricket flushed and nodded his head. "Hello, Chala. I'm happy to meet you."

"He's very cute, Gaddy," Chala said, still holding her palms up against Ricket's.

Gaddy stepped in and grabbed Ricket's wrist. "We're so late. Let's catch up later."

Again, Ricket felt his arm pulled away and they were running toward the central quad area of the university. Ricket turned and waved back at the group. Chala stared back at him with a furrowed brow. Ricket remembered, waving one's hand in the air was a human gesture. He quickly repositioned his hand, palm up. The others did the same.

"Why are we running?" Ricket asked, perplexed.

"That's why," Gaddy replied, running faster now and pointing toward a distant vehicle parking lot.

A convoy of five military vehicles hovered there, and one black, sleek-looking shuttle sat in their midst. On the side of the shuttle was the Craing Empire's emblem of the emperor. Virtually everyone within the confines of the quad rushed in the direction of the awaiting vehicles.

Gaddy, never letting go of Ricket's hand, broke through the crowd of onlookers and approached the official convoy. As Gaddy and Ricket approached, turret-mounted weapons on the five military vehicles tracked their movements. A rectangular hatch slid open on the shuttle and four armed soldiers rushed out; facing outward toward the crowd of onlookers, they took up defensive positions. A Craing female, dressed in a formal officer's uniform, stepped onto the pavement and waited for the two to approach. The woman held up one palm. First Gaddy reciprocated the gesture. Then Ricket held his hand up to hers. He felt no warmth emanating from her skin. He initiated a quick bio-scan with his newly upgraded nano-devices and discovered she was a highly advanced cyborg. There was no visual indication that she was anything other than an organic Craing.

"Hello, Gaddy ... This must be Nelmon ... Greetings. I am May-Five. You may call me May, if you wish. Gaddy, your uncle awaits you at the Emperor's Palace. We must make haste; he has a busy day ahead and has scheduled time to meet with you this morning."

Gaddy and Ricket followed May into the shuttle and took seats next to each other. The inside of the shuttle was plush and smelled good. Ricket touched the seat's soft material.

"Yes, that's the finest leather. Imported from Earth," May-Five said.

Both Gaddy and Ricket nodded and smiled appreciatively.

"You look so much like May-Four," Gaddy noted, in a more serious tone. "Is she still ...?"

"No. She is no longer in service to the emperor."

Chapter 9

It was close to a year since *The Lilly* last entered Washington, D.C. airspace. This time an escort of five Apache Longbow attack helicopters greeted her at the outskirts of the city and guided her to a cleared out space in the Pentagon's west parking lot.

McBride, who had been at the helm the first time, was smiling. Jason knew exactly what he was thinking—the same thing he was thinking himself: *Why not put her down in the Pentagon's center court again, for old times' sake?*

McBride brought *The Lilly* down to several hundred feet above the massive Pentagon building and looked back over his shoulder.

"Not this time, Ensign," Jason said, smiling back.

En route, Jason had changed into his Navy captain's uniform and now, striding down the ship's gangway, a contingent of six armed marines were waiting for him.

Brusquely, without conversation, Jason was hurried into one of the many Pentagon entrances. His footsteps on the highly polished linoleum flooring echoed down the busy corridor. Military personnel scurried in and out of too many offices to count. Heads turned—first with recognition—and then with what he sensed was approval. Back room TVs droned on with familiar voices from Fox, MSNBC and CNN, as TV reporters provided their station's latest information on an inevitable Craing invasion. More than once, Jason thought he heard the words 'hopeless situation' spoken.

After two more lefts and a right, past several alert-looking secret service agents, he was shown into a small, wood-paneled conference room. His father was seated, as was Secretary of Defense Ben Walker. At the head of the table sat President Ross, who, in a rare move, apparently decided to keep their private meeting off White House grounds. No one stood when Jason entered. They were engaged in a three-way heated conversation. The admiral glanced up and gestured for Jason to take a seat.

"That's not what I'm asking, damn it!" the president shouted. "Tell me, in the simplest terms possible, how doing that would help?"

The president waited for Walker to continue, as if what he'd heard so far was not nearly enough.

"For the most part, the world, and that includes America, has been shielded from what's been happening with the Craing: the extent of their military's reach across the universe. Citizens have little concept of how precarious our own existence is."

"That was a unilateral decision. We wanted to avoid mass hysteria."

"We were wrong, Mr. President. Multi-thousands of Craing Empire warships, at this very moment, are converging with the sole purpose of eradicating both Earth and the Alliance."

"So what do you suggest?"

"Everyone, *the world*, needs to know the truth of our situation. They need to understand for themselves that petty power plays will only work against Earth in the end. We were already in the process of declassifying much of what's been shielded from the public. Dismantling the EOUPA will be the first step toward directly involving the American people in the upcoming interstellar war that might very well be our last. Now, we also need to become equally transparent with the rest of the world."

President Ross seemed finally to be coming around and

began nodding his head. The president looked tired and frazzled. He turned his attention to Jason. "It's good to see you again, Captain. How long's it been, a year?"

"Close to that, Mr. President."

"The world's in a similar situation today as it was back then. Only this time we may be facing mass, worldwide, hysteria. I am—we all are—putting our faith in you once again, Jason."

"Yes, Mr. President."

"I've been briefed on the mission you'll be heading up to retrieve the *Minian*. It sounds overtly risky to me. You fail and not only do we not get the *Minian*, but we potentially lose *The Lilly* as well. Wouldn't it be far more prudent for you to stay close to Earth?"

"No, sir, I don't agree with that. Yes, it's risky. But we need to remember, the *Minian* provides advanced technology the Craing could and surely would use against us later."

The president contemplated on that and slowly nodded, "Well, I've made my objections clear. I'll go along with your plan, but you better come through. I hope I'm making myself clear here."

"Crystal, Mr. President."

The admiral slid a folder across the table to Jason. "Review the contents of this folder and be prepared to meet with me again later this afternoon."

"We need to change subjects here, since everything's interrelated," the president said. "As far as bringing the rest of the world up to speed, getting the Earth's populace to unite into a solitary front may be even more imperative, and will require assistance from the media worldwide. We'll need someone to bridge the gap between the media and the populace. Someone intelligent; a communicator; a person who has first-hand experience with the Craing."

There was a commotion behind Jason as more people entered the conference room. But only one person commanded his full attention. Standing there, in an ivory blouse and slim-fitting navy blue skirt—her face tanned and radiant—was none other than Nan Reynolds. Nan and Jason's eyes locked for a brief moment, before she nervously looked away.

The meeting continued for several more hours. Based on her exemplary past work as the legal envoy for the EOUPA, as well as her first-hand experience with the Craing, Nan was to be tasked with heading up both domestic and worldwide interstellar relations. Pretty much anything involving space and the Craing Empire, she would be involved with.

The president looked at his watch and turned to Nan. "I can't stress enough the importance of your position, Nan. Much of what you'll be dealing with for the interim will be media relations. But it involves far more than that. You'll be right in the center of things. It won't be easy."

Nan glanced over to Jason. Her expression showed a mix of stern resolve that also seemed contemplative. "Sir, I have two daughters. Both dealing with things little girls shouldn't experience. I need to be there with them—for them."

"You will have all the support you need. That will extend to your personal life. Nan, this is not an administrative level position. What we're talking about is a new cabinet post." President Ross let that sink in for a moment and continued: "Let me make this clear; even as we sit here, this post is being fast-tracked. Nan, you'll report directly to me and you will start working immediately. Right now."

* * *

The president returned to the White House. Nan and Jason

stood in a Pentagon hallway that swarmed with activity around them.

"How did you get here so fast?" Jason asked.

"One of the Craing cruisers was brought back from the moon and landed in the open space near the scrapyard. I was awakened by military representatives," Nan answered.

"Where are the girls?"

"With me. They're here in the Pentagon, somewhere, being watched over by a Naval officer, someone named Priscilla Miller."

"I was hoping to spend time with you and the girls tonight. Brought *The Lilly* underground yesterday. Thought we could have a barbeque this afternoon."

"That would have been nice," she said, placing a hand on Jason's arm. "Understand, I didn't want this, but ... what do you do when the president of the United States requests your service?" She stared down the corridor as if looking for something. "I'm just worried about Mollie and Boomer," she added.

"They'll be fine," Jason said. "How are they getting along? It must be strange for them. For you."

Nan's expression changed and a smile crept back onto her lips. "They are good together. I mean, sure, they argue and get strangely territorial, but for the most part, they are happy. Happy to have one another."

"I look forward to seeing them ... once things settle down," Jason said.

"You should also know they figured things out for themselves, where they'll be staying."

"Here in Washington with you, I'd imagine," Jason said.

Nan slowly shook her head. "From the start they both knew they wouldn't be living together very long. I don't know how or why they reached their decision, but they're resolute."

Jason waited for her to continue, but a part of him already

knew what she was going to say.

"Mollie will stay with me. Boomer wants to stay with you, on board *The Lilly*. When I suggested to Boomer that she should stay with me and Mollie, she got emotional; said she belonged with you, needed to take care of you."

Jason thought about that for a moment. The truth was, as they'd discovered during recent tumultuous times, living on planet Earth wasn't necessarily any safer than living on *The Lilly*. "If that's what she wants, what they both want, and it's okay with you, too ... then that's fine with me. I miss them when they're gone. We'll get them together as often as possible."

Ben Walker, standing nearby them, seemed to be hovering. "I guess we need to get things moving along now, Jason," Nan said, nodding toward Walker. "I'm scheduled to finish my briefing with the secretary of defense."

"Yeah, and me with the admiral." Jason pulled her into a hug and they stayed like that for several moments. He brought his mouth close to her ear and said: "I'm so glad you're still with us."

She gently pulled away and smiled. "You keep saying that. *This* Nan never left—you can't get rid of me that easily." Her expression became more serious, "Jason ... Um ..."

"What? What is it?"

Nan quickly glanced over her shoulder at Walker and then back at Jason. "There's something else ... Something I'd like to talk to you about. But now's not the time ... or place."

Jason saw the concern in her eyes—the vulnerability. "What is it, Nan? Just tell me."

"I can't right now. Soon, though, okay?" She half smiled and rushed off toward the conference room.

* * *

By the time Jason finished his discussion with the admiral and several joint chiefs, four more hours had transpired. He exited the Pentagon and made his way back up *The Lilly*'s gangway. He felt tired and grumpy. His mind went to the next task at hand: take *The Lilly* and a small convoy of ships to the outskirts of Craing space to the Orange Corridor and locate a planet called Allaria. He knew nothing about the planet or its people. Supposedly, they were not friends of the Craing. But no one knew for sure if they would be found hostile or welcoming.

He stopped when he heard a distant, familiar rumble. He walked back down the ramp and stood on the pavement. He shielded his eyes from the harsh midday sun and saw them approaching, crossing over the Potomac River—a formation of seven Craing light cruisers. They separated from formation and landed where space was available. Only two hours earlier, they'd reached the decision on the implementation of this small fleet to accompany *The Lilly* beyond Allied space, some sixty light-years away.

A convoy of military vehicles arrived and positioned themselves around the cruisers. Men wearing overalls hurried to predetermined stations. Equipment and supplies were hustled from the backs of utility vans. Within minutes the work was underway. A small army had assembled for a simple, but all-important task—painting the U.S. flag emblem over the EOUPA logo. More vehicles arrived and men and weapons were unloaded. They were Marines. Jason knew from his earlier meetings that no less than a thousand men would be divided among the seven warships. Jason turned and headed back up the gangway.

"Dad! Dad!"

Again, Jason stopped midway up the ramp. In the distance, he saw three figures making their way toward him. Running out in front was Boomer. All legs, and with an exuberance of energy, she ran toward him. Behind her was a woman dressed in naval BDUs, and the unmistakable form of Teardrop.

Boomer was up the ramp and coming in for a hug before he knew it. She was smiling and out of breath.

"Were you going to leave without me? Why didn't you wait for us?"

"Well, I don't know. I guess I thought you'd find your own way here, just as you have."

"You need to remember I'm just a kid. I thought you'd gone and left me."

Teardrop swooped by the two of them without a sound and continued into the ship.

The woman NCO stood at the bottom of the gangway and saluted. "Permission to come aboard, Captain."

"Granted."

She hurried up the ramp and stopped. Saluting again, she said, "Petty Officer Priscilla Miller, reporting for duty, sir."

"Why?"

"I'm assigned to your daughter, sir."

"Who made that decision?"

"The secretary of inter-stellar relations, sir," she replied almost apologetically.

"Nan wants you on board?"

"It was one of her conditions for taking the cabinet post, Captain. Boomer's schoolwork needs to be administered; she needs to be better supervised in general, sir."

Jason caught Boomer rolling her eyes and shaking her head. "I don't need a babysitter, Dad. Tell her to go back where she came from."

Jason almost laughed out loud, but held it in. "Look, we've done just fine so far without having Boomer—"

Jason was cut off mid-sentence. "I'm sorry, sir. The secretary said you would argue about it and wanted me to repeat the following words—"

"What words?"

"'My way or the highway. I outrank you now.'"

Both Jason and the petty officer smiled.

"Fine," Jason said, turning and moving up the gangway again. "I'll have quarters arranged for—"

"Already taken care of, sir," she said, brushing past him and Boomer and entering *The Lilly*.

Jason bristled at being interrupted by the woman twice. He shrugged and gave Boomer a commiserate smile. "Sorry, we'll just have to get used to her."

Boomer ran the rest of the way up the gangway.

"Where you off to?" Jason yelled after her.

"Going to the Zoo. I want to see Alice," she said and disappeared into the ship.

Jason stayed and watched as more U.S. flag emblems were added to other Craing light cruisers. He felt a surprising sense of pride as he looked out over the small fleet of freshly painted, bright white ships with their new, contrasting red, white, and blue stars and stripes emblems. A crowd of people from the Pentagon— some dressed as civilians, others in military uniforms—were taking in the spectacle. His father was right. This was indeed America's fight. It always had been.

Chapter 10

The Lilly and her formation of seven Craing light cruisers lifted off from the Pentagon grounds simultaneously. Below, Jason saw many national and local news agencies had their trucks positioned on outlying streets. Camera crews were shooting their departure.

The three hundred and sixty degree overhead display changed from the scene below to an above and forward perspective. Jason watched as his bridge crew went about their business with calm, well-practiced efficiency. Gunny Orion would be filling two roles, as both tactical and acting XO. Ensign McBride was at the helm and one of the Gordon twin brothers, Jason wasn't sure which one, was at comms. He'd given up trying to tell them apart. Typically, they weren't posted on the same shift together.

"Captain," Gordon said, "I'm opening a channel with the interchange. Connection established and in-and-out coordinates have been relayed."

They had no sooner left the outer reaches of Earth's atmosphere when space began to fluctuate, some fifteen thousand miles away. *The Lilly* took up the point position, with a vee formation of light cruisers to her aft.

"Helm, phase-shift all of us to the mouth of that wormhole."

"Aye, sir."

The bridge flashed white as they phase-shifted into position. Then, poised at the mouth of the wormhole, *The Lilly* hesitated briefly—the first ship drawn in.

They'd traveled sixty-five light-years in an instant. Jason had instinctively closed his eyes, wanting to avoid the usual disorientation that would follow. He opened his eyes to a haze of orange amber in the display view. Several planets, both dark and lifeless, took up most of the forward segment of the display.

Jason could smell the familiar aromatic fragrance of tobacco to his right. "How you doing, Billy?" Jason asked without looking over.

"Doing well, Cap. Thought I'd come up and see what this mysterious Orange Corridor was all about."

Jason saw Orion give Billy a quick smile as she moved back to tactical. "Captain ... huh, this is interesting. This planet, Allaria, is really unique," Orion said.

"In what way?"

"By looking at her, you'd think she was a dead planet, but there's life down there." Orion transferred the view on her console to a forward segment on the wrap-around display. The scene of the dark and lifeless planet was magnified and enhanced.

"What's the population?" Billy asked.

"The planet itself is small, about half the size of Earth. The amount of life is so insignificant I'm betting any other vessel would have missed it. There may be microscopic organic life that I'm not picking up."

"How about those bigger than a toaster?" Billy asked.

Orion chuckled at that. "Thirty, forty thousand ... maybe. Very little."

"So those are the Allarians? How is it possible that anything could survive down there? It looks as if the planet's been dead for millions of years," Jason said.

"You're getting into Ricket territory here, but I would surmise that there are areas that are inhabitable, life sustaining,"

Orion said.

The Lilly AI's voice came to life, announcing there were approaching vessels. Orion was back at her console. "Four vessels, Captain ... comparable to the size of Craing heavy cruisers. Better armed than our own Craing ships."

"Seaman Gordon, let's hail them, but friendly-like. We're not here to pick a fight."

"Why *are* we here?" Billy asked. "If you don't mind me asking."

"We're here on our own, light-years from Allied space, in a dangerous neighborhood. Intel suggests the Allarians are looking for new friends. Apparently, they've been bullied by the Craing for millennia—periodically invaded for no reason other than to keep them in line. Truth is, if we hang out here, in open Craing space, eventually we'll be detected. We're hoping they'll be receptive to our dropping in on them."

"Incoming!" barked Orion. "Twenty-four fusion-tipped missiles."

Jason's eyes flashed to the display. *The Lilly* quickly took out six of the missiles with her plasma cannons.

"No response to our repeated hails, sir," Gordon said.

Jason watched as the remaining missiles radically changed course—moving off in different trajectories at incredible speeds.

"That's something new," Billy said.

"Yeah, and I don't like it," Jason said, his eyes never leaving the display.

"Another eight warships just emerged from the planet, Captain. You still haven't given the command to return fire."

"Just keep taking out their missiles ... maybe they'll realize we're not here looking to start a war."

"Aye, sir," Gunny said, not looking too pleased.

"I might have an idea," Jason said, glancing over at Billy.

Gunny looked up at the display. "More missiles coming from the other ships. Counting what's left of the original barrage, that's sixty-six crazy-ass trajectories no one's able to track, including *The Lilly*."

Three missiles zeroed in on one of their light cruisers and all struck her starboard side simultaneously.

"The *Rainmaker*'s shields are down to thirty percent, Captain," Gunny said. "The yields of those fusion tips are amazing."

Both Jason and Billy looked at Orion. "Just saying ... impressive," Gunny said with a shrug.

Their ships were taking direct, near lethal, hits. Jason was well aware that he had mere minutes before his small, new convoy of U.S. ships would be destroyed.

"So what was your idea, Cap?" Billy asked.

"Hold on a second, Billy." Jason had two fingers to his ear and was talking to someone off the bridge. "No, right now would be better. Gunny will forward the coordinates to us."

"Gunny, I need you to lock on to the Allarian command ship, whichever ship you assess that to be."

"I can do that, Cap," Orion replied, working fast at her console.

"Once you have that, I want you to transmit their exact bridge coordinates to me. We're on comms. You have the bridge, XO," Jason said, pushing Billy toward the exit. Together they ran down the corridor toward the DeckPort.

They emerged on Deck 2 and in several strides were at the ship's armory. By the time Jason and Billy had dressed in their combat suits and grabbed up sidearms and multi-guns, Traveler was entering the compartment, heavy hammer in hand. He had three bloody scratches down one side of his face.

"I was up in a tree. I came as quickly as I could, Captain."

As much as Jason wanted to ask him about that, he knew they had no time to spare. "Here's your belt." Jason handed Traveler one of the extra-large phase-shift belts, along with an accompanying wristband. Jason and Billy finished putting on their own belts—both nodding they were ready. Jason contacted Orion. "You got those coordinates for me?"

"Aye, Cap. Check your HUD. You should have them."

"Check ... got 'em," Jason said.

"Cap, all our cruisers' shields are down to ten percent and falling."

"How about *The Lilly*?"

"Eighty-six percent."

Jason acknowledged her and cut the connection. With a quick smile, he looked at Billy and Traveler. "Lock and load, guys." And with that, Jason phase-shifted the three of them off *The Lilly*.

* * *

In a flash Jason, Billy and Traveler phase-shifted onto the bridge of the Allarian command ship. The bridge was large and circular—about the same size as that of a heavy cruiser.

Jason quickly took in their surroundings and, assessing the foreign crew, did a double take. The crew consisted of small, hovering, machine-like creatures about the size of an average table lamp—table lamps with mechanical arm appendages, and hands with five finger-like digits. Their tops were clear, enclosed, egg-shaped containers; inside them sloshed a pinkish, viscous liquid, a full-sized brain, with two extended eyeballs. The creatures, uncertain, hovered around them. Billy and Jason exchanged glances.

"Who is the captain of this vessel?" Jason asked.

Two of the strange aliens raised an appendage and fired at Jason. Protected by his combat suit, the impact was still sufficient to knock him on his ass. In a single stride, Traveler was upon them, batting away one, and backhanding the second with the same hand, knocking the creature's vessel-head to the deck. The alien came to a stop, upside down.

Jason got to his feet and yelled, "Stop! We are not here to fight with you. Please! Haven't you noticed, we've not returned fire toward your ships?"

It was then Jason noticed another brain encapsulated-vessel coming forward, from the back of the bridge.

"What do you want here?" a voice said, sounding surprisingly human.

"I want you to know that we are enemies of the Craing. We only wish to speak to you," Jason said. "Please halt your attack on my ships. I am Captain Jason Reynolds."

The creature's two blue-eyed orbs continued to stare back at Jason ... then they rotated slightly, taking in Billy, and then Traveler. Almost imperceptibly, the vessel-headed alien nodded toward another crewmember, sloshing around the pinkish liquid in a swirling motion in the process.

Jason heard Orion's voice over his comms, sounding relieved, and telling him that the attack had suddenly stopped.

The alien spoke again through a small panel at the bottom front of his head-vessel: "You have invaded Allarian space. Your warships are Craing. That alone speaks for itself—you are our enemy."

Jason shook his head. "Do I look Craing? Does he look Craing?" Jason asked, gesturing toward Traveler. "I don't think so. And those Craing warships were taken from the Craing in a battle—a battle I won. I have close to a thousand others, just like them."

The Allarian, the one Jason now assumed was the leader, looked to be contemplating on that news. Mechanical hands clenched and released several times before the creature answered.

"What exactly do you want from us?"

Chapter 11

They hadn't moved from the same spot on the bridge of the Allarian command ship. Jason had sent Traveler back to *The Lilly*, leaving only himself and Billy to deal with the Allarians. Jason was quickly becoming impatient. He wanted to get his own warships out of sight. He'd been listening to reports from Orion over his comms that several space freighters had moseyed close by within the last few minutes and he felt it was only a matter of time before a Craing warship discovered their small convoy. The captain's name was unpronounceable; even translated, it sounded like gibberish. Jason gave up and simply called him Captain. Once Jason made it clear to them that their ships weren't a threat to the Allarians, but were actually aligned with them in wanting the Craing's presence permanently banished from space, things got somewhat less tense. The truth was, much of their plan hinged on gaining access to this area of space, space that was so conveniently close to the Craing worlds, not only a perfect jumping off point, but a potential allied force if the shit hit the fan.

But communication between him and the Allarian captain was progressing painfully slowly. They were a highly intellectual race, Jason found, but emotionally immature and ultra-sensitive to the point of distraction. More than once, he realized he had hurt the captain's feelings simply by using an inappropriate word or by making an unchecked exasperated expression.

"Please do not mock us, Captain. We have not always been this way. At one time we too were humanoid. It has only been through our own ingenuity and perseverance that we have survived at all," the Allarian captain said.

"Was it Craing invaders who did this to you?" Jason asked.

"Yes."

"Why would they do such a thing? Please don't take offense, but why didn't they simply eradicate, eliminate, your populace, as they have done to so many others throughout the universe?"

"We were always more intelligent and innovative than our Craing neighbors. We too would have been eradicated, as you put it, but they kept us alive to perform a whole slew of tasks—mostly in design and engineering—to support their military efforts. But that changed too, and our populace was eventually killed off, mercilessly ... with the exception of about fifty thousand of us. Select citizenry brains were placed into sub-freezing cryonics storage ... a just-in-case measure, should they be needed later. Then, twenty years ago, a fleet of passing Craing warships fired enough fusion-tipped missiles to decimate our two planets five times over. That was the end of our worlds: Armageddon for the Allarian people."

"Yet you still survived! You are here, talking with me. You have progressed to the point where you have highly-advanced warships of your own," Jason remarked.

"Yes. A handful of our kind lived through the radiation assault and developed the first, very crude, hover prosthetics. Cryo-stored brains were thawed out and, after thousands of failures, they were successful at interfacing with them. I ... we ... are the result of their heroic past efforts and ingenuity."

"Well, I commend you on your people's determination and tenacity. That's an amazing story and it only underscores why the Craing Empire, once and for all, needs to be destroyed."

The Allarian captain became quiet and Jason wondered what he'd said now to offend him. The seconds ticked by. As his crew hovered about, faint sloshing sounds filled the awkward silence.

"Captain Reynolds, we have pulled ourselves back, literally, from death itself. You must understand, trusting you, or any foreign culture, does not come easy. We have no need of friends ... or allies. We built our warships alone, all within the darkness of a dead planet. We live for one purpose ... to one day avenge our ancestors. We cannot afford to trust others. I'm sorry, but you must leave here now and not return."

Jason slowly nodded. Gazing at the deck, he contemplated on what the captain said. He understood and even admired their determination to still go it alone.

"We will leave you then." Jason looked at Billy and then turned back toward the captain. "Um ... you said you were once humanoid."

"Yes."

"And of course you remember what that's like. What that felt like, yes?"

"Of course."

Jason nodded. "My vessel, *The Lilly*, is highly advanced. Far more advanced than the Craing warships, or your own vessels. We have a device called a MediPod. There is a chance that you and your kind could be brought back to your original humanoid configurations."

"That is not possible. That capability does not exist in the universe."

"That's fine. Believe what you wish." Jason slowly looked from one crewmember to the next. "I'm sure you feel perfectly confident to speak for everyone on your planet. Obviously, you haven't a problem condemning your kind to live like this into eternity ... nothing more than thousands of brains sloshing around in glass-enclosed buckets ... and, as the years drift by, your memory of once being corporeal will fade away—one day, all forgotten. So ... have at it." Irritated, Jason moved next to Billy and prepared to phase-shift off the bridge.

"Wait!"

All eyes were on the Allarian captain.

"What would you want in return?"

"First of all, I cannot guarantee that this procedure is even possible. Our medical doctor would have to be brought in ... tests would need to be conducted. But I'm optimistic."

"If it is possible, what would you want in return?"

"For the short term, my small fleet needs immediate sanctuary. Long term, Allarians will join the Alliance. Every effort will be made to keep your existence here secret from the Craing. But when the time comes, you will join us. Fight alongside the Alliance to bring down the Craing Empire."

"You have your sanctuary, Captain. We will fight alongside you and your Alliance."

* * *

It took several hours longer to work through the details and logistics to make it all happen. The decision was made and the Allarian captain, along with two other Allarians, would be the first to undergo the transforming procedure on *The Lilly*. Dira was contacted early on and was in the midst of researching what would be necessary, on her end, to properly reconfigure the MediPod. She was optimistic—if they used the new *Minian*'s MediPod, the one most recently added to Medical.

Jason and Billy walked single file behind the Allarian captain as they were escorted into the bowels of his ship.

"Watch your head up here, Cap—low-hanging crossbeam coming up," Billy instructed, talking over his shoulder.

"See it, thanks." Jason started to feel somewhat claustrophobic in the ultra-narrow corridor. It was clear the Allarians now were many-years-accustomed to their predicament, their unique situation. Although their ship was configured much like any other space warship, there were no seats or chairs, no tables, no bathrooms, no mess hall, no sleeping quarters. Truth be told, a hovering, bodiless, brain-directed being needed none of those things. They walked single file behind the Allarian captain, down several corridors, stooping often to avoid hitting their heads on any number of things.

They finally reached the ship's flight deck. Scores of stacked fighter drones lined the walls. They looked menacing and capable of inflicting lethal damage. The deck was open to space and Jason could see *The Lilly*, and the other U.S. cruisers, off in the distance. Jason spoke into his comms: "Go ahead, phase-shift her over."

One of the smaller shuttles from *The Lilly*'s own flight deck appeared without any warning. Three sets of eyeballs—the Allarian captain's and those of his two crewmembers—bobbled about with the sudden appearance of the shuttle. Slowly, she entered the flight deck.

"Captain Reynolds, this phase-shift process ... That alone convinces me you have the more advanced technology. We would be most interested in acquiring this capability. Perhaps one day ..."

"One step at a time, Captain. But perhaps that's possible," Jason replied.

Once all were on board, the shuttle phase-shifted back to *The Lilly*'s flight deck. The gangway deployed and everyone filed out. Dira was waiting for them below, on the flight deck. She smiled and looked excited. Jason watched as she greeted the three hovering Allarians. Their strange forms turned this way and that, eyes never still.

Dira's expression changed to one of concern as they came closer to her. "Welcome. My name is Dira. I am the medical doctor here on board *The Lilly*."

As Jason and Billy followed behind them, she shot Jason a quick look. In that split second he knew exactly what she was thinking ... *What the hell have you gotten me into?*

Chapter 12

It took Stalls an additional ten round trips piloting the shuttle back and forth between the two Craing warships. Tools and supplies were required, and more help. All twenty-five Craing crewmembers were put to work ... first, to patch the gaping hole in the side of the cruiser and then, one by one, to swap out the large, ruined, oxygen exchange filter units. Apparently, one was still marginally operational. It took several days before oxygen was flowing again throughout the ship.

Stalls' first night living aboard the ship was spent finding the largest, most well appointed quarters, in accordance with the needs of a warship captain. The pickings were few, but he'd found the best of the cabins and took it for his own. Hot water now restored, he spent a good hour in the confined shower space. He released his long braid and washed his hair, then meticulously combed it out and re-braided it. Finding suitable attire was next on his to-do list. His white, somewhat frilly dress shirt was badly soiled. So were his black slacks. For the time being, he would have Craing crewmembers launder them. *Perhaps*, he mused, *there's even a replicator on board*. He'd have to ask Rup-Lor.

The main engines were slowly coming back online. Captain Stalls watched Rup-Lor from across the bridge. He'd been the best choice for XO of the lot, but he didn't trust the little bugger. Nary a one of them. Stalls' nostrils flared.

"Lor! Can't you do something about that smell?"

Rup-Lor and four Craing crewmembers, sitting at consoles around the bridge, looked up and appeared to sniff the air in unison. Stalls watched their own expressions of distaste.

"Decomposition, Captain," Rup-Lor answered, nodding his head.

"Yeah, I know what a rotting corpse smells like. What are you going to do about it?"

"Most of the bodies have been found."

"Have you checked that eat-in church of yours?"

Rup-Lor looked back at Stalls with a horrified expression. "You are referring to the Grand Sacellum?"

"Whatever. That place ... all those disgusting caldrons where you people cook God knows what. Maybe that's the problem. Maybe there's uncooked flesh rotting on those grills. Very unsanitary. Or maybe it's up in those cages. Have you checked each and every one?"

"The Grand Sacellum is a sacred place. Raw flesh is not left lying around. The holding cells have already been searched."

"Well, if you think I'm going to tolerate that odor wafting around here, you're mistaken. Take care of it or I'll find an XO who can."

Rup-Lor rose from his console and hurried from the bridge. Stalls was feeling impatient. His eyes settled on the Craing crewmember sitting to his right. "Drig. How long will it take to bring the engines fully online?"

"Another two hours, Captain."

Stalls nodded. "You there ... What's your name?"

"My name is Trainz, sir."

"You're on comms, right?"

"Yes, sir."

"Okay, Trainz, I'm giving you a most important job. I want you to get an intergalactic message back to my home world. Can you do that?"

Trainz was about to reply when he cut himself short.

Nervously he said, "I'd need more information. A recipient, or perhaps a specific ship? Something we can reference in the database."

Stalls searched his mind. His first thoughts were of his brother, Bristol. Stalls suspected he was dead, or in an Allied prison cell somewhere. That query would have to wait. Most of his fleet was destroyed, but he was fairly certain a few ships had escaped, more likely fled, when things went upside down battling the Allied ships. Giving it some more thought, he remembered someone who might help. As a young pirate, Stalls had served on his ship. He wondered if the old coot was still alive. Stalls turned his attention back to Trainz.

"The *Rangoon*," Stalls said, nodding his head. "Captain Scratch Bonilla on the *Rangoon*. It's a converted freighter. Find the ship and find Scratch, and you'll be nicely rewarded."

"Yes, sir," Trainz said, getting right to work on the project.

"I'll be in my cabin if anything turns up." Stalls stood and headed toward the exit.

Rup-Lor nearly ran into him as he reached the corridor. "We found the, um ... problem, Captain."

"Good for you. Take care of it." Stalls continued down the corridor.

"There is a problem. And an explanation why there are so few crew bodies."

Stalls stopped and turned back toward Rup-Lor. "What? Spit it out. I have things to do."

"Serapin-Terplins. Ten of them are on board."

"Dead, right? That's what's smelling up the ship?"

"Yes ... No. Yes, there are dead, decaying Serapins. We cannot get to the carcasses. They are being protected by ten living Serapins."

Stalls, losing patience with the Craing's constant back

and forth bullshit, thought *why can't these people ever think for themselves?* "Look, go to the armory, wherever that is, and arm yourselves and shoot the beasts. Then throw them out an airlock and be done with it," Stalls ordered in exasperation.

"Please. You will come with me. Let me show you," Rup-Lor said.

* * *

The light cruiser, mostly unexplored by Stalls, was so big it would take him days to see it all. Rup-Lor scurried along in front of him, eventually leading him to the top-most deck. The air was foul—thick and musty with the smell of decay. Distant screeching noises raised the hairs on the back of Stalls' neck. Three Craing crewmembers were waiting for them to approach, each armed with a pulse rifle.

"So what is the problem here?" Stalls asked, then noticed a pair of stubby legs protruding from a hatchway, thirty feet down the corridor. He grabbed a rifle from one of the Craing and slowly moved closer to the outstretched legs.

"You must be very careful, Captain—"

In a jerky flailing motion, the legs were pulled from sight. A smear of blood remained on the decking. Stalls looked at the weapon in his hands, making sure he knew how to use it. He did, and saw that it had a full charge. It was a little small for his large hands, but it should be fine. He moved forward as silently as possible until he was at the open hatch. With the muzzle of the gun outstretched, he carefully peered around the corner. Only feet away, one of the beasts was ripping and tearing the flesh from the slain crewmember's legs. Three more Serapins were rapidly approaching; stringy saliva dripped from long, sharp canines. Jaws snapped open and closed loudly. With their full attention on the crewmember's carcass, they didn't notice Stalls' close presence. Transfixed, his eyes took in the entire scene further back in the compartment. Shredded rags, hundreds of bones, and general filth covered the deck. Seven more Serapins moved about—pacing. But it was the beast in the far corner that made Stalls nearly drop his weapon. Sitting on her backside was a huge female Serapin. Long, stretched teats hung low as Serapin babies suckled. All around the mother, things were moving. At first, he didn't realize what they were: over one hundred small baby Serapins were scampering about—their screeching overpoweringly deafening.

Slowly, walking backwards, Stalls stepped away from the hatch. Once he'd reached Rup-Lor, he let out the breath he hadn't realized he'd been holding. "How many crew have you lost here today?"

"That was the fourth."

"Take me to your armory."

Together Stalls and Rup-Lor walked to another part of the ship. "You must have incendiary devices: bombs. We'll blow that compartment, with the hatch closed. Problem solved."

Rup-Lor stopped in his tracks. Stalls took several more steps before he realized he'd done so. "What are you doing?"

"Female Serapins are sacred. Very rare, not often found in captivity. Captain, harming her cannot be allowed."

"We have barely enough crew to operate this vessel, and you lost four today to those beasts. She's got to go. All of them must go," Stalls said, continuing on. Rup-Lor caught up and several minutes later they were at the ship's armory.

Racks of pulse weapons lined the walls. There were also small handguns, hardened environmental suits, as well as various explosives. Stalls was in the process of determining which armament would be appropriate when a loud series of sounds filled the compartment.

"What is that?" Stalls asked.

"Three gongs—you're being hailed by the bridge," Rup-Lor said, pointing to a panel mounted low on the bulkhead. "You can speak with Drig through that."

Stalls fingered the panel and acknowledged the hail: "This is Captain Stalls."

"Captain," came the tinny sound of Trainz's voice. "I've made contact with the *Rangoon*." "Did you find Captain Bonilla ... Scratch?" Stalls asked excitedly.

"No, sir. Scratch is dead. His son, someone named Crank, is waiting to speak with you."

That would do just fine, Stalls thought. Having this important key pirate commander contact was imperative to rebuilding a mighty fleet of his own—one step closer to sweet revenge.

Chapter 13

Medical was bustling. The three Allarians hovered quietly in one corner, eyeballs following those coming in and out of the room. Dira and Jason were in the lab area—Dira sat at a counter, in front of a terminal.

"I didn't have much warning for today's procedure, Jason. So I attempted contact with Ricket through his NanoCom. We're actually not that far from Terplin ... I gave it a shot."

"How is he? What's going on with his mission?"

"He said he and Gaddy were at the Emperor's Palace; he had excused himself from dinner when he received my hail. So far everything is going according to plan and, depending on the location of *The Lilly*, we should be able to monitor his movements through his newly installed nano-devices."

"What about the procedure?" Jason asked.

"He said it would be dangerous. Growing a lost eye, or even a severed limb is one thing, but an entire body is quite another. The closest we've come to doing that was with Ricket's own transformation, from cyborg to organic being. He told me where to look in the MediPod database—what organic templates to use as a reference. The Caldurians have an impressive database here in Medical, and there are plenty of templates for both Craing and human, but there are very few templates to Allarian, which are similar somewhat to humans. My only guess is that the Caldurians had had only minimal past contact with the Allarians."

"So maybe we tell them no, this wasn't such a good idea on my part," Jason said, now wondering how he was going to back step out of this mess.

"We're not starting from nothing. We have their individual DNA codes from whatever bio-mass still exists. The truth is, the human body is comprised of eleven primary common elements: mostly oxygen, carbon, hydrogen, and nitrogen. The MediPod has access to an entire organism's fully constructed body, from just one cell. The problem comes down to the template that's stored in the database. How similar is it to these three beings? We have four Allarian templates ... we use the wrong one and we're ... they're ... screwed."

Jason, looking up, realized the Allarian captain was hovering at the entrance to the lab. He glided forward and stopped in front of the terminal.

"We will move ahead with the procedure. I understand the risks. For our kind to survive, to live life with any semblance of normality, of what it once had, this must be done."

Dira pursed her lips and stared at the hovering Allarian. "One in four odds isn't great, Captain. Perhaps with more time we can do further testing and make a better determination. Now that I have samples of your DNA—"

"We will move forward, and do so now, if possible. Understand, the three of us, our lives, would be a small price to pay, in exchange for the procedure's potential success, and the benefits it will bring to all the Allarian people."

Jason understood where he was coming from. Hell, how they'd kept functioning, not wholly living, he couldn't imagine. The alternative to success, death, was not such a leap. Jason nodded. "Who's first?"

"We have discussed this at length and although I believe I should be the first to undergo the procedure, it will be my second-in-command. She will go first, then me, then Phloridaaamict—"

Jason held up his palm. "Please ... Your names are very hard for us, even with translation ... for the time being, may we call you by alternate names?"

The Allarian captain paused, his eye orbs moving back and forth between Dira and Jason. "You may call me Captain, or Chromite; my second is Graphite; and third in command is Silicate. Will that nomenclature suffice?"

"Yes, thank you," Jason replied. "Dira, please ready Graphite for the MediPod."

* * *

As the clamshell closed with a sucking *thump*, Graphite could be seen through the small observation window atop the MediPod. Although her hover prosthetic had been removed, her brain matter still resided within its clear vessel; the MediPod would deal with any foreign material in much the same way it had dealt with Ricket's cyborg-mechanical materials during his procedure.

Dira kept her focus on the MediPod terminal and Jason could see stress lines on her pretty face. She was quiet, double- and triple-checking her settings. Eventually she looked up and noticed Jason, Chromite and Silicate staring at her.

"The process has begun. If everything goes according to plan, in twenty-four hours Graphite will—"

A muffled *splat* sound emanated from the MediPod. All eyes turned toward the observation window. There, within the clear vessel, was what looked like pink pudding. Her brain. Graphite was no more.

Dira stood with a hand to her mouth. Tears swelled and cascaded down her cheeks. "I'm so sorry. So so sorry." She looked to the Allarian captain and then to Silicate. "This is too dangerous. There's too much I don't know or understand. This was a mistake."

"No. Not a mistake. You were clear about the odds of success. She gave her life willingly for a greater cause. She will be remembered as a hero to our people."

Jason and Dira nodded, both looking defeated. Jason was unsure how to proceed. He would transfer the two Allarians back to their ship and find some other way, an alternative to receiving sanctuary on Allaria.

"Please prepare this device for my biological settings," the Allarian captain said.

Before Jason could say anything, Silicate spoke: "I will go next. You must allow me to go next!"

Jason hadn't heard the third Allarian speak until then and was surprised to hear another female voice. There was strong emotion there. These two were more than fellow crewmembers.

The Allarian captain turned to Silicate and hovered forward until the clear vessel enclosing his brain was touching hers. Their eye orbs were now as close as they could be and they maintained focus on each other for a long moment. He said, "No, I will."

Dira wiped at her moist cheeks and, standing before the terminal, she began changing the settings. The MediPod began to open and soon came to a stop. Chromite, the Allarian captain, hovered in close and used his two robotic arms to pick up the clear vessel that once contained Graphite's brain. He hovered before Jason, with outstretched arms: "Please take this and destroy it."

Jason wanted to ask if he was sure. Perhaps they could take her remains back to their planet—have a memorial service. Jason said nothing; he simply took the vessel and deposited it back in the lab. When he returned, Dira was already placing Chromite's vessel into the MediPod, in the exact same location where Graphite's had rested only moments before. Silicate moved in close to the MediPod, her orbs locked on to Chromite. Gently, Dira ushered her back. In moments the MediPod clamshell began to close. Dira's eyes stared at the terminal. Her fingers held still, but poised to enter the initialization command. She turned to Jason, her expression a mixture of sadness and guilt.

"Do it," came the voice of Silicate. "You have to do it."

Jason stepped in closer to Dira and placed a hand on her shoulder. "It's okay, it's what they want."

With one touch on the terminal the initialization process for the Allarian captain began. The seconds ticked by. Jason tried to remember how long it took before Graphite's procedure had gone so terribly wrong ... He waited, anticipating hearing the same awful *splat*.

Three minutes into the procedure no *splats* were heard—nothing catastrophic had happened.

"Everything seems to be progressing normally," Dira said, looking away from the small screen and attempting a weak smile. Silicate continued to stare into the small observation window at the top of the MediPod.

Chapter 14

Boomer ran until she felt her lungs would burn right through her chest. Her hair was wet with sweat that kept running into her eyes. She stopped and tried to catch her breath. She listened. She knew he was back there somewhere, in the thick jungle foliage. Boomer stared at the trees. *Had something just moved there, off to the right?*

Today was her first out-in-the-real-world test. Woodrow had made it clear—he would not go easy on her. Being only nine years old would not factor into his assessment of her passing, or failing, today's exercise. His rules were simple. First, track her prey through HAB 4; second, get in close enough to kill it; third, return with the carcass. Oh, and one more thing: "*Accomplish this before I track and capture you.*"

She'd never been this far into the jungle, not even riding the big elephant, Raja. Could she find her way back? Something was definitely moving up ahead. Was it the same wild boar she'd been tracking for the last three hours? For the umpteenth time, Boomer checked her trio of throwing knives; each was secured within a leather hilt at her belt. She crept forward, doing her best not to make any undue noises. Mosquito-like insects hovered in a cloud around her face and she instinctively slapped at her cheek—another bite.

Snorts and squeals. Definitely the wild boar was up ahead and on the run again. Boomer gave chase. The ground was moist and her steps were slowed by the wet sucking of her boots. She kept as low to the ground as possible, below wide leaf and fern foliage.

She wondered if spiders were falling onto her back. Boomer hated spiders—she scratched at her neck, feeling something bug-like. She held back a scream as she looked at her fingers and saw blood. *Is that mine or the bug's?*

Boomer ran on and saw a small clearing coming into view ahead. There it was! The little, black, pig-looking thing had yellowed tusks protruding from its snout. She slowed and again did her best to control her rapid breathing. She replayed Woodrow's words in her head: *You must kill it and bring its carcass back with you.* She watched as the small boar rooted around in the dirt. Boomer knew it was dangerous, could probably even kill her. But right now, it looked anything but feral. In fact, it was kinda cute. Boomer continued to watch the animal as it used its two front hooves to dig into the soil. Then it lay on its back, wiggling in apparent ecstasy. *You must kill it and bring its carcass back with you.*

Boomer's eyes filled with tears. She looked back the way she'd come. Woodrow could be watching her this very moment and she'd never know it. How important was passing this test, anyway? Boomer thought about that as she continued to watch the boar wiggle-wiggle-wiggle up ahead. The tears stopped. Resolve replaced fear and guilt. Without looking down, Boomer pulled the first of her throwing knives from her belt. She felt the cool hardness of the blade between her fingers. She felt the weight of it and its familiar feel in her hand. Staying low, she entered the clearing. The boar had ceased rolling about, its head now turned sideways, listening. Boomer paused—she stopped breathing. She was twenty feet away. She'd hit targets farther than this, but not every time. She'd get only one throw ... miss, and the boar would dart away into the jungle for good. Slowly, Boomer brought her arm back, the hilt of the knife pointing backwards over her shoulder. Her arm was taut and coiled back, like a spring. She took one step, then another, and then another. The wild boar snorted and quickly regained its feet. It was running for the jungle. Boomer threw the knife, anticipating the distance and the fleeting second it would take to fly across the clearing. The knife struck the boar with a resounding *thunk*; caught right behind its neck, the blade was buried to the hilt.

Both the boar and Boomer stood motionless for several beats. She watched as the animal slowly wavered and dropped halfway to the ground. It was suffering. *You must kill it and bring its carcass back with you.* Boomer quickly moved in behind the boar, straddled it, and pulled another knife from her belt. In one fluid motion she cut the boar's throat, slicing it ear to ear.

* * *

Carrying the animal was out of the question—far too heavy. It took a little trial and error, but in the end Boomer simply dragged the beast behind her—holding on to the boar's hind legs. That worked best. After first cleaning and then replacing the two knives back into their hilts, she wasted no time heading back the way she'd come. Her own tracks were deep and easy to follow. Coming to terms with what she'd done had been surprisingly easy for Boomer. At one level, sure, she felt sad about it, but it was necessary. Woodrow had made a good point: *If you can't kill a wild boar, how, then, will you kill a man, or take on something else intent on killing you?* Kill or be killed.

Boomer's pace was brought to an immediate halt. The carcass was caught on something. She tugged with both hands and yanked, but it wouldn't budge. She dropped the legs and walked around it to see what was the problem. She made a face when she saw the boar's head caught between a Y-shaped tree root protruding up from the ground. The thought of touching the boar's head made her hesitate. Instead, she used the toe of her boot to dislodge it, and that seemed to work. Then she heard a low, deep, growl.

Boomer kicked at the boar's head until it came free and, in a rush, re-grabbed its hind legs. She quickened her pace. Looking back over her shoulder she saw the red swath of blood from the dead boar's cut throat trailing back the way she'd just come.

The growling was louder now—a deep rumble from a large animal. She knew that sound—had heard it on TV and at the wild animal park she'd visited with her mother. Her hands were wet and slippery with sweat and the boar's hooves slipped from her grasp. Frantic now, she wiped her hands on her pants and reached again for the two hooves. It was then she spied the splash of orange and black.

The tiger stood motionless, only its big head visible through the dense foliage. Boomer backed away. Dragging the boar was no longer an option. "You can have it," Boomer said aloud. For every step she now took backward, the tiger took a small pounce forward. Coming into full view, it was immense. Boomer looked from side to side, hoping to find some place to escape to. The beast growled so loud Boomer screamed. The large cat's mouth opened into a wide snarl; its teeth and tongue glistened red and wet where it had licked the trail of blood. The tiger, no longer hesitant, moved faster and with purpose.

"Take the boar! Just take it!" Boomer screamed, moving with all the speed she could muster while continuing to run backward.

The tiger paused at the boar, sniffed it, and then looked toward Boomer. It left the boar and pursued Boomer, who began to scream at the top of her lungs, "Help! Help!"

She turned and ran forward, all out, as fast and far as her young legs could take her. The tiger's menacing presence—its breath, the thumping of its large paws hitting the ground, was so close Boomer no longer believed she could survive this. She kept running by sheer instinct. She thought of her mother and father and then of Mollie. At least they'd still have Mollie.

Chapter 15

Jason was amazed by what was happening within the MediPod. The captain, Chromite, had become more than a singular brain residing in a clear vessel. His vessel was dissolving and all about the brain, a head, with a face, was taking shape, and the elements of a body were forming.

Jason backed away to let Silicate take his place at the observation window. He wondered what she was thinking. How the procedure was going to change their lives. Then he heard her speak.

"I've almost forgotten what he looked like. He was so handsome. Far more handsome than I was pretty." Her orbs turned toward Jason. "If I could cry, I'd be crying. Crying and smiling. It will be nice to do those things again, Captain."

"I'm very happy for you. I'm happy we are able to help," he said. Startled by a noise, he looked toward the entrance.

Petty Officer Priscilla Miller stormed into Medical, her face pinched and flushed red. Jason involuntarily grimaced when he saw her storming toward him.

"Petty Officer, how can I help you?"

She barreled in closer to Jason than he liked. "Did you authorize an off-ship training for Boomer?"

Others in Medical looked startled by her outburst and then looked nervously away.

"Take one full step backward, take a breath, and remember who you are addressing," Jason said in a stern voice that made no attempt to hide his annoyance.

The petty officer stayed put for several seconds before moving back one step. That alone was insubordination, as far as Jason was concerned.

"Boomer is not on this ship. Did you know that? I have clear, definitive orders from the secr—"

"Yes."

The petty officer's expression turned to a look of confusion. "Yes?"

"Yes, I authorized *my* daughter's real-world training exam. But she is not off-ship."

Face flushing red, she retorted, "I asked the on board artificial intelligence ... Boomer is currently off the ship! You are in direct violation—"

"AI, is Boomer currently in HAB 4, on board *The Lilly*?"

"Yes, Captain Reynolds, Boomer is located approximately one mile from the Zoo portal entrance. Would you like me to contact her?"

"No, not at this moment, thank you."

The petty officer did not look in the least placated. "I demand you tell me where she is and exactly how to find her."

"You demand this, huh?" Jason said.

"I don't think you understand the seriousness—"

Jason held a pointed finger between them. Then, holding two fingers on his other hand up to his ear, he said, "Security? Yes, I need two men to escort a hostile to the brig."

Her eyes widened. Anger gave way to disbelief. "You wouldn't dare."

Jason held his temper and looked away from the woman glowering up at him. Ten feet away, Dira leaned against the MediPod behind her and shook her head. She traced an extended finger across her own throat, letting him know the obstinate petty officer deserved exactly what was coming to her. For some reason

Jason found that particularly funny and had to fight to keep his face expressionless.

Two armed security officers rushed into Medical. Both brandished multi-guns and looked poised to kill, if necessary. Jason held up a palm. "Hold there, please." He looked down at the petty officer, hoping to see some level of regret for her actions, but saw none. "Take Petty Officer Priscilla Miller into custody. She is to remain in the brig until further notice."

"I'm sorry, Captain. I was out of line," she said at the last moment.

Jason stared at her for several seconds before waving the security officers off. "You and I need to come to an understanding, Petty Officer. You're walking a thin line and I won't tolerate insubordination."

"Yes, sir. I understand. It won't happen again."

No sooner had the two security officers and Petty Officer Miller left Medical than Jason received a frantic hail.

"Dad! Oh God, Dad! Help me …"

"Mollie! Boomer! What is it? What's wrong?" Jason yelled into his NanoCom.

She sounded out of breath and he heard what sounded to him like running feet. Boomer was shrieking now: something was chasing her … something about a tiger.

* * *

Within two minutes Jason made it to the Zoo and was running into HAB 4. Raja was right where she usually was, her long trunk pulling foliage from trees. She stopped chewing as Jason flew by her. He had Boomer on his NanoCom: "Just try to stay calm."

"He's so close. He's going to eat me, Dad. Help me!"

Then Jason heard the low, unmistakable growl of a nearby tiger through his NanoCom. Jason ran into the jungle, bowling over leaves larger than himself. "Where is Woodrow, Boomer?" She was either too out of breath to answer or she didn't hear him. Jason repeatedly tried to contact Woodrow and got no response. The AI indicated he was alive, but injured.

"Dad!" She was crying and so out of breath her words came out in choppy bursts. "He's ... here ... next ... to me."

Jason ran until his own chest was on fire. There! Up ahead he saw her—his little girl—so small and vulnerable. The tiger was the biggest one he'd ever seen. It was circling Boomer, with blood on its face. *Is that Boomer's blood?* Boomer turned to see her father approach and screamed out, "Dad! I don't know what to do ..."

Jason noticed the tiger had the handle of a knife protruding from its chest. The knife looked small and insignificant compared to the overall mass of the big cat. Boomer held two more knives, one in each hand.

Jason had no weapon, no way to fight the tiger. He slowed to a walk and approached them both. At thirty feet, the tiger moved in even closer to Boomer, snarling in Jason's direction and swiping the air with a claw the size of a baseball mitt. The tiger was conveying its message clearly: the small human was its dinner and it wasn't sharing the meal. Jason stood and looked for something he could use as a weapon. A stick, a rock ... anything! There was nothing.

"Dad, please help me ... please-please-please."

"I will. I'll help you, sweetie." Right then Jason decided he'd take her place. He'd willingly let his little girl escape into the jungle while the tiger took him instead. Others would step up, if required, to take his place leading the mission ... he had an amazing crew. Nothing was more important than saving his little girl.

He took several steps closer, then crouched down to the ground and crawled forward. "Come on, tiger ... here I am, easy prey."

The tiger snarled again and then moved toward him, low to the ground; its muscles tightened as it made ready to spring.

Boomer cried uncontrollably as the tiger left her—her arms tightly wrapped around her knees.

"Get ready to run, okay? Don't look back, sweetie ... Just keep running."

The tiger was less than eight feet from him. They stared at one another for a long moment. This was it. Jason only hoped death would come fast.

A rustling sound came from his left. It wasn't Boomer. Had Woodrow found them? In a blur something black moved into Jason's peripheral vision and in a split second Jason recognized something familiar about the creature's running, awkward, gait.

Alice sprang at the tiger from ten feet out. Teeth bared, it landed on the cat's back and ripped at the tiger's neck with amazing ferocity. The tiger reared back, nearly bucking the six-legged *drog* from its back and hindquarters. Alice held tight and continued her onslaught. First one ear, and then the other, was ripped from the tiger's head. The tiger's head and neck soon looked like bloodied ground beef. It was making a high-pitched yowl that made Jason almost feel sorry for the beast ... almost.

The tiger lay dead on the ground in less than a minute. Alice was quickly at Boomer's side, licking her face and wagging her tail like the playful animal Jason remembered. He rushed to his daughter's side and put his arms around her. Boomer cried into his chest until Alice started running around the two of them. Boomer scolded her but reluctantly was made to laugh. Jason, relieved, started to laugh as well. They both watched as the funny-looking animal continued to run in and out of the jungle.

Chapter 16

Woodrow would live. He spent the next day in Medical, much of that in a MediPod, recovering from his injuries. Jason stood at his bedside. Woodrow's eyes fluttered open. When realization hit him where he was, he frantically tried to sit up. "Boomer!"

"She's fine," Jason said, not doing a very good job keeping the contempt from his voice.

Woodrow looked up at Jason. "I didn't know. She was never supposed to be in any real danger. I was never far away."

"Apparently, HAB 4 isn't the docile jungle habitat everyone thought it was," Jason said.

Woodrow rubbed his eyes, now coming fully awake. "There were three tigers, each bigger than any I'd ever seen. Maybe they'd moved closer to the portal, in search of game ... I don't know. One was upon me before I realized what was happening—it nearly took my arm off. I managed to put a plasma bolt into its head. I no sooner killed that one when another tiger was right there, moving in for the kill. I got a shot off, but it was already on me. Before I passed out I felt his claws ripping at my face."

Jason watched Woodrow relive the events and saw the fear on his usually confident, even cocky, face.

Dira had mentioned Woodrow was mauled beyond recognition. When they'd found him he was seconds away from completely bleeding out.

"Captain, I am sorry. I deserve any punishment you deem appropriate. Just know I would never do anything to harm

Boomer. She's an amazing little girl."

Jason continued to look stone-faced at Woodrow. When he spoke, his words were measured and soft. "What happened was nearly catastrophic. You've taken this training too far. You placed my daughter in a life-threatening situation."

"Yes, sir."

"But you may have inadvertently saved her life, as well."

Woodrow looked perplexed. "I'm not following, sir."

"Both Boomer and Mollie have played in HAB 4 on a daily basis for nearly a year now. We've gotten so used to her hanging around in there she seldom has any supervision."

Realization crossed Woodrow's face and he slowly nodded. "Three tigers running loose, looking for game. It would only be a matter of time before ..."

"So, as furious as I am today about your conduct, I'm surprisingly also in your debt."

Woodrow eased somewhat, a weight lifted from his shoulders.

"We'll talk more. Recover so I can properly kick your ass later," Jason said. He left the hospital section of Medical and joined Dira near the MediPods. She was speaking to the Allarian captain. He indeed looked human and healthy. Medium height and middle-aged, his blond hair fell to his shoulders. He was wearing spacer overalls.

When the Allarian captain saw Jason, he smiled broadly. "What you have done ... for me, our people, will not be forgotten, Captain. I am, and will always be, in your debt." He looked over at the largest of the MediPods and his eyes welled up. "She is almost restored back to her original self. I never thought ..." His words got caught in his throat.

Jason put a comforting hand on the Allarian captain's shoulder. "Look, once things settle down I'm hoping we'll be able to help the rest of your people as well. When Ricket, our science and technology officer, returns I'll have him construct for you a MediPod of your own."

Jason was being hailed.

"Go for Captain."

"Captain, we have a situation on the bridge," Orion said.

"On my way."

* * *

Entering the bridge, Jason was startled to see a disturbing, gaping, open-mouthed face staring back at him from the wrap-around display. He recognized the Mau female officer he'd learned to admire over the last few months.

"Admiral Ti," Jason said, taking a seat in the command chair.

"Captain Reynolds. I have important information."

"Go ahead."

"From what I understand from your tactical officer, you are unaware of events currently taking place within the Allied worlds."

Jason shook his head. "What events?"

"The Craing. Six fringe planets have come under attack within Allied space: Lapoine, Coral-19, Halperon, Vori, Lear-Escott, and Jhardon."

Jason stood, feeling his pulse quicken. "No! Don't tell me they've been destroyed."

"All but Jhardon, but there are casualties there on a massive scale. The others are gone. Disintegrated to space rubble."

"How is that possible? Destruction of a planet ...?"

"A Craing fleet of six dreadnaught warships. We've heard rumors about them, but never knew they were anywhere near ... what you refer to as ... Allied space. They're known as the Vanguard fleet."

"They destroy planets? That's their objective?" Jason asked incredulously.

Ti nodded. "What's special about these warships, similar to Craing dreadnaughts, is that each carries a large, ultra-powerful plasma cannon, specifically designed for extended long-range bombardment. Take in mind, Captain, the Vanguard attack as a group, single out one planet at a time, and together concentrate their plasma beams on it. The result is nearly always the same—complete and utter planet annihilation."

Jason brought the conversation back to Jhardon. "Have you talked to Admiral Reynolds? What's being coordinated to rescue survivors there?"

"Captain, we have problems of our own—our own survival being the most relevant. Yes, we have talked to the admiral—in fact, pleaded with him for assistance. Carz-Mau is, most assuredly, the Vanguard fleet's next destination. Like those six planets, we lie directly within that same directional course. I'm sorry, but all Mau vessels have left the Allied fleet. We're currently en route to Carz-Mau, to protect our home world."

Jason nodded in understanding, but was distressed four hundred-plus advanced warships had left the fleet.

"Captain, others within the fleet have also left ... some were too afraid to go up against the Craing; others left, as we have, to protect their home worlds. *The Lilly* may have the capacity to go up against this Vanguard fleet. Captain—Jason, we desperately need your help. That's why I've contacted you directly."

Jason needed to talk to his father. "Give me some time. Let me come up to speed. I'll do what I can, Ti, I promise."

Even before Ti's face disappeared from view, another face popped up on another display segment.

Jason said, "Dad! What the hell's happening?"

The admiral looked terrible, his face flushed and sweaty,

and some kind of commotion was taking place behind him. "What's going on is fucking mayhem. Five planets have been demolished—"

Jason cut him off. "I heard. So what's happening now? What's the situation with the Allied fleet?"

The admiral looked angry and ready to explode. "Allied fleet? What fucking fleet? The Mau just hightailed it back to Carz-Mau; the Malgos have officially revoked their membership, hoping they can get back in the Craing's good graces, and we're facing massive desertion on board fleet vessels. Three ships are verging on mutiny. Pure and simple, everything we've accomplished over the past year is coming apart—going to hell in a hand basket."

"Okay, take it easy, Dad. You don't look so good. What exactly do you want me to do?"

"My first impulse is for you to bring *The Lilly* to the Allied worlds, or head off to intercept this Vanguard fleet."

"I can do that."

"No! Just be quiet! I'm still thinking out loud." Then the admiral spun around and reprimanded someone behind him. "Hold on ... Give me a God damn second, will you?" He turned back to face Jason. "What's left of the fleet is scattered. Over the next twenty-four hours we'll regroup and converge back in Allied space. I'll do what I can to help Jhardon."

"So you want us there—"

"Look, the successes we've had defeating the Craing over the past year haven't gone unnoticed. The Craing are mobilizing fleets brought in from multiple sectors—we're getting reports of Craing warships converging at two locations. The first is within an area of Orion's Belt—more ships are arriving there every day. They're also converging in the Craing worlds. A multi-pronged attack is coming. Some kind of sweep ... Earth ... the Allied planets. Hell, these might be just the tip of the iceberg. My guess, they're cleaning house within the entire sector. They're looking to make an example of us. Look at what they did to those six outer-fringe planets? We're talking about mass destruction on a whole different level." The admiral took a breath and wiped a hand across his chin. "Add in the present spate of Allied worlds withdrawing from the Alliance and we're in serious trouble. Acquiring the *Minian* is more important than ever. I'm serious, Jason. It just might be the differentiating factor between survival and extinction of the human race. Complete the original mission and get me that damn ship!"

Chapter 17

Ricket and Gaddy were the first to arrive at the emperor's personal dining hall. Gaddy had hand selected suitable attire for Ricket and told him how handsome he looked. The table was long and narrow. Ricket counted the empty chairs around them. Twenty-two. Were twenty-two guests joining them for dinner?

Ricket felt awkward in social situations. Yes, physically, he was now a one hundred percent living, organic, being. The problem was he'd spent close to two hundred years as a functioning, highly effective cyborg, not having to deal with the constant confluences of emotion and ego. Ricket was so out of his comfort zone, and he wondered if it was obvious to those around him. His analytical mind was constantly monitoring his every movement: *Should I smile or look more interested? Where do I put my hands? Am I communicating correctly or being too introspective?* He was currently thinking about something Gaddy had repeated more than once—just be yourself. Terrific. *So, who am I?*

They'd been at the Emperor's Palace for two days now. Other than a quick meet-and-greet the day he and Gaddy arrived, they hadn't spent more than a few fleeting moments with the acting Craing Emperor, Lom. That was about to change in the next few minutes.

Gaddy reached across the white tablecloth and took one of Ricket's hands in both of hers.

"Relax, you look nervous."

"I'm not nervous, I'm uncomfortable."

"Same thing," she said. She leaned forward and pulled Ricket in close. "Have you spoken to anyone?"

She was referring to anyone on board *Her Majesty*. That was another thing—Ricket's total lack of progress with the mission so far was hanging over his head like a bag of rocks.

"I'm due to contact *Her Majesty* with an update," he said, trying to match her smile. Ricket sat back in his chair, letting his hand pull away from hers. Wait staff were bustling around behind them. He heard distant sounds of kitchen activity—clanging of metal pans and pots, excited voices, the sound of meat hitting a red-hot grill.

"Isn't this beautiful? Look at those tapestries. That one there," she said, pointing past the far end of the table. "Close to two thousand years old. Those are my ancestors, battling the Micronials."

Ricket thought their illustrated depictions looked almost cartoon-like. All the Craing warrior faces were almost identical. Hundreds of ornately dressed Craing—riding atop galloping Serapins—arms raised, swords pointing skyward, while the poor Micronials ran about naked, weaponless, and cowered in a nearby forest.

Ricket didn't hear the acting emperor enter the room. Dressed in a long, green silk robe, he now stood between the charging Craing and the fleeing Micronials. Gaddy was out of her seat and running into Lom's outstretched arms. As he embraced her, his eyes never left Ricket.

Lom looked the same as Ricket remembered. Beneath the arrogance, gaudy robes and jewelry, was the same deceitful, cowardly Craing leader. Ricket watched Gaddy, almost beaming and acting childlike. She'd retaken on her persona of years past—acting just as Lom would remember her. Ricket wondered if she'd forgotten her recent days as a student dissident—the fearless young Craing who helped Captain Reynolds and his team bring down the wormhole loop on Halimar, and who'd escaped into HAB 12. But as Gaddy returned to her seat, Ricket knew in a glance. Her eyes were cold and lifeless. She truly hated Lom.

Ricket stood and placed his own palms against the acting emperor's waiting palms. Both bowed their heads while maintaining eye contact. Lom was the first to step away. He took the seat at the head of the table, sitting where he had their first time together.

"This is so nice, but I must apologize for the little time I've had to spend with you both. I'm not normally so busily engaged, but amazing things are happening within the empire that will guarantee a most brilliant future for my beautiful niece." Lom reached out and placed his palm against Gaddy's cheek.

Lom turned his attention back to Ricket. "I must say, I've been racking my brain where I've seen you before. So familiar. It will come to me ... I have a near perfect memory."

Ricket saw Gaddy's eyes lock on her uncle, her easy smile looked forced.

"I must have sent you a picture, Uncle. Isn't Nelmon handsome?" Gaddy asked.

Lom continued to look at Ricket, still trying to place where he'd seen him. "Gaddy tells me you're a post-graduate student, is that right? Information technologies ... computer programming?"

Ricket glanced at Gaddy and then nodded toward Lom. "I'm about ready to publish my doctoral thesis."

"Really? What area are you most interested in?"

"Artificial intelligence, sir."

"He's an amazing scholar, Uncle. I've never met anyone so ridiculously smart," Gaddy said with bubbling pride.

There was a commotion at the other end of the room. A young and pretty hostess was leading a large party of individuals into the dining hall. Wait staff pulled chairs away from the table and gestured for the guests to sit. Lom stood and, with open arms, greeted the newcomers. "Welcome ... welcome all of you. Tonight a feast awaits you." Lom turned toward the chef who now stood near his side. "Tell us, Posh-hok, what are you preparing for us this evening?"

As the chef continued on about the culinary delights in store for them, Ricket was having a hard time keeping his eyes off one of the recent additions to the table. Granger, sitting tall and confident, sat four seats across the table from him. His eyes left the yammering chef and locked on to Ricket. In that instant, Ricket was almost positive the Caldurian knew exactly who he was. A bead of sweat trickled down Ricket's cheek. He swiped at it with his napkin and looked nervously toward Gaddy.

Eventually the meal was served, all five courses. Ricket picked at his food, not hungry in the least. Conversations stayed light and removed from anything remotely controversial or specific to the Craing Empire's expansion movements—that is until two of the Caldurian guests talking with Granger in hushed voices turned angry. Granger never lost his composure, even as they abruptly stood, threw their napkins onto the table, and stormed out of the dinner hall. Ricket assumed they were emissaries from the nearby Crystal City ships.

The night was winding down and Gaddy was clearly getting impatient. More than once she had attempted to bring the conversation back to more relevant issues: What was going on with the new warships in Craing space? Who was her uncle meeting with this week? But Lom would have none of that, casually smiling and waving away her inquiries as tedious business he'd like to forget for the night.

One by one, guests thanked their host and adjourned to their quarters for the night. Ricket watched as Granger stood.

Thinking he too was leaving, Ricket was surprised when he moved closer and sat down to Gaddy's right.

Lom made the introductions. Granger was charming and at ease. He asked Gaddy about her life at school and then turned his attention to Ricket. Soon the conversation turned to the specifics of his doctoral program.

Never one to consciously lie or even embellish, Ricket was forced to pull from real life experience and knowledge. Without a doubt, acting-Emperor Lom had Ricket completely checked out upon their arrival. Subsequently, prior to coming to the planet, Ricket had hacked into his cover alma mater, the Craing Empire University's student database, and inserted not only the name Nelmon Lim as a graduate and postgraduate student there, but also technical details of his abstract research. Research, Ricket speculated, that was far more advanced than that of any of the scientists currently working on the *Minian* would be able to match.

This area he was conformable with. The more technical Granger's questions were, the better, more confident, Ricket started to feel.

"I'm impressed. Highly impressed." Granger and Lom exchanged eye contact. "Nelmon, I am not an engineer by any stretch; I'm what you'd call an implementer. I'm meeting here with Emperor Lom in that capacity. With his approval, I'd like to show you something you may find quite fascinating." Granger looked as if he was holding back great inner excitement.

"I think my niece and her young suitor would enjoy seeing what you have to show them," Lom said, standing up from the table. "Unless you two are tired and would rather adjourn to your rooms for the night?"

"Are you kidding? We're young and ready for anything," Gaddy said enthusiastically.

* * *

Ricket and Granger walked together along an enclosed temporary construction causeway while Gaddy and her uncle followed close behind. It had taken them about fifteen minutes once they'd left the palace, boarded the emperor's space yacht, and flown up to the space platform they referred to as the Ion Station. Craing security was tight and Ricket saw emperor's guard soldiers wearing green battle suits stationed throughout the station, as well as guards moving about on continuous patrol. Considering her importance, Ricket understood why there was an even larger security force guarding the *Minian*. That could be a problem, later.

As tall as a human, but brandishing features that were more Craing-looking, Granger led Ricket and the others through a maze of winding turns. Their visibility to see far ahead was curtailed by temporary high-reaching barricades. It was only when they'd reached the farthest boundary of the construction zone, and passed through another heavily guarded checkpoint, that Ricket could confirm to himself where they'd been led. Through a temporary way station of sorts there was now an unobstructed view of space beyond.

The *Minian* was secured several hundred feet out from the platform by two sturdy-looking, metal, cross-beamed scaffolds. They seemed to secure the vessel in place and had more of the same enclosed causeways, like tunnels, leading to the ship's starboard egresses. Another potential problem—dismantling the scaffolds.

Ricket was reminded how similar the Caldurian vessel looked to *The Lilly*—though closer in size to a Craing dreadnaught ... no less than a mile in length, from bow to stern. Then his eyes took in what lay beyond the *Minian,* farther out in open space. There was a tight formation of parked dreadnaughts. Hundreds of them—maybe thousands.

Granger looked down, watching Ricket's expression. "Magnificent, wouldn't you say?"

Both Lom and Gaddy joined them and also took in the spectacle suspended before them.

"She's beautiful," Gaddy said.

"I've never seen anything like her," Ricket lied.

But Lom's attention was elsewhere, his eyes scanning an area of nearby space. Then suddenly, looking furiously toward Granger, he said, "The Crystal ships! They're gone ... what did you say to them? Tell me, where have they gone, Granger?"

"Just as I recently have, they too were informed about your plans ... regarding the *Great Space.*"

Lom's expression said it all—something clandestine, something Lom wanted kept secret, had been discovered. Ricket watched the exchange between them and put two and two together. The pair of Caldurians that abruptly left the dinner table were actually from the Crystal City ships. Whatever this secret *Great Space* plan was about, it was enough to cause the Caldurians to quickly flee to their Crystal City ships and leave Craing space.

Lom tore his eyes away from Granger and, with more than a little effort, composed himself. "How would you like to come aboard?" Lom asked, already maneuvering to the front of the group. "This way. Careful, this is a construction zone—watch your step there."

The trek across the scaffolding took several minutes. By the time Ricket reached the *Minian*'s forward starboard hatch, he was already initiating his new, recently added, nano-devices to talk to the *Minian*'s AI.

"Looks like this ship is being modified, maybe retrofitted?" Ricket asked Granger.

"This is a Caldurian Dartmouth-class ship. Perhaps she's one of *the* most sophisticated space exploration vessels in existence. With that said, Nelmon, much of her technology is beyond me. It just so happens a major stumbling block for us is the AI. We'll need a much better understanding of that technology before we can even think about reproducing and incorporating it on new Craing vessels."

They entered the ship and Lom continued on for Granger: "What's happening here is basically investigative work. Reverse engineering is a slow and complex process. From the advanced propulsion systems in engineering, there's fantastical multiverse interfaces for such things as moving between decks in the blink of an eye, and the capability to phase-shift across tens of thousands of miles in space. All this technology, once produced and understood, will be reproduced. You're looking at the prototype for future Craing super-warships, the first of thousands to be deployed throughout the universe."

Gaddy made a face of sheer astonishment. "Oh my God, Uncle. How exciting! I had no idea."

Ricket thought Gaddy was over-playing her role a bit.

"How far have you gotten, deciphering the technology?" Ricket asked.

"Not as far as we'd like. But we're making progress. With Granger's help, we should be able to begin new construction within several months."

That was actually much sooner than Ricket would have guessed, not good news for the Alliance. It did seem like they'd made some progress on the engineering front, but it was difficult to tell. "Do you think it would be possible for me to take a look at the AI? Perhaps I could give you my perspective ... although this technology is probably far more advanced than anything I'm familiar with."

They were now making their way forward and heading toward a DeckPort. Lom looked pleased by Ricket's inquiry. "We would love to have a smart scholar such as you take a look," Lom said to Ricket, giving Granger a reassuring nod.

Ricket could see the DeckPort was active, which meant the AI was probably still online. He used his nano-devices to make his first low-level inquiry. Ensuring that he used a pseudonym-login, Ricket quickly accessed the *Minian*'s core processes—evaluating the state of the ship's spaceworthiness.

They approached the DeckPort and Gaddy, again overacting, tried to look tentative about walking through the opening.

Lom took Gaddy by the arm, and then took Ricket's as well. "Let me show you how this is done." He escorted them through the DeckPort where they immediately exited out onto another deck level. "Keep in mind, this is all highly classified. What you're seeing here tonight cannot be discussed with anyone."

"We understand," Gaddy said.

They were approaching the bridge. *Perfect*, Ricket thought. This would be the deciding factor as to the likelihood of absconding with the ship, and if it was even remotely possible for him to do so.

Ricket saw Lom slowing down. He'd yawned more than once and it was only a matter of minutes before he'd want to head back to the comfort of the palace and his awaiting bed.

They entered the bridge. Nearly twice the size of that of *The Lilly*, it was a shock to see. Ricket's hopes fell. Much of the bridge was torn apart. Consoles were dismantled—optical cable and phase-junction wires were hanging loose, like scraggly vines.

Even Granger looked surprised by the mess. "It's hard to picture what this normally looks like, but this is the ship's bridge,"

Granger said.

Both Gaddy and Ricket wandered around, mouths agape. Lom moved close to Ricket. "How would you like to work right here, on this amazing ship?"

Ricket paused, then regarded the Craing acting emperor. "You mean, like a job?"

"Well, that's up to you. We have the finest Craing minds working to unravel the mysteries of this wonderful vessel. You'll be in good company. She is the most important technological discovery in Craing history. But we need help. From what Granger tells me, after only a few minutes of your speaking together, he knows you have the high level technical mind we need on our team."

Ricket looked over to Gaddy, who looked overjoyed, both hands balled up into fists and a smile from ear to ear. "Can you imagine, Ri—"

Ricket quickly cut her off before she continued uttering his name. "Yes! I would be honored and, of course, gladly offer my services, to assist you in any way possible."

Ricket wasn't sure, but he thought he saw Granger do a double take. Had he now figured out who he was? That something wasn't right? Ricket looked at Gaddy, who had quickly turned away, looking at something on the bulkhead. He saw that the back of her neck was somewhat flushed.

"It's getting quite late for me," Lom said. "I'm not young like the rest of you. Nelmon, I want you and Granger to meet again in the morning. Talk. I'm hopeful you will be the expert to crack this vessel's AI." He joined Gaddy and put an arm around her waist, and together they headed for the bridge exit.

Granger was quiet, introspective. He took in a slow, long breath. "Yes, yes, yes ... Nelmon, we should meet first thing in the morning. How does that sound? I'm sure we can come to a mutually beneficial arrangement."

Ricket said, "I'd like that. I can't wait to talk to the ship's AI."

Granger put a reassuring hand on Ricket's shoulder and together they followed Gaddy and Lom toward the DeckPort. Ricket's mind was not on Granger or Lom or Gaddy, he was fully interfacing with the *Minian*'s AI and bringing up the necessary systems that would take her into space.

Chapter 18

The Lilly and the convoy of seven U.S. spaceships were now safely hidden on the surface of Allaria. Jason had phase-shifted onto *Her Majesty* and had arrived on her bridge twenty minutes earlier. Ricket began transmitting, via his recently altered nano-devices, POV visual and auditory feed during acting-Emperor Lom's two hour long dinner party. They watched as the evening events unfolded on the primary display. During the less interesting dinner conversations, Jason had time to bring Brian up to speed on the dire events taking place in Allied space, and the Allied fleet's dwindling numbers. Brian said he was up to date on some of this from earlier ship-to-ship communications.

"How did Dira react to news about Jhardon?" Brian asked. "She must be going crazy worrying about her parents ... hell, her home planet."

"She wants to return home. She's frustrated she can't do more for her people. She was able to connect and speak briefly with her father and mother. Both were off-planet during the attack but returned to find near total devastation. Some areas are uninhabitable due to radiation; others were leveled, with zero life-sign readings. I've promised I'll get her home as soon as *The Lilly* is freed up here."

"Talk to me about those dreadnaughts," Jason asked, pointing to a smaller display above the console where Perkins was sitting.

"Yeah, we've been watching them move in from all directions over the last thirty-six hours. Makes you wonder. Where are they manufacturing them? I think we've underestimated the Craing's military might."

"You think?" Jason responded sarcastically. "You're sure the cloaking device on this ship is totally failsafe?"

A voice came from behind them. "Nothing is totally failsafe," Bristol answered, entering the bridge. "We're lucky this monstrosity of a ship hasn't taken a dump before now. But the one thing that I'm fairly certain *will* keep working is the toric-cloaking device."

Apparently the dinner party was breaking up and Ricket was seen talking directly to Granger on the display. Jason followed the conversation and was encouraged by both Granger and Lom's apparent interest in Ricket, *Nelmon*'s, impressive technical, artificial intelligence, background. Truth was, Jason hadn't had much faith the plan would ever work. There were just too many variables. But now, listening to Ricket speak, he was encouraged. His knowledge was vast and it was obvious to anyone he met he was not only a genius, but sincere and humble about it. Jason's biggest fear was he would come across as too perfect a fit—filling more than their needs demanded—that having so much knowledge could bring on suspicion.

The bridge went quiet as everyone watched, from Ricket's POV, the group's trip from Terplin, to the space station, to the *Minian*. Jason and Brian looked at each other and smiled.

"We're on the ship ... we're on that damn ship!" Jason barked, sounding astonished. The display changed to a split-view—one side showing Ricket's POV, the other a code of some kind ... thousands of lines of meaningless, scrolling, code.

Bristol walked up closer to the display and turned toward Jason. "The little guy has interfaced to the *Minian*'s AI—he's talking to her, bringing up her systems." Bristol continued to stare at Jason, then made a flabbergasted face. "Don't you get it? He's doing it now! He's stealing that big fucking ship ... stealing it right now!"

"No, look, they're leaving the *Minian*," Perkins interjected. Granger and Lom were indeed heading off the ship and onto the scaffolding, with Ricket and Gaddy following close behind. Then Ricket reached a hand out for Gaddy, getting a grip on the back of her gown. She turned, surprise in her eyes, which turned to confusion. Ricket stepped back, pulling Gaddy back into the ship with him. Both Granger and Lom turned around, smiling and looking like they hadn't a care in the world, then watched with confusion as the *Minian*'s forward starboard hatch slid shut right before their eyes.

"Captain," came Ricket's voice through his NanoCom.

"I'm here, Ricket."

"I didn't think I'd get this opportunity again."

"You did the right thing. Can you phase-shift the *Minian* out of there?"

"No, Captain. That function is offline. Almost everything's offline."

"I don't understand. How were you planning to get the *Minian* away?"

Ricket didn't answer for several beats. "The only thing I can think of is *The Lilly*. Phase-shift her into the *Minian*'s hold and together we'll phase-shift both ships to open space."

"Can *The Lilly* even do that, phase-shift both—"

Bristol, now standing close to Jason, shook his head in irritation. "That's not going to work. Far too much mass for *The Lilly* to compensate for. Can't generate that kind of power."

Ricket was speaking at the same time as Bristol and Jason wasn't tracking what either said. "Wait. Hold on, Bristol. Go ahead, Ricket."

Ricket said it again. "There's more than enough power being generated by the *Minian*. Get *The Lilly* on board and I'll interface the two ships."

Jason conveyed what Ricket said to Bristol, who thought about it for a second and slowly nodded, answering, "Yeah, that might work."

Bristol sat at a console tapping at a terminal, and soon Ricket's voice could be heard by those on the bridge.

"There's one more minor problem," Ricket said. "Two problems, actually. One, getting *The Lilly* in close enough to phase-shift. Two, getting the *Minian* separated from the two scaffolding constructs. They extend out from the space platform and completely surround the *Minian*'s hull."

Brian said, "Ricket, there's hundreds of dreadnaughts and other warships all around us in surrounding space. We're talking twenty, thirty thousand miles of tightly packed warships. Multiple phase-shift jumps with *The Lilly* will surely be detected and there goes our element of surprise. As of right now, Granger and Lom are probably thinking something abstract's happened. I doubt they've put two and two together ... that you're actually planning to steal the *Minian*."

"Yeah, who'd be that stupid," Bristol threw in, without looking up from his console.

Jason continued, "We'd have limited time to deal with the scaffolds, not to mention those security forces on the space platform. No, we need to get *The Lilly* into the *Minian* without triggering suspicion or alarms."

Betty put a new diagram onto the main display, which depicted the location of Terplin and the space platform, as well as surrounding formations of other space vessels. "So look," she said, "I've plotted a course through the dreadnaught formations. It would be tight, sometimes no more than one hundred yards clearance, but *Her Majesty* could probably get in fairly close to the *Minian*. Close enough to eventually phase-shift *The Lilly* from one ship to the other."

"That is, if you don't first crash into one of the fifty or sixty dreadnaughts along the way," Bristol answered, giving her a lopsided smile.

Brian scowled. "Wait ... okay, you're thinking since we're cloaked we can hide *The Lilly* on board and deliver her in close?"

"Yup, just like UPS," Bristol said.

Betty nodded and brought up the schematics of *Her Majesty*. "Sorry, Brian, there's not one single hold large enough to phase-shift *The Lilly* into. But here and here," she pointed, "there's adequate space, if we think creatively. It'll still be tight."

"Terrific. Go ahead and ruin a perfectly fine ship." He looked over the diagram. "I see the two adjoining forward holds, but that area there ... those are the officers' quarters and over there is the ship's mess. You're talking about destruction of nearly three entire decks."

"It looks like a one-way trip for *Her Majesty* anyway, Brian," Jason said apologetically. "Hell, what are our chances of making it through that maze of dreadnaughts anyway?"

Chapter 19

Her Majesty was piloted back to Allarian space and was currently in high-orbit around the dark and desolate-looking planet. Ricket's impromptu actions aboard the *Minian* moved their timetable up—everyone was scurrying around, double-time.

Jason finished securing his helmet and watched as the familiar, glowing, three-dimensional HUD came alive and hovered before his eyes. Stepping over to the bulkhead, he passed Rizzo a multi-gun from the armory's equipment rack and then selected one for himself.

"What kind of defenses are we talking about, Cap?" Rizzo asked.

"From what I saw on the feed, and from what Ricket has relayed to me, the emperor's security forces are all over the place. They're well armed and we can expect them to be better- trained than the typical Craing combatant." Jason paused a beat before walking out of the compartment. "Don't underestimate the Craing; that's bitten us in the ass more than once. Remember, securing that platform is paramount. We'll need time to uncouple and take the *Minian*."

"Got it, Cap. We'll get it done."

Jason made his way down to the mess, where Billy was inspecting his team of one hundred and twenty men—all outfitted in the latest hardened battle suits and carrying a multi-gun. About half the armed men were Navy SEALs and this new mission was just one of the many ops they'd been called up on while serving aboard *The Lilly*. Jason stood back and watched Billy move through their *at-ease* formation, stopping periodically to speak to someone, then moving on down the ranks. Many, Jason recognized, including Chief Petty Officer Woodrow, who looked no worse for wear. The others were hand-selected by Billy, from the thousands of new recruits who'd recently come aboard the convoy, at the Pentagon. They were mostly elite Delta Forces personnel—all eager to join the action in space—training at what was previously the EOUPA, but now solely a United States base in the Chihuahuan desert.

Heads turned toward Jason as he walked to the front of the assembled men.

"Some of you fought side by side with me on Earth, and in space, over the past year. To you, I say thank you for your service and continued commitment to fighting the Craing. Others of you are certainly not new to combat and have fought for your country with honor, and no less a commitment, to defending first your country, and now planet Earth. If there's one piece of advice I can give you today it is this: Don't underestimate the enemy. They tend to let others do their fighting for them, preferring to hide in the background. But that doesn't make them any less dangerous. They're cunning and will stop at nothing to secure all known space for themselves. The planets they don't annihilate—turn into space dust—they invade, and subjugate the inhabitants into either slavery, or fighting for the Craing Empire—under threat of destruction of their homes and families. I want you to know the importance of this mission, what's at stake. Recently, five Allied planets were singled out and destroyed; another is on life support. We're talking billions of people dead, in a matter of hours. The Craing are looking to make an example of what happens to a world when they go up against Craing tyranny. The Alliance is a mess. Worlds we thought were allies have decided it's safer to leave and go it alone ... hoping to stay in the Craing's good graces. Others, such as the Mau, have taken their fleet home to defend their own planet. The Mau withdrew four hundred advanced warships, and we're seeing similar actions from others. Recently, the Craing obtained a vessel of such technological superiority that it's unthinkable what devastation may come about as a result. This ship, the *Minian*, just might be our single best hope in defending not only the Allied worlds, but all known space."

Jason, while addressing the men, had observed others from around the ship filing into the rear of the mess hall, including bridge, engineering, medical, security personnel, and others, until crewmembers were overflowing into the adjoining corridor.

"They say the darkest hour is just before dawn. We have arrived at that darkest hour. What dawn will look like completely depends on us—individually, and as a team. Team leaders, prepare for battle."

Jason walked over to where Dira was standing, at the back of the room, and saw Boomer and Petty Officer Miller standing there as well. Dira looked tired, but brightened as he approached. Their eyes met and Jason smiled. Boomer looked up at her father and said, "That was super depressing. Aren't you supposed to motivate your soldiers?"

"Yes, I'm supposed to. Not so good, huh?"

"Give your dad a break, kiddo. I thought your talk was plenty motivating, Jason." Dira gave him a half-hearted smile and a thumbs up.

Miller wore a pinched expression and rested a hand on Boomer's shoulder. "You're not thinking of keeping your daughter on board while you go into battle, are you, sir?"

"What you'll find is there's really no perfectly safe place in war. Even back on Earth ... it's only a matter of time—"

"I don't accept that. Captain, I'd like to keep Boomer on one of the convoy ships. It's all a matter of degrees."

Boomer squirmed away from Miller's hand and stood next to Jason. "I'm going where my father goes. Why don't you stop sticking your big nose in other people's business?"

Jason held up a hand. "Hold on, little one. Where *The Lilly*'s going won't be safe. You can stay with Petty Officer Miller. I'll contact the *Cutlass*, one of our cruisers. If all goes well, we'll be back before you know it. That work for you, Petty Officer?"

"The truth is ... it should have been your suggestion in the first place. But yes, that will do."

* * *

Jason stood on *The Lilly*'s bridge and waited for Brian's final confirmation that all was clear for them to phase-shift into the bowels of *Her Majesty*. He felt bad for his brother. The only time Brian had been given his father's trust and the heady responsibility to captain his own ship. Now he'd be forced to watch as his ship was gutted and piloted off to all too imminent destruction.

Up on the wrap-around display, Jason could see Brian standing with his arms crossed, looking somewhat resigned. In the background, never far away, the hopper lurked—keeping its protective vigil.

"We're all set here, Captain. All aboard who's coming aboard."

Jason nodded toward McBride at the helm. "Phase-shift when ready."

A white flash and they phase-shifted into *Her Majesty*. *The Lilly* shuddered and then everything outside her hull shifted—the sound of metal twisting and scraping came from all directions. The three hundred and sixty degree display above showed *Her Majesty*'s exposed crossbeams and bulkheads—metal was twisted in some places and completely sheared clean where *The Lilly's* hull had displaced overlapping matter. Jason turned clockwise on his heels, studying *Her Majesty's* mangled, internal skeleton. He wondered if there was adequate structural strength left, or would the big ship implode at the slightest nudge.

Both Jason and Rizzo used their battle suits' belts to phase-shift onto *Her Majesty's* bridge. Startled, Brian's hopper clicked and hissed until it recognized Jason's face behind his visor.

"You're all going to need battle suits."

"Yeah? And what about him?" Brian asked, pointing to the hopper.

"I'd suggest we move him to *The Lilly* temporarily. There's a really good chance this ship will breach at some point."

Brian, who hadn't yet looked up from the console he was working at, glanced over to the hopper. "I don't tell him what to do."

"That's fine. I don't have a problem telling him," Jason said. "Does he understand what we say?"

Brian shrugged. "I suppose. When he's interested in what's being said."

Jason approached the hopper. "We need to move you to a safe place. It's only temporary. I promise, we'll bring you back to Brian as soon as possible. Gunny, phase-shift with him into one of *The Lilly's* holds."

Orion gave Jason a sideways glance and stepped up to the hopper, tentatively placing a hand on its arm. The hopper's black forked tongue flicked in and out and the clicking sound grew louder.

"My guess, he's not warming to that idea much," Brian said, a bemused expression on his face.

"Best make it quick, Gunny," Jason said.

"On it, Cap. Just need to set my HUD phase-shift location

to Hold 2." In a flash they were both gone.

Within two minutes Orion was back on the bridge—lying on her back. She got to her feet and said, "Hopper wasn't very happy with your decision. Came right at me with those claws flexing, knocked me on my ass, and tried to bite me through my visor."

Jason turned to Brian. "This is your ship, Captain. Take us into the maze."

Chapter 20

Betty was at the helm of *Her Majesty*. With her extensive time on board numerous large freighters, she had the most experience piloting big, lumbering vessels. Actually, space travel was virtually all computer or AI controlled, though a ship's pilot constantly oversaw pre-plotted course data and, if necessary, overrode those plot computations—sometimes at the very last second, if time permitted.

The large, cloaked, luxury liner turned warship entered the maze of parked, mile-long dreadnaughts.

"Crap!" Betty said.

"Well, slow us down," Brian barked.

"Obviously," Betty snapped back. "AI, compensate for all drones and other small vessels within the plot route. Add them to the display."

The live video feed with plot-line overlay was refreshed with hundreds of tiny new icons moving like insects back and forth between the dreadnaughts. Jason watched in silence. It wasn't the AI's fault; Brian had only specified that dreadnaughts be logged and plotted.

Brian glanced at Jason. "Relax. We got this."

Jason nodded. "I know you do." The view on the display reminded Jason of driving through Manhattan, with its high-rise buildings. Although here the buildings, as such, were above and below them, not merely on the sides—a three-dimensional maze that, from their bridge perspective, looked impossible to traverse. At no point were the dreadnaughts closer to each other than five hundred yards, but *Her Majesty* was almost that long herself—so a constant pitch, yaw, and roll action was necessary to maintain adequate clearance. Jason caught himself looking up only to remind himself there was no three hundred and sixty degree view from here as there was on *The Lilly*.

"We're coming up to our first course change," Betty said.

"I understand we're visually cloaked. But you're sure we won't be picked up on any proximity sensors?" Jason asked.

This time it was Bristol who spoke. "What do you think cloaked means? It's not singularly based on aspects of the spectrum of light, or visual information."

Jason chewed the inside of his lip, but didn't say anything. There was a total disregard by crewmembers to exhibit proper military respect and conduct on this bridge. It was bringing up his ire, and it took more than a little self control not to publicly reprimand and discipline Bristol. Truth was, it was up to Brian to set a higher standard of command.

An alarm sounded from the helm console. The display showed *Her Majesty* making the course change, while pitching at a thirty degree angle and rolling ten degrees starboard. The maneuver put *Her Majesty* between the aft and forward corners of three massive dreadnaughts.

"It's okay, Captain Reynolds," Betty said with a confident smile. "As long as we don't get ourselves into a pinched span that's less than four hundred thirty yards, we should be fine."

She entered something at her console and a dynamic proximity counter displayed. The numbers made no sense to Jason. Before he could comment, she said, "Oops," and the numbers changed to yardage measurements. The readout was hovering between five hundred, and five hundred ten yards. From Jason's perspective they could be moving along at too rapid a clip—not allowing for the possibility of necessary, but unexpected, course changes. But this was Brian's bridge—his call, though it was still taking longer than he'd earlier imagined it would. He looked at the overall distance they'd need to traverse within the maze before getting close enough to phase-shift *The Lilly*. He wondered if Ricket would be able to hold off the emperor's security forces that long.

Jason hailed Ricket.

"Go for Ricket."

"What's your status?"

"Granger is working at an outer hull access panel. Normally it would allow him to open the forward starboard hatch. I'm doing my best to jam the control logic, while building an AI subroutine that will do this automatically."

Jason was amazed at Ricket's ability to multitask. Even now, he was writing code while they conversed back and forth.

"It's a temporary measure, though, Captain. Eventually, he'll access that or another hatchway into the ship. I suggest you hurry."

"Doing our best. What's the status on bringing up the *Minian*'s systems?"

"Not good. Although the AI is indeed operational, many of the various access terminals that control or even monitor ship functions have been disconnected."

"What are you telling me? She can't move under her own power?"

"Neither move nor navigate. As we discussed, phase-shifting via *The Lilly* will be our only option." Ricket then added, "I'm looking for a suitable hold location and a way to interface the power couplings between the two ships. There are problems doing that as well."

"What kind of problems?" Jason asked.

"*The Lilly* is several technological generations behind the *Minian*. I'll need to manufacture a new anti-matter power coupling."

"I'm guessing for that you'll need the *Minian*'s phase-synthesizer to be operational."

"... and that's another problem. I haven't had time to check, but it seems to be disconnected," Ricket replied.

"Then we're screwed," Jason said with resignation.

"Maybe not ... I could use the phase-synthesizer on board *The Lilly*. I'll have everything ready, but it will still take time once you phase-shift her on board."

"This is becoming a cluster fuck," Jason said, more to himself than to Ricket.

"One more thing, Captain. Both Crystal City ships have left Craing space."

Jason's attention was brought back to *Her Majesty*'s bridge—a second, even louder, alarm was sounding. The dynamic proximity counter was flashing, with the readout wavering between four hundred fifty and four hundred seventy yards. In the midst of the new course change, there were now four dreadnaughts to navigate through.

"What's the problem?" Jason asked.

Betty looked irritated, glancing at the display. "That!"

"What the hell is that?" Brian and Jason asked together.

"It's another delivery drone. But this one's bigger and it's sitting right inside our plot path."

Jason looked at Orion, who had sidled over to the tactical console. "Cap, I've got a lock on it. Give me the word and I'll make it disappear."

"Do that and you may awaken the beast," Brian said.

"Can we back off, try a different plot path?"

All eyes went to Betty as she did the calculations. "Sure," she said, tilting her head and pursing her lips. "But you'll add forty minutes to the timetable." She looked over to Brian. "What do you want to do, Captain?"

The seconds ticked by while Brian watched the display and the bulbous, beetle-shaped drone sitting several hundred yards off *Her Majesty*'s bow. Jason asked, "As far as they're concerned, we're not even here. Is there any chance they'll conclude it malfunctioned?"

"No chance in hell," Bristol said. "Plasma firing signatures are distinct. They'll know in an instant what has happened and every dreadnaught will awaken into full battle-station mode."

Jason heard Ricket talking; he'd forgotten to cut his NanoCom connection. Holding two fingers to his ear, he said, "Can you repeat that, Ricket?"

"Captain, I suggest someone board the drone and phase-shift it out into open space."

"Orion, what's that drone's mass?"

"Not much, maybe eight hundred pounds. Added to that, three hundred pounds of freight, so let's say eleven hundred pounds, give or take."

* * *

After a quick phase-shift to *The Lilly*'s armory, Jason hailed Orion. "You got those coordinates for me?"

Jason saw his HUD's instant update. "Okay, got 'em."

"Use the same coordinates in reverse for the way back ... except for the last one, which will be here, on the *Minian*. Good luck, Captain. You sure you don't want me—"

"No, Gunny, I've got this. Anyway ... seems pretty straight forward, so what can go wrong?" Jason didn't wait for an answer and phase-shifted away, using the first coordinates provided by Orion.

He reappeared, standing on the back of what looked like

a giant deer tick. Having seen them countless times as a kid growing up in San Bernardino, Jason hesitated at the uncanny resemblance.

"You need to move it along, Captain," Orion urged into his NanoCom. "Remember your life signs are no longer cloaked."

"Copy that," Jason said. Immediately he felt he was being watched—scanned by countless sensors, his life form targeted by any number of dreadnaught plasma cannons. He angled his visor to look over his shoulder, and took in the closest of the cube-shaped behemoth warships. Its sheer size was overwhelming. Everything—including himself—seemed insignificant in comparison. Jason consciously slowed his breathing—taking deep breaths.

He slid the oversized rhino-warrior phase-shift belt he'd brought along from around his shoulder and looked for a place to attach it. There were nothing but arcing, gentle curves. Looking over the side of the drone, Jason lost contact and started to float off into open space. His fingers grasped for a handhold, but everything was smooth. He held his breath as he drifted out of reach. At ten feet out, Jason phase-shifted again, only this time he changed the coordinates to reach the bottom side of the drone. Here there was a more angular surface. He pulled himself along the hull and eventually located a protruding C-shaped flange that he could place the rhino belt around. The multiple phase-shift coordinates had already been programed into it—all he had to do was press the *Activate* button on the belt's corresponding wristband display. He'd attached the rhino wristband around his thigh since it was far too large to fit around his own wrist. He took one last look around before tapping the button.

In a series of flashes, Jason experienced incremental phase-shifts along the same plot path *Her Majesty* had recently navigated. Even the larger rhino belt didn't have anywhere near the same phase-shift distance capabilities as a full-sized ship, and soon Jason felt disoriented. It was like watching rapid, stop-go film edits; he closed his eyes until he felt stable again. Sure enough, he and the tick-shaped drone were now floating somewhere in deep space—many thousands of miles from *Her Majesty*.

Technology he didn't want lying around in open space to be found by the Craing or anyone else, he replaced the large rhino belt around his shoulder. Without the added mass of the drone, Jason would use his own HUD-controlled belt for the return trip. He double-checked the coordinates and prepared himself for another sickening ride back.

He was being hailed.

"Go for Captain."

Ricket's voice sounded far away and only a few words were intelligible: "Captain ... *Minian* ... being breached ... hurry."

Chapter 21

Jason stared at the distant planet and imagined the scores of dreadnaughts surrounding her. He needed to change things up. He hailed Orion.

"Go for Gunny."

"Ricket's in trouble and we're about to lose that ship for good."

"He hailed me after you, Cap, and we're still an hour away from being close enough to phase-shift *The Lilly*. From what Ricket said, Granger's seconds from getting that hatch open."

"Let me ask you, Gunny—was there any indication my presence was detected when I was out there?"

"Not that I can see. Things still seem pretty dead as far as the dreadnaughts are concerned. Guess a single, momentary, life form in space was too inconsequential to attract much attention."

"Good. Let's hope five more of us are just as inconsequential."

"I'm not following, Cap."

"Have Billy and a small team suit up. They'll need to bring along big rhino belts for extended phase-shifts."

Orion was silent for a moment. "That's a long way to go and a whole lot of phase-shifting. I'm not real sure anyone can withstand that kind of—"

Jason cut her off: "We're out of time. Pre-program all the belts, including the rhino belt I have with me. I'll meet them on board the *Minian*, in her corridor outside the bridge. Let me know when I'm good to go."

Jason cut the connection and waited for Orion to update

the belts with the new multiple phase-shift coordinates. The belt display was refreshed and ready for him to press *Activate*. He took a deep breath, tapped the button, and closed his eyes.

* * *

Their updated belt configurations were capable of only so many phase-shifts before needing them to stop and wait for the belts to recharge several moments. Jason eventually remembered his standard battle suit belt was still around his waist, so he continued to make shorter distance phase-shifts in between recharge times. He'd already thrown up in his helmet twice and was at the point where non-stop dry heaves were ravaging his gut. Tears obscured his vision. He heard a voice in his NanoCom— someone speaking to him in an excited voice, but he was incapable of making any sense of what was said.

On the verge of blacking out, Jason tumbled into the corridor outside the *Minian*'s bridge—gravity abruptly bringing his nightmarish ride to a halt.

He unclasped his helmet, pulled it from his head, and dropped it on the deck. He inhaled fresh air and realized he wasn't alone.

Ricket stood before him, holding a piece of equipment that Jason didn't recognize. Ricket looked at Jason's messy helmet on the deck and made a face. "Captain, are you all right?"

"Don't ask. What's the situation here?"

"I take it you didn't hear my last transmission. The ship's been boarded. I've got the DeckPorts disabled but it's a temporary fix at best."

"Where's Gaddy?"

"I have her running around looking for things I'll need. She's helping me bring crucial systems back online." Ricket looked more distraught than Jason had ever seen him. "Captain, there's something else. The *Minian*'s phase-synthesizer—it's gone."

"What do you mean gone? That thing's huge ... took up a whole compartment."

"It must have been taken off-ship in large segments, then phase-shifted close by—heavy as it is."

"We have one on *The Lilly*, we can leave it."

"No. In some ways it's more important than the *Minian* herself. There's virtually nothing it cannot synthesize ... including another ship. Don't forget how we completely rebuilt the *Minian*'s bridge, not so long ago."

Jason stared down at Ricket, feeling a bad situation was getting worse—much worse.

There was a flash and Billy appeared sixty feet down the corridor. "Best we get out of the way, Ricket. There's a few more coming," Jason said, and he and Ricket stepped back in the direction of the bridge as two more of the team arrived.

Rizzo looked annoyed and a pale shade of green. "Thanks for the heads up this was going to be a puke-ride, Billy."

Three more team members showed up simultaneously. With the exception of Billy's, all visors were clouded with vomit. Their helmets came off, followed by gasps for fresh air. Jason was surprised to see Dira among the arrivals, as well as two of the new Delta Force guys.

Dira joined Jason and Ricket. "I know you didn't ask for me to be here. But the sooner we complete this mission, the sooner I can get home. I'm also looking for a little payback."

Ricket took Dira's helmet from her, reached inside, and within several seconds the visor started to clear. "Instigated a nanite cleanse." He handed it back to her and then did the same thing to Jason's helmet.

Jason looked inside his helmet and nodded. "Handy feature.

Looks like you have a few more who need their helmets tidied up." He put his helmet back on and assessed the moving groups of life-icons on the deck three levels below their own.

"I'm counting at least fifty Craing down there," Jason said. Adjusting to a wider perimeter setting, he saw too many life-icons to count moving in from other areas of the platform. "Our presence has been discovered," Jason informed the team. "Dira, I want you to stay here and help Ricket and Gaddy. Whatever they need; it's imperative we get this ship operational."

He noticed she was less than thrilled about staying behind, but she didn't say anything.

"Billy, we need to clear Deck 4—give Ricket more time to work. We'll pair up and utilize our biggest advantage: our ability to phase-shift."

Jason brought his attention back to his teammates. He noticed the SEALs and Delta Force guys remained separated, each keeping to his own group. He caught Billy's eye and opened a channel: "Is this going to be a problem?"

"I figured it best to let them work it out on their own. Some things you just can't force."

Jason pointed to someone on the Delta Force team: "What's your name, Sergeant?"

"Jackson. Toby Jackson." He was black, muscular, and over six and a half feet tall. He grinned, revealing a gold front tooth.

"You're with me. Hold on."

Jason hailed Orion.

"Go for Gunny."

"How's your progress?"

"Better than expected. Betty's been able to increase speed through the straight-aways. ETA's still thirty minutes out."

"That'll have to do. I want you to query *The Lilly*'s AI for 'Ion station.' The *Minian*'s phase-synthesizer has been removed.

There's a good chance it's here, on the space platform above Terplin. Platform's as big as a city. Try querying space traffic and planet networks. I'll need any specs you can dig up that will shed some light on where they'd most likely keep the thing."

"I'm on it, Cap."

"Captain, Gaddy's overdue and there's no way to hail her. My nano-devices are picking up a bio-signature from her. Most likely she's in the area around Medical. Would you mind checking on her?" Ricket said, looking concerned.

"No problem, you're sure she didn't leave this deck?"

"Not possible. DeckPorts are offline."

"Okay, we'll find her, I promise. In the meantime, utilize Dira's help."

Another hail was coming in. "Go ahead, Gunny."

"Not much info available on the platform. I've uploaded two items to your HUD. The first is a schematic ... more like a general layout ... sorry it's not very detailed. The second item is more interesting. It's a bill of lading form intercepted from a Craing freighter several months back. Typically, equipment is brought into any one of a dozen port stations on the planet. But this form specifically designated the space platform as the port of delivery."

"So how does that help me?"

"The equipment is primarily geared toward power generation. Like fusion generators. Perhaps the type of equipment one would need to power a ginormous phase-synthesizer? Now if you look back at the first diagram, you'll see there's really only one compartment on the platform that one, has the necessary space required, and two, has a number of sufficiently-rated power conduits."

Jason looked at the schematic and saw where Gunny had highlighted an area toward the center of the platform. "Good job, Gunny. Go ahead and send this on to the rest of the team."

"Aye, Cap."

Jason continued to look at the diagram. The platform really was a city unto itself. Easily ten miles in circumference, it had multiple landing pads as well as eight different hub ports—one presently in use by the *Minian*. The majority of the facility was environmentally sealed off from outer space, an enclosed habitat. Basically rectangular in shape, each corner had a revolving turret with a mounted plasma cannon. There were also barrack-like structures that could accommodate hundreds, if not a few thousands of security personnel.

All the crew had paired up—Billy, paired with the remaining Delta Force soldier, had his virtual notepad out, and a 3D holo-display of Deck 4 hovered several feet in front of him. Within three minutes, Jason and Billy laid out cover positions and a basic plan of attack to clear the Craing insurgents from Deck 4. Something caught Jason's attention from within the bridge. Now his attention wandered as he watched Dira helping Ricket jostle one of the open consoles closed, then she scurried off out of sight. That's all it took—right then and there, Jason had come to a decision. It was time to tell this amazing violet-skinned woman from Jhardon how he felt—how he was so over-the-top—

He caught himself mid-thought. Dira was standing at the entrance to the bridge, staring back at him as if reading his mind. He heard her lightly accented voice over his NanoCom: "Don't you have some Craing to kill, or something?"

Jason didn't answer, somewhat embarrassed he'd been caught staring—especially in light of what was needed of him now. He shrugged and smiled.

Billy finished talking and closed down his holo-display.

"Let's do this," Jason said, and one by one, the paired teams phase-shifted to their designated positions, three decks below.

Chapter 22

Ot-Mul listened to the distant whirling sound coming off the ship's two drive propulsion units—it relaxed him and helped him to think. He was finding it hard to comprehend what had just occurred.

They were back within the protection of the Sector 6300 Craing fleet, and the fifteen hundred warships it comprised. He thought back to his last hour's conversation with his Eminence. Even the acting emperor had referred to his six black dreadnaught warships as the *death squad*. A reference he'd heard before, but not by anyone he had actually spoken to face to face. He couldn't deny the name was aptly appropriate; the total grand number of lives lost to his Vanguard fleet was quickly approaching five hundred billion. If there had ever been a more successful arbiter of death than he and his death squad, he was not aware of them. But what Lom was proposing, not only to him but also thousands of fleet commanders, was beyond his own hardened sensibilities. He replayed the interstellar comms conversation in his mind one more time:

The acting emperor was dressed in his typical green robes and tall headdress. "Emperor Lom, you grace us with your presence." Ot-Mul bowed his head toward the display before him.

"It is I who am honored, Commodore. What you have accomplished throughout multiple sectors is nothing short of spectacular."

Again, Ot-Mul bowed, showing proper humility and respect to the one who would shortly become the Craing Empire's

137

final supreme leader. Soon, he'd complete the *transformation of eternity*, supposedly a process that had been perfected, and would allow the Craing leader to live well beyond earlier mortal restraints of mere hundreds of years, in a less than perfect cybernetic body. Soon, he would return to his physical youth and rule, unencumbered, virtually until the end of time itself ... at least that was the latest gossip among fleet personnel. Ot-Mul was not sure how he felt about such a contrivance. Although he'd never spoken of such things out loud, Ot-Mul had higher aspirations for himself—why should becoming the Craing Empire's supreme emperor be out of reach for himself?

"Commodore Ot-Mul, welcome back to Sector One. Let's not waste any more time with pleasantries. By now, I'm assuming you've had time to review my directives. The *Great Space* will set Sector One apart from other sectors within the universe. It will set the example of Craing dominance and safeguard the Craing worlds for millennia to come."

Ot-Mul had indeed reviewed the top-secret directives. The *Great Space* was a profound and staggering undertaking. With the exception of the seven Craing worlds, there would be systematic removal of all other celestial bodies within the sector. Problematic neighboring star systems, such as the Allied worlds and numerous others becoming more and more rebellious, would simply cease to exist. The *Great Space* would be an exemplification, a monument, for all to witness across the universe: a no man's land that guaranteed safety and isolation of the Craing Empire, once and for all. Only through wormhole travel would one have access to Craing space. Those civilizations across the universe which had the same capability were even now being systematically destroyed. Acting-Emperor Lom, beyond doubt, was procuring a universe for himself that best supported his *transformation of eternity* and his everlasting rule.

"You have been chosen, Ot-Mul. Wear your new uniform with pride. Display your medals upon your chest. As the emperor's Chief Military Commander now ... all empire fleets report directly to you. With the exception of myself, and the High Priest Overlords, no one will hold greater influence or power within the universe. As we speak, Craing fleets have been recalled to Sector One. Your Vanguard fleet of six dreadnaughts will become the model for hundreds if not thousands just like it. Your efforts moving forward, Ot-Mul, are key to implementing my vision ... the *Great Space*."

Ot-Mul returned to the here and now and let the distant whirling sounds bring balance back to his disrupted consciousness. He surveyed his bridge crew. They, too, were aware of what lay ahead as they unleashed a wrath of death and destruction that would guarantee, for each and every one of them, a very special place in Hell for all eternity. *So be it.*

"Chief Commander, we approach the worlds of Mangus and Trumach," Helm Master Phom said. "Shall we alter course around them?"

Ot-Mul didn't answer. He knew the acting emperor wanted to scale back small altercations ... at least until the fleets converged at one of their two designated deployment zones— an area within the star system of Orion's Belt, and another at the Craing worlds. Only then would they conduct a systematic, coordinated, outward attack. An attack he would command.

"How much time would that cost us?"

"No more than three hours, Chief Commander."

Ot-Mul let the makings of another rare smile pull at his lips. He had been appointed Chief Commander for all Craing Empire fleets. This was to be his first command, holding this most prestigious position. "No. Three hours is three hours too many, Helm Master. Signal the rest of the fleet. The Vanguard

Death Squad will be making a short detour."

* * *

Ot-Mul leaned back in his seat and was surprised at his own feelings of exhilaration after so many years, so many annihilated worlds ... soon he would take his rightful place in history as the greatest Craing military leader of all time. A leader that understood power. He was the arbiter of death across the universe. Now, he would be the true unifying force across space. Eventually acting-Emperor Lom, too, would be brought to his knees. First, Ot-Mul would need to do something none of his recent predecessors had been able to accomplish. Something spectacular. He'd bring down the rebel Allied forces in one fell swoop. Again, Ot Mul smiled to himself. No. He would not be taking his Vanguard *death squad* directly to the rally point on the Orion's arm, as ordered. First he would slice the head from the snake ... Destruction of Earth and Allied fleet command was imperative. By doing so, he alone would claim responsibility for bringing down the Alliance.

"Sir, we've entered Trumach space."

It had been a long time since Ot-Mul had seen not one, but two planets possessing their kind of beauty. The closer of the two, with her emerald green continents, surrounded by bright, azure-blue seas, was marginally superior to the other one, a perfect landscape, yet completely void of technology. Two virgin worlds—unspoiled—and for all intents and purposes, neither was a threat to them. But the primitive beasts inhabiting these worlds were warriors of unmatched strength and courage. Reports of great rhino-beasts fighting alongside Allied combatants within this sector were becoming the origins for future great fables, or historic lore ... No ... best to quell that nonsense right now.

"Helm Master, bring us into a high-orbit formation around Mangus."

"Yes, Commander."

The bridge became quiet—perhaps more quiet than usual. Ot-Mul prided himself on being an approachable leader. Not overly dictatorial. He knew each of the Craing officers—their family dynamics, their personal aspirations. All of them, with their similar black tufts of hair and rutty complexions, had a brotherly connection. Maybe, though, they were more than that, Ot-Mul thought, for the atmosphere within their confined space had taken on a more rigid, in fact, a downright somber, mood. Due, perhaps, to their knowledge that neither of these worlds showed any semblance of posing some military offensive against them? Even Jhardon had had a fortified space station.

Having a conscience could prove to be an enemy, all unto itself. With the inevitability of what lay ahead—the systematic destruction of millions of similar worlds such as these—there would be nil room for sentiment. No, best they get used to it, here and now.

The tactical officer, Gi-Mul, a distant cousin to Ot-Mul, turned in his seat and said: "Sir, we're in position, and all six Vanguard vessels are charging weapons. There is much water content here. Atmosphere has high refractive characteristics. As you know, we have not had particularly good success—"

Ot-Mul interrupted the tactical officer. "We target the land formations first. We will make an example of the rhino-warrior beasts. We will pound their world over and over and over, until the seas boil and turn to steam. We will pound their world, until the land melts into red-hot rivers of lava. Fire at will, Tactical Officer Gi-Mul."

The sound of the plasma energy generators was akin to an engine revving up; a progressive, high-speed pitch; a whining sound that everyone on board the Vanguard vessel registered, through a tightening of shoulder muscles and a clenching of teeth. The eventual climatic expulsion of energy shuddered the vessel. The sound, although dampened by any number of technological devices, was still noisome enough to make everyone flinch.

Ot-Mul was disappointed with the first wave of plasma fire. The first of the two worlds was not destroyed—not completely. With his eyes focused on the bridge display, he ordered the tactical officer to recharge the weapons. It took three additional, concentrated plasma strikes to dematerialize the world's mass into cloudy, multi-colored dust.

The sudden lack of sound within the command ship's bridge was deafening. None had dared let out his breath.

"See. Not so impossible. Helm Master, bring us into high-orbit around Trumach. Tactical Officer Gi-Mul, prepare to charge weapons."

* * *

Many light-years away, within an arid, desert-like landscape known as HAB 17, three rhino-warriors abruptly stopped what they were doing. Few Words, First Reflection, and their leader, Traveler, were all paralyzed with a most horrific realization ... their home world, Trumach, was no more.

Chapter 23

Jason and Sergeant Jackson phase-shifted onto Deck 4, directly into an equipment storage compartment, midway down the deck's primary corridor. Similar to those on *The Lilly*, hatchways were virtual, and they could either materialize or dematerialize—an option that was AI controlled. Like the rest of the ship, the function was now offline and all hatchways were left wide open.

Noises were coming from the forward area of the ship and Jason chanced a quick glance down the corridor. Eight security personnel wearing green battle suits were casually standing around; several were leaning their backs against a bulkhead. Definitely not on alert, they seemed unaware the *Minian* had been boarded by Jason and his team. Granger was at the center of their grouping—crouching down in front of a recessed command panel. He knew similar panels were located on every deck. Granger was probably attempting to access the AI; perhaps modify parameters that would allow them access to the DeckPorts. He'd already bypassed the many restrictions placed on the exterior hull access, so it was conceivable he'd be able to do the same here.

Jason opened a channel to the assault team. "Go! Take the deck."

Jackson moved past Jason and took up a crouched, defensive position, with his multi-gun sighted on the still unaware eight Craing security forces idling down the corridor. Jason moved past him, keeping close to the opposite bulkhead. The two guards, whose backs leaned against the wall, noticed Jason and began to react—bringing up their pulse weapons. It was too little too late, and they were shot in the chest, both falling down onto the deck. Jackson fired six bursts and took out the rest of the Craing from his crouched position. That left a startled-looking Granger, the only survivor, to hold up his hands as he slowly stood up.

In the distance, Jason heard more plasma fire, coming from ahead and from behind. One by one, combatant life-icons disappeared from his HUD. As Jason closed in on Granger, the tall Caldurian's expression turned from one of concern to one of recognition and then to relief.

"Captain Reynolds. I had a feeling you'd be showing up right about now."

"I should burn a hole in your skull ... right about now."

"Do what you have to do, Captain."

Jason stood less than a foot from the Caldurian, his eyes holding steady on Granger's.

"We trusted you ... I trusted you, Granger."

Jason looked for some sign of regret, or self-reproach, and for a fleeting moment thought he saw them on the Caldurian's face.

"Do you know the repercussions you caused by altering Earth's time realms? How many lives were lost?"

"Lives were never meant to be lost. If anything, it was a way to save lives. By interfering with those drones before they'd completed their task, it was you who, inadvertently perhaps, caused the loss of life. Yes, Earth would have been sent, technologically, into an earlier time era, but it was temporary. Easily reversible. With the capabilities of the *Minian*, I could have just as easily destroyed your planet. And isn't your wife alive now, or is that not important to you?"

Jason swung the butt of his multi-gun into Granger's solar plexus, forcing him to double over and gasp for air. He reached out and grabbed Granger's throat and tightened his grip. Bringing him up onto his tiptoes, he pushed him against the bulkhead. Jason's mind replayed the devastating events occurring over the previous month caused by this deceptive alien shit, and he continued to squeeze. As life started to fade from Granger's wide, terrified, eyes—Jason released his grip and let him fall to the deck.

It was several minutes before Granger could talk. The assault team, having secured the deck, stood alongside Jason, staring down at Granger.

Unsteadily, Granger got back to his feet. He rubbed at his throat and swallowed with a wince. "I suppose I had that coming."

"No, I should have killed you. That's what I should have done," said Jason.

"Captain, I made the mistake of trusting the Craing. Understand, my intentions were quite honorable in the beginning. The technology I've given you is beyond anything your society would have advanced to in a thousand years. But in the end, the Craing had far more to offer. The Allied worlds, including Earth, were to be ours: a new home for wayward Caldurians, such as myself."

"Planets for you to rule over? To subjugate? Hell, you're no different from the Craing."

Billy, who'd lit up a stogy sometime in the last few moments, moved closer to Granger—their faces inches apart. "I would have killed you. I want you to know that. I would have ripped your fucking head off your shoulders and shoved it up your freaky alien ass." Billy stayed put, and let the smoke from his cigar rise and cloud around their faces. "Someday, I'm going to make that happen, and that's a promise from me to you."

Granger returned his stare as Billy stepped back. "Captain," he said, "I'm afraid you have far worse problems than me."

Jason waited for him to continue.

"Lom, soon to be elevated to full-fledged Emperor of the Craing Empire, and who already commands fleets of warships extending to the far reaches of the universe ... is fearful. You, your actions over the past year, have greatly contributed to that. I speculate he dwells on them to the point of distraction. He's infatuated with the prospect of his own immortality. His impending *transformation of eternity* is only effective if he keeps safe, here in Craing space."

"Is there a point to all this or are you going to ramble on indefinitely?" Jason asked him, looking bored.

"It's why the Caldurians fled in their Crystal City ships. It's why, after uncovering their plan, I ceased providing any meaningful, technical assistance to them. Captain, you've seen it yourself—the massive accumulation of Craing forces. It's all part of Lom's secret plan, the *Great Space*."

"The *Great Space*? I don't get it ... what does that even mean?"

"It means that Lom no longer wants to control and subjugate the planets in this sector, the sector where the Craing worlds reside. No, he wants to empty it—completely clear the sector of anything and everything. Every star system within hundreds of light-years of where he resides will no longer exist. Captain, it's already begun."

"And you gave him not only the *Minian*, but the phase-synthesizer as well. Perfect. All he'll need to make this *Great Space* bullshit of his come about that much quicker."

"I knew the Craing, Lom, was ruthless. I didn't know his insane plan. I wouldn't have ..."

"Well, it's too late now for woulda-coulda-shouldas. The question is: What can you do to help?"

"Take a look around, Captain. Hundreds of dreadnaughts, spread out thousands of miles, surround this planet, this ship.

The only vessel that could possibly prevail against them is the *Minian,* and she's half torn apart."

"Where's the phase-synthesizer?" Jason asked.

"It's here, on the platform. But it's protected."

"How?"

"Battle droids, Caldurian designed; one is unbeatable, five's overkill."

"So there are five battle droids patrolling the platform. There has to be a way to bring them down. You're Caldurian ... you can help us figure it out."

Granger nodded but didn't look overly confident. "One question, Captain. How did you get here? How did you get past the dreadnaughts, without alerting the Craing?"

Chapter 24

Granger would stay alive as long as he continued to be of use. After that, Jason assured him, Billy would be happy to rearrange his body parts. So far, Granger was doing everything asked of him, and more. He'd resealed the forward outside hatch and was now being led to the bridge to help Ricket.

Jason remembered he'd promised to check on Gaddy and phase-shifted to the corridor outside Medical. Even before entering, he knew something was wrong. Gaddy was yelling:

"Get out of my way!"

"Get out of my way!"

"Get out of my way!"

"Get out of my way!"

"Stop repeating what I say!"

"Stop repeating what I say!"

"Stop repeating what I say!"

"Stop repeating what I say!"

To Jason's utter surprise there were four Gaddys, all identical to one another. They looked the same, with identical clothing, and they sounded the same. Positioned around the forward Medical compartment, they turned their four faces toward him as he entered the room.

It was easy to see which one was the real Gaddy. She was the first to say or do anything. The other three Gaddys lagged a second or two behind her.

"Shoot these fucking things!"

"Shoot these fucking things!"

"Shoot these fucking things!"
"Shoot these fucking things!"

Jason couldn't help but laugh out loud. For some reason, perhaps due to the stress of the last few days, he lost it. Now laughing uncontrollably, Jason had to hold on to the closest MediPod while he regained his breath. Gaddy, followed by the other three Gaddys, stood with her arms crossed over her chest and her head tilted to one side. Straight faced, she saw nothing funny about the situation, and that made him laugh all over again. She started tapping a foot and soon there was a chorus of foot tappings.

Jason raised his multi-gun and pointed it at the closest of the impostors. "Okay, fun's over. Why don't you get back into your enclosures?"

All three smiled and hurried off toward the back of the compartment. One by one, they morphed back into their original forms. Octopus-like, with multiple arms, having hundreds of suction cups, they jittered up the sides of three glass enclosures and dropped into the clear liquid within.

"How did you do that? I've been standing here for an hour trying to get through to them," Gaddy asked incredulously.

"I've had contact with those little devils before. I think they're harmless."

Gaddy was already striding out of Medical. "Well, I'm glad you found this all so funny."

Jason was being hailed.

"Go for Captain ... what's your status, Gunny?"

"We're three thousand feet off your port."

"Any problems?"

"Quite a few close calls. Came within eight feet of a dreadnaught. All in all, Betty did a great job navigating us through that maze of ships."

"Good to hear it. Have *Her Majesty* sit tight, right where she is. I need you over here. Seems we have another—unplanned—mission that will require your expertise."

"I'm on my way, Cap."

* * *

The alarms sounded as Jason entered the bridge. Their presence was no longer a secret. "Well, it was only a matter of time," Jason said. "I suppose fifty of the emperor's security forces gone missing would be anything but subtle."

Gaddy, standing next to Ricket, still looked perturbed.

Jason noticed things were looking better—more like an actual bridge, with several consoles now seeming operational. Similar to *The Lilly,* the overhead three hundred and sixty degree display was presenting them with a magnificent view of space beyond the ship. One by one, the encircling dreadnaughts were coming alive—thousands of small lights winking on in a matter of seconds.

"Oh good, Captain, you're back." Ricket looked up at Jason. "I'd like to jump back to *The Lilly* to get several components manufactured on 4B. Granger has offered to help. It would save us some time."

"Granger doesn't go anywhere without an armed guard in tow." Jason nodded toward Sergeant Jackson, who was standing off by himself. "Sergeant, don't let him out of your sight. If he tries anything, shoot him in the head."

Granger made an unpleasant expression, but kept his mouth shut. Ricket put a hand on Granger's wrist, as well as one on Jackson's: "I've got this." In a flash, the three were gone.

"Captain," Orion said from the far side of the bridge, while Billy and Petty Officer Woodrow were huddled in front of a console. "Granger's provided us with the specs on the battle droids. I've never seen anything like this. Hold on."

She transferred the spec sheet, with a detailed vid-image, to a segment on the main display above. Everyone stopped what they were doing and stared at the menacing-looking battle droid. What caught Jason's attention first was the highly reflective nature of the thing. Every aspect of the droid was like a mirror reflecting itself.

"That's about its actual size, Cap," Orion said.

It was no taller than the average man but much wider, with four squatty-looking legs, a barrel-like torso, four arms, and a circular turret of a head. Every surface was covered with thin, razor-sharp plates that constantly moved, not unlike old-fashioned push-mower blades.

"So what makes this thing so hard to kill?"

"For one thing, Cap, it utilizes the *Minian*'s same phase-shift tech. Individual sections, as well as the whole construct, can phase-shift into the multiverse and back at will. Fire a plasma bolt, or a micro-missile, or throw a rock at it, and it will phase-shift away. It possesses a wide array of offensive weaponry. Try to touch it, anywhere, and you'll be sliced into bits with those constantly moving mower blades. It has three small integrated plasma cannons on the torso and the equivalent of a turret-mounted rail gun ... it's right there, that thing that looks like its head. Oh, and this battle droid is completely autonomous, with its own highly advanced AI."

Jason looked back at Orion blank faced.

"It's beyond badass, Cap. Did I mention there are five of them?"

"Yes, I think so. Work with Ricket and Granger. I want a course of action for defeating those things within the hour."

"Cap, there's just no—"

"Within the hour, Gunny."

Jason held up a hand to Gunny; he was being hailed.

"Go for Captain."

It was McBride on *The Lilly*. "Captain, it's the admiral. You're needed over here—something's happened to the rhino-worlds."

* * *

Jason told McBride to transfer the connection to his ready room. Sitting at the conference table, Jason hardly recognized his father's face on the display. His eyes were red-rimmed and he hadn't shaved in several days.

"They're both gone, Jason. The rhino-worlds."

Jason stared at the screen and let that sink in. "You're saying Mangus and Trumach have been attacked?"

"They've been fucking annihilated! Don't you understand English? We're talking space dust."

"What happened?"

"The same thing that happened to the other five planets and almost to Jhardon. A fleet of six huge black vessels, believed to be dreadnaughts. They move into some kind of formation around a planet and pound it and pound it and pound it until it disappears."

Jason closed his eyes and nodded his head.

"You knew about this?"

"Not the specifics. Not that it was the rhino-worlds. But yeah, I know what's happening."

"Do tell."

"It's something the Craing call the *Great Space* ... I heard that it had already begun, at least to some degree."

Jason proceeded to bring his father up to speed on what had occurred over the past twenty-four hours. By the time he'd relayed the news regarding the *Minian*'s deconstructed condition and the battle droids protecting the phase-synthesizer, the admiral looked downright suicidal.

"It's all falling apart, Jason. The Alliance is a joke. We've lost more than half our fleet, and now you're telling me the Craing are going to create an empty space-like mote around their worlds that will destroy Earth, along with all the Allied planets."

"We'll think of something," Jason said.

The admiral inhaled and almost smiled.

Jason changed the subject. "Tell me, have you heard anything from Nan?"

The admiral brightened. "In fact I have. She's the one bright spot in all this ... taken her post to a level none of us expected. She's the conduit for the masses, Jason. Earth is no longer kept in the dark regarding events happening in space. She's downright beloved—approval ratings beyond any president's, living or dead. Son, Earth stands behind what we're doing. Enrollment into the military is off the charts."

"That's wonderful, Dad. I always knew Nan was destined for great things."

"She told me to remind you that she needs to talk to you. It's something important."

"I will. Just as soon as things aren't so crazy."

Chapter 25

After cutting the connection with the admiral, Jason decided he needed a shave, and he definitely needed a shower. He had a feeling there wouldn't be many such opportunities in the coming days. There was only so much time before the emperor's security forces would figure a way to breach the *Minian*'s hull. He removed his battle suit and padded his way into the head where he got the water going. As soon as he stepped beneath the steaming hot spray, he felt the tension in his shoulders start to relax. Jason willed his rambling thoughts to cease—his brain to shut down, even for the few minutes he stood beneath the shower's heat; he'd needed this short respite.

By the time Jason returned to his ready room, he saw a video message from Mollie. He sat back and pressed *play*.

Mollie was smiling, looking cute with a mouthful of braces, and her hair pulled into two lopsided ponytails at the top of her head. "Hi, Dad. Mom said she didn't know when you were coming home. I miss you. Mom's always busy lately, doing her new job for the president. She's on TV a lot." Jason saw her smile fading away and she began to look melancholy. "I wish I'd stayed on *The Lilly* with you, Dad. I'm going to school in Washington, D.C., and I hate it. Anyway ... I'm looking forward to seeing Boomer. And Raja, and Alice, and Dira, and everyone. Mostly you, though. Come back soon, okay?" The video ended and froze with Mollie looking into the camera, wearing the same scolding expression her mother had also exhibited countless times in the past. He continued to look at his little girl and wondered if he'd ever see her again. Would Earth soon fall to the Craing as so many other worlds had of late?

* * *

Jason left his cabin and walked *The Lilly*'s corridors, moving from one department to the next. He stopped and talked to the crewmembers—listened to them, querying about their issues and fears ... big and small. Being seen among them, one of them again, Jason was doing more than building ship morale—he was letting them know he hadn't given up. Enemies had underestimated *The Lilly* and her crew before—a mistake that often led to their own demise.

By the time Jason made it to Engineering, he was feeling better about things. Truth was, nothing had really changed. The Craing were amassing a contingent of ships beyond comprehension— worlds were being extinguished in the Craing's *Great Space* pursuit. But, surprisingly, there was evident hope here, among the crew of *The Lilly*. They certainly hadn't given up—and there was the expectation that their captain would lead them to victory, as he'd done so many times before.

Engineering was quiet. Chief Horris sat at his desk, feet propped up, reading a paperback

book. Startled, he nearly fell backward off his chair when Jason entered his small office. "Captain ..."

"Don't get up, Chief. Enjoy some free time while you still have it. Soon enough, *The Lilly* will be back in open space."

"Aye, Captain. Truth is, I'm going a bit stir crazy with so much down time."

"You know ... last I heard the *Minian*'s propulsion system was still offline. Maybe you can help Ricket. I'm guessing he's a bit overwhelmed."

Chief Horris jumped to his feet, moving fast for a man of

his robust size. "Aye, Captain. You know, the *Minian*'s antimatter drives are not so different from *The Lilly*'s. If Ricket's having a problem getting them initialized, I could probably give him a few pointers."

"Well, then, I think it best you head over there, first thing."

Jason watched Chief Horris scurry about Engineering, grabbing several portable test equipment devices before heading out of the department—presumably to get himself fitted with a phase-shift belt.

Jason had one more stop to make. Entering HAB 17, Jason was accosted by sudden darkness. As his eyes adjusted, nighttime stars, and two distant quarter moons, helped illuminate his long walk toward the rhino-warrior camp. Several miles in, off in the distance, a campfire blazed—a flittering amber glow danced upon nearby domes.

Three rhino-warriors sat upon wide tree stumps, each seemingly immersed in his own thoughts. As Jason took a seat in front of the fire, he assumed Traveler had watched his movements into the camp. He could see that the dire news he'd come to deliver was unnecessary. They already knew.

The fire crackled and popped. *What does one say at a time like this?* Finally, Jason said, "I'm very sorry."

The three rhinos pulled their eyes away from the fire and leveled their gaze upon Jason.

Traveler shifted his weight and let out a labored breath. "Our time—the time of the rhino-warrior—has come to an end. The three of us are but a fading echo ... a distant call into the wind. Soon ... no one will be left to remember our once proud and honorable race."

"Many will remember you. I will remember you. You are, and always will be, true friends ... but I want you to know that you won't be bothered here again. You have my word on that. There's

156

nothing more you need to give, now that everything has been taken from you. Hunt the local game, fish ... live out your lives in this place you've come to call home."

Jason met Traveler's steady stare. Tears flowed freely from his small dark eyes. As Jason prepared to leave and let his friends mourn in peace, he noticed the three rhinos were dressed for battle. Their plasma weapons and heavy hammers lay on the ground, close to their feet. Traveler, Few Words, and First Reflection stood up and secured their weapons, attaching their heavy hammers to leather thongs at their sides. One by one they approached the campfire and pulled burning timbers from the blaze. Unsure what was happening, Jason watched as the three warriors hurried off toward the domed structures surrounding the campsite. Traveler was the first to reach the largest of the domes. He stopped and looked to the heavens as if praying, or perhaps making a promise. Then, without further hesitation, he held the burning timber beneath the dome's wood frame. In seconds the structure was burning—soon, fully engulfed in fire. The three moved with purpose from one dome to another, until all the domes were on fire.

They returned to Jason at the campfire. "We are not deserving of a home. No, we will not hunt and fish here. The honor of our people fully resides within the three of us. Only us."

"What do you want to do?" Jason asked, getting to his feet.

To Jason's surprise, the three rhino-warriors looked happy and were smiling. Traveler spoke for all of them: "To avenge their deaths and die in battle with honor. We will fight at your side, Captain Reynolds. We won't stop until the Craing are beaten down by our heavy hammers and we, too, join our brethren in the great beyond."

Chapter 26

Dressed again in his battle suit, Jason phase-shifted back to the *Minian*. As soon as he entered the bridge, Dira looked up. "You took a shower. That's not fair!" She was sitting at a console next to Bristol, who must have phase-shifted over from *Her Majesty*.

"Status?" Jason asked, already noting there was substantial progress.

Ricket emerged from beneath a console. "Good! Progress is good, Captain. DeckPorts are online."

Jason walked over to where Ricket was working and picked up a metallic device about the size of a toaster.

Ricket took it from him, and put it back on the console. "We manufactured this power-interface coupling back on 4B. Once connected, it should provide *The Lilly* with enough power to phase-shift the two ships together into deep space."

"Well, don't let me hold your progress up," Jason said, looking around the bridge for Orion.

"She's in the armory, Captain," Dira said.

Jason tried to remember if he had ever been in the *Minian*'s armory.

"I'll show you the way." Dira stood up and looked relieved to get off the bridge. She grabbed a battle suit helmet and headed for the exit.

"That one's mine," Bristol said irritably.

Dira stopped and took a closer look at the helmet. "Oh, you're right." She tossed the helmet back to him and grabbed her own.

Together, they left the bridge and headed toward the closest DeckPort.

"How you holding up?" Jason asked.

"Anxious to get home. Annoyed that I can't be there. Basically, I'm staying busy to keep my mind off things. I guess my biggest worry is I'll never make it back before ..." She couldn't finish her sentence.

Jason stopped and guided her into an open compartment off the main corridor. He pulled her in close. He looked into her eyes and spoke softly. "Not only will we get through this, I'll come home with you. I want to help out any way I can."

She shook her head. "I don't know, Jason. Be realistic. You've got your own family to worry about ... Mollie, Boomer, even Nan. We both know it's only a matter of time before Earth is in just as much danger."

He kissed her. He didn't want to talk about the perils of their two worlds right now, or anything else for that matter.

She pushed him away with a hand on his chest. "What are you doing, Jason? Why now?"

"You really don't know?"

She stared up at him with those amazing *Jhardanian* eyes, with their flecks of violet and amber. She looked down—her long lashes fluttered—then back into his eyes as if searching for something.

The words were out before he realized he'd said them. "I love you, Dira."

She continued to look into his eyes, not saying anything. She placed her hands on his face and, ever so gently, pulled him forward. She kissed him—the most tender, gentlest of kisses. She continued to hold his face close to hers, her lips touching his. "You know ... I've always been yours, Jason ... I think I always will be. I so so love you, too."

With eyes locked on each other, they kissed again, and again, and again. Gentleness gave way to passion and soon their hunger took them past caring about anything but having each other ... being one with each other. Together, they slid down the bulkhead to the floor. Their battle suits came off with surprising ease and they held each other close, experiencing each other's complete nakedness for the first time. Jason had never wanted anything as much as he wanted her—right now. Passion turned to quiet, slow intimacy. She guided his hands, his fingers, to explore her body ... its physiology wasn't exactly human—in some ways, the same; in other ways, quite different. He took in the sight of her smooth, violet skin and it stirred him. She was the most beautiful being he had ever seen, or could ever imagine. She watched his face—his every expression—with a bemused smile on her lips.

Dira put two fingers on Jason's lips and whispered into his ear, "I want it to be special. If you can wait, let me give myself to you at the right time."

Jason smiled and brushed the hair away from her forehead. "Of course, I'll wait. I'd wait a lifetime for you." She kissed him again and pulled him close one more time.

Eventually they parted. They helped each other into their battle suits and made their way back to the main corridor. To Jason's surprise, Gaddy emerged from a nearby DeckPort just as they exited the open compartment.

"Seriously? Again?" Gaddy said, shaking her head.

Both Jason and Dira looked puzzled, as if they didn't know what she was talking about.

"Whatever. Orion's looking for you ... in the armory." Gaddy headed off toward the bridge.

* * *

The *Minian*'s armory was larger and more akin to a technical lab setup than the armory on *The Lilly*. Orion was seated on a tall stool and leaning over a counter. No less than six three-dimensional holo-displays were active, hovering in front of her. "There you are. Was wondering if we needed to send out a search party." Orion wore a condescending smile she made little attempt to hide. It was clear to Jason she knew exactly where they'd been. Gunny's eyes shifted back and forth between the two and then refocused on the hovering displays. He was glad she didn't say anything further on the subject. But he wondered how she knew and how many others knew?

"What do you have for me, Gunny?"

Jason and Dira joined her on either side and looked at what she was working on. It was obviously a battle suit—actually, multiple iterations of the same suit.

"Captain, while you were ... busy, I started to think how I was going to come up with a means to destroy those battle droids. Nothing I came up with would do the trick. Perhaps with one exception—just nuking the whole platform. Unfortunately, the phase-synthesizer would be destroyed along with it."

"So tell me about this battle suit. You're thinking it can stand up to one of those things?"

"Yes and no. Ricket was here a while ago and showed me some interesting add-ons. For one thing, these suits have the same capability to phase-shift into the multiverse that the battle droids have. It's so fast—instantaneous—that the user wouldn't even notice."

"What does that mean when going up against the droids?"

"It means they can fire plasma bolts, or even rail-gun munitions at you all day—but you, your physical self, wouldn't be around to take the hits."

"I like that," Jason said.

"Yes, I do, too. The only problem is, the droids have the exact same capability. That's sort of where I'm at with all this."

Dira pursed her lips and looked as if she wanted to say something.

"What is it?' Jason asked. "Don't be shy."

"I'm not tech-savvy about such things but, well, I was wondering where do the droids actually go? You know, in those flashes when they jump back and forth into the multiverse?"

Orion shook her head. "The multiverse is endless—an infinite realm of possibilities."

"But that doesn't necessarily mean the droids are shifting to an arbitrary place," Jason said. "We already know the Caldurians have the ability to move back and forth to specific locations within the multiverse. And they don't, typically, leave things to chance. Why, then, wouldn't the instant, projected, multiverse location the droids go to, be a real, specific location also?"

"I suppose they do, but why would that matter—" She cut herself short. "I think I know where you're going with this. If we can't destroy them here, on this plane of existence, perhaps we can do so on another."

"Yes," Jason said excitedly. "Here, we have more to worry about than just the battle droids. We're trying to keep ourselves alive, and not destroy the phase-synthesizer in the process. That whole ... nuking ... plan to eliminate the damn things might be a possibility after all."

"I can work with that. I'll need Ricket's help. Thanks!"

"Don't thank me," Jason said. "It was Dira's idea, not mine."

Orion gave Dira a quick fist bump. "Oh, here's something extra about these new battle suits." Orion selected one of the floating holo-displays and enlarged it. With several more taps on the input device, the suit came alive and, in animation, turned three hundred and sixty degrees, doing a myriad of functions as it slowly turned on a vertical axis. "No more cumbersome and separate segments." She placed a small, metallic-looking device, about the size of a pack of cigarettes, on the counter. "See this? This is your battle suit. You wear it on your belt at all times."

"What do you mean this is the battle suit?" Jason asked, looking confused.

Orion stood up from her stool and stepped into the center of the room. "Watch ... don't blink or you'll miss it." She clipped the device onto her jumpsuit's belt and squeezed its two longer-side edges inward—toward each other. Building upon itself, segment by segment, all in the span of two or three seconds, a hardened, red and black battle suit took form around her body. The last section to engulf her was her helmet.

Jason got up and walked around her. It was a radically more advanced suit than he'd ever seen. The damn thing looked lighter, even aerodynamic. "Looks like the thing can fly," he said.

Orion smiled behind her new amber visor, and then her helmet segmented, reversing, and disappeared into the back of the suit. "No more carrying around your helmet, Cap. As for flying, I think it actually can do that. Again, I'll need Ricket's help with some of the exotic configurations. I know that phase-shifting is all integrated and the suit will configure to all sizes."

"Even someone the size of a rhino-warrior?"

"I suppose so, if you can convince one to use it," Orion said. She pressed a small indentation on her wrist and the battle suit continued to segment backwards; in seconds it was self-contained, encased in the small metallic device on her belt.

"See, you're in and out of your suit in seconds," Orion said, giving a quick wink to Dira.

Dira smiled and looked at Jason. "Hmm, I think I like that feature."

Chapter 27

As Jason listened to Ricket explain what would be needed in the hours ahead, his high hopes for the new droid-fighting battle suit were quickly being dashed. There was one snag Orion had neglected to mention. With the exception of the one prototype she had demonstrated, manufacturing the actual suit was only possible using the *Minian*'s phase-synthesizer.

"So we're really no closer finding a solution to steal back the phase-synthesizer?" Jason asked irritably, quietly cursing Granger again for the colossal mess he'd gotten them into in the first place. He'd deliberately left Granger on the bridge under guard when he requested Ricket to join them in the armory.

"Not necessarily, Captain." Ricket plucked the battle suit cartridge off Orion's belt and looked at it—flipping it over several times in his hands. He appeared to be contemplating something. He looked up at Jason and then around the *Minian*'s armory. "This battle suit cartridge—"

"I call them SuitPacs ..." Orion interjected.

"This SuitPac is fairly basic. Doesn't provide for the re-modifications you'd mentioned. With that said, it is still a remarkable piece of technology."

"So what are you thinking?" Jason asked.

Ricket started to pace the floor, still flipping the SuitPac around in his small fingers. "If someone could covertly breach the platform's security—make their way to the synthesizer—he may be able to initiate a manufacturing process."

"Start cooking these things right under their noses, you're

saying?" Jason asked.

"Why did you say *he*?" Orion asked. "Why not a *she*? I have more experience manufacturing battle suits than anyone here, other than perhaps yourself, Ricket."

"In all likelihood, this will be a suicide mission, Gunny." Jason shook his head. "I'm not willing to throw you into the mix."

"Cap—"

"It's not open to discussion, Gunny."

Jason could see Orion was fuming, but she'd just have to deal with it.

"I was thinking neither one of you, Captain," Ricket said.

"Don't even think that I'd let you—"

"No, Captain. Not me. Whoever will be going up against one or more of the Craing battle droids will be at a tremendous disadvantage. Granted, the suit's micro-servos greatly enhance one's strength, but neither of you has one-tenth of the raw power that one of these droids possesses. And if you consider the matched defensive and offensive weaponry aspects, it may very well come down to hand-to-hand combat."

"So where does that leave us?"

Ricket did not answer right away. He didn't have to.

"No. Absolutely not. You do realize, don't you, that they are the sole remaining members of their species, right?"

No one said anything while Jason stewed on the prospect. He kept hearing Traveler's words in his head: "*To avenge their deaths and die in battle with honor. We will fight at your side, Captain Reynolds. We won't stop until the Craing are beaten down by our heavy hammers and we, too, join our brethren in the great beyond.*"

"I'll leave it up to them, specifically to Traveler," Jason finally said, although he already knew what the rhino-warrior would say.

* * *

Traveler, Few Words, and First Reflection made the expansive armory's confines seem significantly smaller with their large presence. As Jason expected, Traveler was excited by the proposed mission, the prospect of fighting, even dying, honorably.

"I will fight this mechanical beast. But no, I will not wear this fancy costume you propose."

"Why not?" Jason asked.

"There would be no honor wearing such a strange garment. For millennia we have fought with this, this, and this," Traveler said, referring to his hammer, his leather breastplate, and his fist, which he raised high into the air.

"You have to wear the suit, Traveler. No suit ... I can't let you go. I'm fine going myself and taking my chances."

Traveler became agitated and repeatedly snorted. He walked from one end of the armory to the other, eventually stopping in front of Jason, his fists resting upon his hips. Jason and the others waited quietly until he settled down. The rhino-warrior looked from Jason to his brethren but got nothing from them. "I do not know how to use such a device. I am not comfortable with technology. I cannot learn this—I will surely fail."

"Can you use a plasma weapon?" Jason asked.

"Yes."

"How about a phase-shift belt?"

"Yes, I am getting better with that device."

"Then maybe you should give this suit a try. Hell, you may have some fun along the way," Jason said with a shrug. He turned his attention to Ricket. "Are you sure this thing, this SuitPac, will expand to cover Traveler's ... um ... girth?"

"The actual technology of the device, the suit, no longer exists locally. Think of it like cloud computing, only now it's the multiverse where the massive amounts of programming data is stored." Ricket held up the small metal cartridge. "This is merely an interface to the multiverse." With that said, Ricket moved in closer to Traveler and looked up at him. "Want to give it a try?"

Traveler snorted again and simply looked straight ahead.

"I'll take that as an affirmative," Ricket said, and secured the SuitPac onto Traveler's own large belt. Noting that Traveler's fingers were too large to compress the two micro-switches on the device, Ricket reached up and did that for him.

Immediately, the device started to expand out, segment by segment, until Traveler's legs, torso, and head were completely encased in the hardened battle suit. Somehow, the helmet conformed perfectly to the peculiar contours of Traveler's head and horns. Instead of being red and black in color, his suit was all dark gray. Only his visor had the same amber color configuration of the first suit.

Traveler looked down at his arms and legs, appraising the hardened material that encased his body. To everyone's surprise, when he snorted, as all rhino-warriors inevitably do, the suit somehow compensated for the snort with no apparent diverse effects.

Traveler flexed his arms and lifted his legs—testing his mobility. He reached over and took back his heavy hammer from Few Words, who was holding it for him. With no warning, Traveler swung the weapon from high above his head down onto the deck plates. A resounding *clang* filled the armory, causing everyone to flinch and reach for something, or someone, to hold on to. Where the hammer struck the deck, an oblong three to four inch deep dent was evident.

Traveler rose to his full height, staring down at the ruined deck plate.

Although it was impossible to see if he was smiling, a difficult prospect in any situation, Jason could tell the big rhino was pleased.

"I will wear this costume."

"Good," Jason told him, but his feelings were mixed, sending his friend into battle by himself. "Ricket, stay with Traveler until he's completely familiar with all aspects of the suit. Practice until everything is second nature to him. You got that?"

"Yes, Captain, I will do my best," Ricket said.

Jason was being hailed. "Go for Captain."

"Captain Reynolds, we've got a development here on the bridge," Sergeant Toby Jackson said. "Granger would like you to join us here."

"On my way."

Jason left the three rhinos in Ricket's care and he and the others phase-shifted into the corridor outside the bridge. In less than ten seconds Jason entered the bridge.

"What do we have, Sergeant?"

Granger spun on his heels and faced Jason. "What we have is a concentrated effort to breach the *Minian*."

"I didn't think that was possible."

"Normally, that would be true, it wouldn't be possible. At least not with the technology the Craing possess."

Studying the overhead display, Jason saw the problem. Three now familiar-looking battle droids were situated on the platform's scaffolding, directly outside the *Minian*'s forward hatch. Near-blinding pinpoints of light, with cascading showers of sparks, were concentrated from three separate locations along the perimeter of the hatch. It was clear the three droids were attempting to cut through the ship's hull.

"How long before they breach?" Jason asked.

"At this rate? No more than one hour and twenty minutes," Granger replied. "You understand, once they enter the ship, there will be nothing to stop them."

"Yeah, and you just remember who gave them those killing machines. They breach this ship, I'll make sure you're the first to die ... that I promise you," Jason said, still watching the droids' deliberate progress.

Orion joined Jason at his side. "I think Traveler's training time just go a whole lot shorter."

Chapter 28

Two dreadnaughts and a cluster of five heavy battle cruisers had moved in closer to the *Minian*; one cruiser was parked precariously close to the still-cloaked *Her Majesty*. Each of the Craing warships had their weapons systems charged and were targeting the *Minian*. The message was clear as far as Jason was concerned—Lom was making every effort to recapture the *Minian*, but if all else failed, he was willing to destroy the ship and maybe the Ion Station as well. With the *Minian*'s shields still inoperable, she would not withstand a prolonged attack.

Jason, back in the armory, looked for Traveler. He hailed Orion. "Where are you?"

"Firing range, Cap. One second," Orion answered. Across the compartment, one of the few mechanical non-virtual bulkhead hatchways opened, and Jason saw Orion wave and gesture for him to come in. "In here, Captain. Traveler is getting acquainted with the battle suit armaments."

The firing range was anything but typical. More like *The Lilly*'s small Zoo habitats, Jason took in his surroundings: a large, circular, hub-type affair, with a central station and a selection of compartments around its outside perimeter.

"There are four dynamic combat environments here. Each can be changed to virtually any battle condition or landscape required. There's tons of templates to choose from, or you can build your own environment based on an existing template."

"What's this?" Jason asked, pointing to the central hub station.

"Typically, you can select and manufacture any weapon imaginable on demand." Orion tapped on a 3D holo-display and paged through numerous hand-held weapons ... handguns, pulse weapons, and various plasma rifles. "Unfortunately, this is typically tied to the ship's phase-synthesizer, which, as we know, isn't on board anymore."

"Where's Traveler?" Jason asked.

"There just so happens to be a combat template for the Ion Station. Ricket's working with him in bay three," she said, pointing toward an entrance to one of the periphery environments. Although he could see movement within, detail was obscured—out of focus. Orion checked a small display on the bulkhead outside bay three. "The current combat scenario ends in ten seconds."

They waited until the display signaled it was safe to enter. Orion tapped in a combination of virtual buttons and led Jason inside. It was as if he were back inside the platform station. Everything was holographically reproduced—down to the smallest detail.

Traveler, wearing the prototype battle suit, stood in front of a paused-in-mid-motion battle drone. Ricket was pointing to something on the drone and shaking his head.

"Traveler, there are few vulnerable areas on these drones. This area here has one-inch-thick composite material plating. Most other sections of the drone have one point five-inch plating. A blow from your heavy hammer here, and the drone may be incapacitated."

Jason looked at the area Ricket was pointing to and wondered how Traveler, or anyone else, could possibly manage a blow to that highly protected section of the droid's mid-section. The battle droid's four arms were composed of sharp, highly reflective mower blades. Seeing the thing up close, Jason estimated the droid to be as tall as Traveler and even wider. Those mower blades looked capable of slicing through bone and flesh with ease.

As Jason approached, Ricket and Traveler looked in his direction. "How's progress coming?" Jason asked.

"It's only been thirty minutes, Captain. Traveler is fairly familiar now with how the plasma weapons are fired and what the various HUD readouts are. He would need many more hours of training to be proficient with the technology."

"Have you reviewed the steps necessary to access the phase-synthesizer? Get the thing building more BSCs?" Jason asked.

"We haven't had time."

"Well, we're out of time." Jason looked over to Orion and then up at Traveler. "Ricket, give me the basics on how to work with that synthesizer. You can guide me via my HUD, once I'm actually in place."

Orion was incensed. "You can't think you're going in there alone—"

Jason held his palm up. "Calm down. Traveler and I will do this mission together. He'll be the muscle, keeping the battle droids occupied, while I access the phase-synthesizer."

Ricket was shaking his head. "Even wearing a conventional battle suit, all it would take is one plasma hit from one of those droids and you'd be atomized."

"Well then, I guess Traveler better be up to the task of protecting me."

"I should be the one going, Captain," Orion said.

"You will be. I want you playing courier. You'll be phase-shifting back and forth, from here to the *Minian*, delivering the SuitPacs. That reminds me, Ricket: once the synthesizer is up and running, how long will it take for these things to reproduce?"

Ricket thought about that for several seconds. "No longer than a minute for each."

"I was hoping it would be quicker than that. I want Billy and his team outfitted in these new suits as soon as they become available. Orion, you'll have to do double-duty—giving them the basics on their use and operation, in between shifting back and forth from here to the platform."

"Aye, Captain. I can do that."

* * *

By the time Jason and Traveler were ready to phase-shift onto the platform, another ten minutes had elapsed. The three battle droids, working at the *Minian*'s hatch, were a mere thirty minutes away from gaining access to the ship. Billy, commanding seventy-five SEALs and Delta Force combatants on board *The Lilly,* was bringing them over in teams. Once on board the *Minian,* they would be outfitted and deployed as soon as the new BSCs became available.

Jason had purposely kept Dira away—having her prep Medical for the possibility of incoming injuries. In light of their developing relationship, the last thing he needed was his attention diverted by her presence.

Both Ricket and Orion were wearing conventional battle suits. Ricket was prepared to phase-shift in, if anything happened to either Jason or Orion. Jason looked at his HUD and saw three red battle droid icons still working at the *Minian*'s forward starboard hatch. Another droid was making its way around the platform on security patrol, while a fifth droid stayed close to the phase-synthesizer unit, located toward the center of the space platform.

Jason moved their center of operations to one of the more expansive *Minian* hold areas. Billy and his team, newly arrived, were now at the ready and awaiting their SuitPacs. There was ample space here to phase-shift in and out of the *Minian*, with less chance of landing on top of one another—although safeguards were built into the belts to minimize that possibility.

"You ready?" Jason asked Traveler.

"Yes, Captain Reynolds, I am ready."

Jason double-checked the settings on his multi-gun. Ricket suggested he utilize the weapon's micro-missile settings. Jason and Traveler phase-shifted out of the *Minian*'s hold and, in a flash, appeared inside a massive compartment, thirty feet from the building-sized phase-synthesizer unit. From all appearances, it seemed to be assembled and functioning. Several rows of small glowing lights blinked on and off on various panels. The primary user holo-display was active and Jason wasted no time moving toward it. The necessary SuitPac construction data would be available as soon as Jason set up what Ricket had referred to as a *remote multiverse I/O exchange*. Nothing—no external data drive, or any other type of hardware on this plane of existence—would be capable of holding the amount of data that would be forthcoming. Connecting to the multiverse required Jason to follow Ricket's instructions exactly. He'd be accessing what was, in effect, a micro-wormhole channel. As long as the channel remained open, data would move back and forth to an alternate plane of existence, with zero lag time.

As Jason reached the holo-display, Traveler was heading in another direction. He couldn't think about that right now. Jason's first step was to attach a small iPod-sized device to a connecting port, somewhere near the holo-display.

"I don't see the port, Ricket," Jason said into his NanoCom.

There was a flash and Ricket appeared at Jason's side. He took the small device and attached it to a small port nowhere near where Jason was looking.

"Okay, get out of here," Jason said.

Ricket looked over at the stacked-high components of the phase-synthesizer and hesitated.

"Now!" Jason barked. Ricket disappeared.

The holo-display came alive with a menu prompt asking for user input. It was just as Ricket had described and Jason quickly began making menu selections as he'd been instructed.

Plasma fire erupted in bursts so bright the nearly dark compartment was transformed to daylight-bright with each strobe flash. Jason saw Traveler and a battle droid firing at each other from fifty feet apart. Continuously firing from what looked to be wrist-mounted plasma weapons, Traveler ran toward his opponent. Ricket was right. Jason certainly didn't want to get in the middle of that firefight. The *thud thud thud* pounding of plasma fire shook the compartment and made the deck plates beneath Jason's feet vibrate. The rhino-warrior and battle droid were upon each other. Traveler's hammer poised to strike, they circled one another.

The holo-display indicated it was accessing the data stream. The phase-synthesizer came alive with the definitive sound of parts moving within it. "Huh, I guess it's working," Jason said aloud, as he brought his attention back to the two combatants.

Traveler was slow compared to the droid. In addition to the sounds of plasma fire, there was now something far more disconcerting—the sounds of mower blades making contact with Traveler's battle suit. Sparks erupted from Traveler's arms as he fended off the constant assault from four constantly slashing, and thrusting, mechanical appendages. Jason could see Traveler trying to strike back with his heavy hammer, but his attempts to do so were totally ineffective.

Traveler was driven backward. Exhaustion was overcoming the rhino-warrior and he was wavering on his feet before falling on his back. The battle droid moved in for the kill, firing a continuous barrage of plasma fire toward Traveler's helmet. Traveler, perhaps as a last resort, kicked out with one gargantuan kick, connecting to the droid's torso. It staggered backward and hesitated for several moments. When it attacked again, it came for Traveler with near-blinding speed. Traveler kicked again but this time the battle droid was ready and a significant section of Traveler's foot was sheared off. Traveler roared in pain as a stream of blood sprayed like a fountain into the air.

Plunk.

The sound drew Jason's attention to the output tray. He had gotten so caught up watching Traveler and the battle droid fight, he'd forgotten his whole purpose for being there. Lying atop the synthesizer output tray was the small metallic device. Before Jason could reach for the SuitPac, a second battle droid entered the compartment.

Chapter 29

The second battle droid approached Jason cautiously—moving at a relatively slow pace: perhaps sizing up the situation, or perhaps seeing no reason to exert itself against such an unworthy opponent. Jason knew he only had a split second to make a decision. If he didn't do something, he was seconds from being killed. He took what he feared would be the stupidest course of action. Ducking behind the support construct of the holo-display, Jason quickly unlatched the clasp beneath his helmet, pulled it free, and tossed it toward the oncoming droid. The mechanical beast stopped and turned its attention toward the bowling-ball helmet rolling away into the darkness. Jason, busy removing the rest of his battle suit, never took his eyes off the droid. The droid was again heading right for him. With no time to think, Jason leapt to the output bin and snatched up the newly manufactured SuitPac. He sprinted forward and quickly darted around the nearest corner. Plasma fire continued buffeting past into the air. Once behind the twenty-foot-thick wall of stacked phase-synthesizer components, Jason lost his footing and went down on his side. Up on his feet again, he ran into the darkness. Jason fumbled the device, nearly dropping it, before clipping it to the front of his spacer's jumpsuit.

There was another roaring scream from the other end of the compartment and Jason could only imagine what tortuous pain Traveler was now enduring. As he ran around the back side of the phase-synthesizer, having no idea where the second battle droid was located, Jason compressed the two micro-buttons on either side of the SuitPac device. Immediately something started to happen. In the span of several seconds, new suit segments expanded outward—quickly covering his entire body as he ran. The helmet section was the last to take form.

Jason realized he'd been holding his breath and gasped to fill his lungs as the amber HUD filled his vision.

The new suit's HUD was substantially different from the one he was familiar with. *Shit*, he needed to know two things: *How do I phase-shift and where's the fucking weapon menu?*

Jason hailed Orion.

"Go for Gun—"

"How do I call up the weapon menu on the new suit?"

Her hesitation seemed endless as she tried to figure out what he was requesting. "You're wearing a new—"

"No time! Just tell me!"

In as few words as possible, Orion talked him through the use of the new HUD and weapon- access menus. There was no time to figure out the phase-shifting aspects and by the time Jason came around the back side of the phase-synthesizer, the second battle droid was waiting for him. The droid's torso spun as multiple plasma cannons fired bright bursts of energy toward him. As Ricket had surmised, the new suit compensated for the plasma fire onslaught and he was apparently no worse for wear. Jason lifted his right arm and found the pressure-sensitive trigger mechanism. He fired, and pulses of energy erupted from the micro-plasma cannon integrated into the forearm of his battle suit.

The battle droid seemed unaffected by the plasma fire, but its progress had definitely slowed, and that was exactly what Jason wanted.

"Gunny, get in here. There should be several SuitPacs sitting in the hopper tray by now. Keep your head down."

Jason didn't have time to verify if Orion phase-shifted in because of two things: First, Craing security forces wearing green battle suits were filing into the compartment. Second, the battle droid was making a new move in his direction. Frustrated that firing micro-missiles had little apparent effect on the battle droid, Jason called up the weapons menu and, one by one, tried alternative munitions selections. Although the integrated battle suit weapons design was convenient, it didn't seem to offer the same level of *wallop* that his multi-gun could dole out. As the battle droid slowly but steadily advanced, Jason maneuvered back to where he'd left his weapon. There it was. Leaning against the holo-display support column. He flashed through several more menu screens looking for the phase-shift functions, but came up short. Jason ran, diving for the multi-gun. He snatched it up with one hand and rolled into a one-knee firing position. Relieved to see his HUD munitions menu had automatically refreshed and was now synchronized to his multi-gun, Jason selected the rail-gun munitions option and fired.

The battle droid's progression slowed—then ceased. Jason got to his feet and cautiously stepped closer. The droid seemed to be having difficulty fending off the relentless stream of micro-rail ammo. *I always liked this weapon*, Jason thought to himself. But his self-congratulation was short-lived. The droid re-compensated and was making forward progress in his direction. The Craing security forces, easily one hundred armed combatants, had moved into position behind the droid and were unleashing a constant barrage of plasma fire directed at him.

Crap! A new HUD warning message flashed: Jason's phase-shields were down to ten percent and falling fast. One by one he tried other munitions options—some seemed to be ones he'd used before, but others were definitely new. For the most part, he ignored the Craing security forces and was focusing his attention on the battle droid. But their rapid fire was starting to take its toll on his battle suit.

Three selections down, Jason noticed an odd-looking option called *Expansion Gum*. He selected it and fired. This time there was no loud percussion sound. No recoil or kickback. The multi-gun acted more like a high-tech squirt gun. *What the hell is this?* A viscous stream of brown sludge spewed forth from the muzzle of his multi-gun, sending out short squirt bursts. Ready to change to an alternate selection, Jason noticed the sharp reflective mower blades on the battle droid's arms were slowing. *Squirt-squirt-squirt.* Jason continued pumping the stuff into the inner workings of the battle droid. Sure enough, the blades were seizing up and the viscous liquid was hardening into a spongy, gooey-looking mess.

With its blade defenses deactivated, the droid seemed to only double its plasma fire efforts. Again, it steadily advanced on Jason, forcing him, one backward step at a time, to retreat. Suddenly, with his back against the phase-synthesizer, he had nowhere left to go—no way to escape the pounding onslaught of plasma fire. Jason's HUD continued to flash warnings; his phase-shields had dropped to one percent. Then, as his phase-shields finally gave out, Jason felt the full force of the plasma fire pummel his battle suit. He was being relentlessly knocked against the phase-synthesizer behind him. As the heat from the plasma barrage increased, his battle suit started to glow red and steamy waves of heat rose up into the air. Feeling his flesh start to blister, the pain quickly became unbearable. Gritting his teeth, he stifled a scream. Jason was on the verge of losing consciousness—his vision starting to fail.

To his relief two new HUD life-icons appeared. Had the cavalry arrived? Yes and no. Unfortunately, it was too little too late. Orion and Billy had joined the fight, but both were battling the Craing security forces, as well as the battle droid Traveler had gone up against earlier.

Clang!

Something obscured Jason's vision. *Clang! Clang! Clang!*

Jason wondered if his sight had finally gone—blinded now by the relentless plasma fire into his visor. No, that wasn't it. There was movement in front of him. A dark gray form was making strange, repetitive motions. A hammering motion. As the form slowly moved away from Jason, he was able to see more detail. It was Traveler, arching his heavy hammer from above his head and hammering it down, again and again, upon the battle droid. He was pounding away at the droid's weak spot. Three more spectacular strikes by Traveler's hammer and the battle droid ceased firing. It had been destroyed.

Jason let his back slide down the phase-synthesizer to the deck. He watched as Traveler gave the incapacitated battle droid several more hits from his heavy hammer before he turned his attention toward Jason. Limping, he joined Jason, then sat next to him on the deck.

They watched as three more friendlies joined the fight against the second retreating battle droid.

"I thought you were dead," Jason said.

Traveler was quiet for a while. "A powerful opponent. I could not match its speed, its strength. I had come to realize this was going to be an honorable death—I was prepared to die."

Jason saw a section of Traveler's left foot was missing, as well as most of his left hand. Gouged and scratched, his battle suit no longer had the same smooth surface as his own.

"So what happened?" Jason asked.

"I am almost ashamed to say ... preparing to die, I curled into a ball. I tucked in my arms and legs and waited. Doing this, the battle droid was unable to slice off any more body parts. I believe it grew disinterested in me. Once the others arrived I was able to join your fight."

"Thank you. I thought I was a goner—one more time you've saved my life, Traveler."

Jason hailed Orion. Out of breath, she said, "Go for Gunny."

"Try the *Expansion Gum* setting."

Within several seconds Orion and Billy were squirting brown liquid goo into the workings of the battle droid. Its defensive mower blades slowly ground to a halt. More of Billy's assault team arrived—each equipped in a new battle suit.

He heard the familiar hail tone in his ear. "Go for Captain," Jason said. "What's up, Ricket?"

"Captain, those three battle droids have breached the *Minian*."

Chapter 30

Still on the Ion Station, Jason and Traveler needed healing time in a MediPod, but that would have to wait. As it was, their nanites were already busy at work—repairing Jason's scalded skin blisters and reconstructing Traveler's missing bone, blood vessels, muscles, tendons and flesh.

Orion and Billy, along with six others of their team, successfully brought down the second battle droid. The *Expansion Gum* did the trick. It took a while longer to defeat the remaining Craing security forces, but eventually they too were defeated.

Billy phase-shifted back to the *Minian* to lead the squad in fending off the three remaining battle droids. Orion returned to *The Lilly,* back to manning her tactical post. Things were heating up in local space and Jason needed her presence there to keep him abreast of the situation.

For now, the immediate issue was how to deal with the phase-synthesizer. Pocked with numerous blast holes from the recent fighting, the thing was still operational and continued to manufacture SuitPacs, one after another.

Ricket, wearing one of the new battle suits, stood in front of the repositioned lower holo-display.

"So how'd they get this thing here in the first place?" Jason asked. "They certainly didn't carry it. Even broken down into segments, there isn't a hatchway on the ship big enough to accommodate them."

Ricket glanced over to Jason, who'd moved closer to his side. Traveler, in the process of standing, grunted, then began hobbling around as he tried to put weight on his injured foot.

"Granger informed me how it was first done," Ricket said in a matter of fact tone. "I expected as much—each of these segments is equipped with an individual, integrated, phase-shift circuit." He rapidly screened through the menu. "Ah, it's all listed here. I simply need to reverse the last phase-shift command parameters. I think it's best if I move everything at the same time. That's what Granger did. Getting it set up on the platform in the first place."

Jason heard two hails coming in and answered them in the order received. He was surprised to hear his brother's voice.

"Jason ... things are heating up."

"What's up, Brian?"

"Combination of heavy and light cruisers are about to make port on the Ion Station. Within the next few minutes you're going to have some company. There's a crew of thousands on board those ships. You need to get out of there ... like right now, Brother."

Jason heard a commotion. "What's that, Brian?"

"Oh, shit. I've got to go. Looks like we've been side-swiped." Brian cut the connection.

Jason answered Orion's hail: "Go for Captain."

"Multiple forces are unloading onto the station, Cap."

"I know. We're in the process of moving this thing, I hope." He looked over to Ricket, who nodded his head without looking up from what he was doing.

"What's going on with *Her Majesty*?" Ricket asked.

"One of the heavy cruisers, en route to a nearby hub-port, winged her bow. There's actually a section, looks like the starboard bow, that's now visible ... no longer cloaked."

"We need to get those people off—"

Orion cut him off. "Cap, the heavy cruiser's firing. *Her Majesty* is under attack."

Jason interrupted Ricket. "You have one minute to show me how to access the phase-shift setting on this damn suit."

* * *

Prior to phase-shifting directly onto *Her Majesty*'s bridge, Jason grabbed up two handfuls of freshly manufactured SuitPacs. No sooner than he got on board, the ship jerked and he was thrown down onto the deck plates. Alarm klaxons bellowed from above and everyone was shouting to be heard.

"We're taking multiple direct hits to our forward starboard hull," yelled Perkins, manning the tactical console.

"Bring all guns online ... fire at will," Brian yelled.

"Shields are down to thirty percent, Captain," Perkins reported.

Jason rose to his feet and watched the mayhem around him.

"Two more Craing light cruisers just joined the fight!" Betty yelled over the noise.

Jason felt thunderous pounding, the vibration making it hard to stay on his feet. Brian glanced over to him with a sardonic smile. "This baby has some big-ass cannons."

"The light cruiser's lost her shields and ... she just imploded," Perkins looked up from his station, smiling.

"Our shields holding at thirty percent. The heavy cruiser is losing her aft-shields."

"Don't let up," Brian commanded.

Betty looked up, unable to speak for several beats. "Our toric-cloaking system just went down. They can see us ... they can see every inch of us."

"Bristol! Get that thing working or we're toast," Brian yelled toward the floor.

Jason hadn't noticed that Bristol was even on the bridge,

then spied his legs beneath a nearby console. His muffled voice answered back, "It's fucking fried." Bristol crawled out from the console and shook his head. "There's nothing I can do."

Her Majesty violently jerked three times in rapid succession.

"Shields are completely down. All of them! Multiple hull breaches—we're venting to space."

Jason put a hand on Brian's shoulder. "It's time, Brian. We knew this was going to happen." Brian stared back. Jason could see he wanted to argue ... to insist the old luxury liner still had some fight in her, but realization set in and he simply nodded.

Jason handed everyone on the bridge a SuitPac. Bristol looked at it with disgust and scowled at Jason. "What am I supposed to do with this thing?"

"Those of you wearing a conventional battle suit, go ahead and phase-shift to *The Lilly* right now."

Neither Brian nor Bristol was wearing a battle suit. Jason snatched back the SuitPac from Bristol's still outstretched fingers and clipped it onto the front of his jumpsuit. Jason then triggered the device, and within seconds the SuitPac had expanded and segmented out—covering Bristol from head to toe.

"Cool," Bristol said. Within five seconds Bristol flashed away, apparently a lot better at figuring out how to use the new HUD menu than Jason had been.

It took another few minutes before Brian and Jason were alone on the bridge. "Time for us to go, Brian. All departments are clear. No one's left on board but you and me."

Brian, now wearing his own new battle suit, took another look around the bridge. The klaxon was still howling and all ship systems were failing. He nodded and then stopped and looked at Jason. "The hopper!"

"Where is he?"

"In the hold," Brian said.

"*Her Majesty* is on the verge of imploding ..."

"I can't leave him!"

"Fine! You're not going to be able to figure out the suit's HUD menu. Take my arm." It took Jason close to a minute to configure the proper destination coordinates before phase-shifting them into *Her Majesty*'s hold.

* * *

The attack came from behind. The hopper went for Jason first, knocking him to the deck and with raking motions used his outstretched claws to rip at his back. The suit, nearly impregnable, saved Jason, who quickly got back on his knees. Surprised by the added strength the suit provided, Jason was able to get a fist around the hopper's neck and squeeze.

"Don't hurt him!" Brian yelled.

"I'm trying not to but he won't stay still. He's squirming all over the place."

"Just hold him down for a second, will you? He's probably scared."

Jason got a better grip and slowly brought the struggling creature down to the deck. Its arms were jerking this way and that and its tail whipped with such force Jason nearly lost his grip again.

Brian was at Jason's side, looking down at the struggling hopper. "Hey, look ... It's me!"

The hopper's eyes were wide with fear and still not looking up in Brian's direction. Brian got down to the hopper's level, putting his visor only inches away. "See? It's me."

The hopper stopped struggling. Jason released his grip and slowly took his weight off it.

"You better get us all out of here," Brian said. "This ship's about to blow."

Chapter 31

Jason phase-shifted himself, his brother, and the hopper onto *The Lilly*. By the time Jason made his way onto the bridge, *Her Majesty* was in large pieces floating separately in space. McBride was already in the process of phase-shifting *The Lilly* into the largest of the *Minian*'s cargo holds.

"Status," Jason asked, as he took the command chair.

"As you know, *Her Majesty* has broken apart. We got everyone off in time," Orion said.

"What about the *Minian*?"

"I sent Bristol to help with getting her shields up. So far, no one's shooting at her, but I think that's about to change."

"What about Ricket? Has he gotten the phase-synthesizer back on board yet?"

"Not yet. Some sort of technical problem. Billy and a squad are there, holding off the arrival of new Craing security forces."

Jason glanced through the three hundred and sixty degree display, seeing into the dark confines of the *Minian*'s hold. He stood, realizing there wasn't much he could accomplish staying here. "Keep me apprised, Gunny."

"Where you off to, Cap?" she asked.

"To motivate Granger." With that, Jason phase-shifted over to the main corridor on the *Minian*. He came out of the phase-shift and made it into the bridge in three long strides.

Bristol and Chief Horris were leaning over a console having a heated discussion while Granger casually sat in the command chair, his arms behind his head, his fingers interlocked. Jason pulled the tall Caldurian to his feet and punched him hard across the face.

Granger stumbled sideways and slowly recovered his balance—blood trickled at the corner of his mouth.

"There's little reason to keep you alive, Granger. But never let it be said I don't give second chances. This is yours. You either help or you die. It's up to you."

"What would you like me to do?"

"First, get the shields up on this ship. Do it now. Then we can talk about bringing minimal, at least, propulsion back online."

All eyes were on Granger. He paused, then casually moved to the same console Bristol and the chief were standing by. He knelt down and inspected the work Bristol had started and slowly shook his head. "No. You've got this misconfigured."

Bristol, his helmet retracted into the back of his suit, looked ready to spew more of his typical profanity, when Granger added, "It's close, but you neglected to use a trion-matrix coupler." Granger pointed to an obscured section of the inner console that Jason couldn't see from his position.

Bristol went down on his knees to inspect the area Granger was indicating and came back up to stare at him. Jason wondered if it was admiration he saw in Bristol's expression. "Why the fuck would that be removed in the first place?" he asked, while moving to a similar console positioned against the bulkhead on the other side of the bridge. Within several minutes he was back, holding up a small device. Optical cables of some sort hung from it. "Will this work?"

Granger nodded. "For now."

As Bristol went to work on the shields, Granger glanced toward Jason, then turned his attention toward Chief Horris. "Propulsion. Let's head to Engineering."

The chief looked over to Jason, who offered him a quick nod.

Jason then nodded toward Sergeant Toby Jackson, indicating he needed to stay with them.

* * *

Jason phase-shifted back to the Ion Station, to the compartment where he'd left Ricket and the phase-synthesizer. Billy, Traveler, and ten or more SEALs, plus a few of the Delta Force guys, were engaged in a firefight at the entrance to the compartment. Billy, catching Jason's eye, turned and held his hands out to his sides as if to say, *what's the holdup?*

Jason shrugged and stood beside Ricket. "I thought you said you had this?"

"I was wrong, Captain. Apparently the device was damaged while fighting the battle-droids."

"It's time to go, Ricket. We'll blow this station, along with the synthesizer, from the *Minian*."

"This equipment is irreplaceable. Far more advanced than what's on *The Lilly*—"

Jason cut him off. "It won't do us any good if we're all dead."

Ricket's fingers continued to rapidly input data even while looking up at Jason. Then, with a final pronounced key tap, each section of the immense phase-synthesizer flashed to a blinding white and disappeared.

"Let's just hope you sent it back to the right place," Jason said.

Ricket smiled. "Ye of little faith."

Jason hailed Billy, looking at him from across the compartment. Making a twirling motion with a raised finger, he said, "We're out of here."

* * *

Jason supposed they were making progress on the *Minian*,

but it seemed things were moving along at a snail's pace. The shields were still offline and Engineering was reporting it would be another ten minutes, at least, before even minimal propulsion would be possible. Jason sat in the command chair, drumming the fingers of one hand onto the knuckles of the other. Periodically Bristol looked up from what he was doing and, scowling in Jason's direction, would disappear again beneath a console.

Lieutenant Commander Perkins was back on the bridge, resuming his role of XO, while Orion remained full-time on tactical. Last he heard, Brian, Betty and the hopper were in *The Lilly*'s mess, grabbing a bite to eat.

Jason found it hard to keep his eyes off the overhead display. Above and beyond the hundreds of dreadnaught warships filling space as far as the eye could see, scores more Craing warships were arriving all the time ... space cruisers, destroyers, various gunships, and other vessels he wasn't familiar with. He was pretty sure, with few exceptions, they were actively targeting the *Minian*—only waiting for the command to unleash a hell storm of firepower.

Jason hailed Ricket.

"Go for Ricket."

"We're going to need to hightail it out of here sooner rather than later. What exactly is involved in coupling the *Minian*'s power source to *The Lilly*?"

"I'm encouraged, Captain. Perhaps if Bristol could assist me?"

"He's still working to connect the ship's shields interface."

"I'll keep going then, Captain."

"Fine. Keep me abreast of your progress," Jason replied, cutting the connection. Shaking his head he went back to drumming his fingers.

"The last of the scaffolding has been cut away, Cap," Orion

announced. "Both the forward and aft space-bridge gangways are adrift in space—physically, we're clear. "

That had been a bigger obstacle than anyone figured on. In the end, it was a combination of directed plasma fire and sheer brute-force strength that did the trick. With nothing else to do, Few Words and First Reflection were more than willing to be on the space-walk team and lend helping hands toward dismantling the scaffolding support beams and various crossbeam members.

"Thank you, Gunny," Jason said. *Now we can just drift in space until we career into a cruiser or maybe a dreadnaught ...* Jason thought, brooding to himself.

"Cap, I think that triggered a reaction. All Ion Station gun turrets are charging weapons."

Orion no sooner made her report than the *Minian* came under attack.

The bridge shook violently, knocking several crewmembers off their seats.

"Report," Jason yelled.

"All four station plasma cannons are firing. Hull integrity is down to twenty percent, Captain. Temperature out there's starting to spike—I'm seeing heat-related damage in multiple areas."

Jason wondered why only the platform was firing on them. He instinctively looked out, toward the heavens above, and the ever-growing fleet of Craig warships. Jason smiled. "They're not prepared to destroy their Ion Station. At least not yet." Although the *Minian* had indeed drifted, she was still close enough that a stray shot, or even a resulting *Minian* explosion, would be catastrophic to the platform.

The Ion Station's plasma cannons continued to pound the *Minian*'s outer hull. The inside temperature on the bridge was now markedly warmer. Jason looked over to Orion. She simply shook her head. They both knew the hull was mere seconds from being breached. What more needed saying?

Jason stood—he'd already waited over-long to move everyone back to *The Lilly*. She'd saved his ass more than once. Hell, with a little creativity, maybe they'd manage a combination of quick phase-shifts—find obscure hiding places—and eventually wend their way out of Craing space. But one glance out toward the view of countless hovering Craing warships dashed his hopes. Truth was, Jason hated the idea of losing the *Minian*—a vessel that just might be Earth's only hope against inevitable Craing attack.

"Try it now," Bristol said, his head reappearing from beneath the same console he'd been working on.

Orion didn't need to be asked twice. Within two seconds the *Minian*'s shields were coming online.

Chapter 32

The pounding continued. The shields were holding steady at nearly 99 percent. That would change as soon as other ships got into the fight.

Looking around the *Minian*'s bridge, something else occurred to Jason.

"Bristol."

"Huh?" said Bristol.

"No, not 'Huh' … it's either Sir or Captain," Perkins interjected from across the bridge.

"Okay, Captain. What is it?"

"What's the condition of the *Minian*'s communications?"

"We're feeding everything through *The Lilly*."

"That's not what I asked," Jason said, beginning to lose patience with him.

"All consoles are mirrored. Comms can be accessed from anywhere on the bridge. But there's only one primary interface. That's what the Craing fucked with. Like they did with the shields. They got their grubby little fingers into the workings of things and left the ship a total   fu—"

"I've got the idea, Bristol. Again. What's the status of getting comms up and running … here … on the *Minian*? We're going to need a way back home. *The Lilly*'s lost connection to the interchange. Maybe the *Minian* will be a different story. According to the admiral, other allied ships are still able to call up wormholes at will."

"I didn't know you'd lost connection with the interchange.

That's bad," Bristol volunteered.

"You were on *Her Majesty* at the time," Jason told him.

"Why don't I take a look at what's going on with *The Lilly* first? Maybe it was one of those idiot comms twins. Or both of them. I'm pretty sure they're both mentally impaired."

Jason saw Orion tilt her head and give just the tiniest of nods.

"Let's not start disrespecting other crewmembers. But yes, that sounds like a good plan. Stop by and see if you can help Ricket first. He's there, in Engineering."

Bristol collected some tools and small test devices and left the bridge without another word.

"Cap, we're taking fire from three Craing gunships. They've positioned themselves directly above the Ion Station."

Jason raised his eyebrows.

"Still at ninety-nine percent. It would take a few of those dreadnaughts' fire to negatively affect the status of our ships' shields."

Jason let out a breath. "Keep me updated. I'll be back in my ready room on *The Lilly*. XO, you have the bridge."

* * *

Realizing there was nothing he could do until propulsion was restored, Jason grabbed a few minutes of down time. Checking his messages, he saw that there were thirty-seven that were marked 'important.' He scanned the senders' names and saw one vid-message from Nan and one from Boomer. He clicked on the one from Boomer first. She wasn't happy. With her hair pulled back in a tight ponytail and wearing her customary dark gray spacer's jumpsuit, she looked so different from Mollie, he had to remind himself that they were actually, genetically, the same person. She looked older, more confident, and there was something else there, too, something Jason couldn't quite put his finger on.

"Hi, Dad. Where are you? You need to come and get me. I can't go to the bathroom without that crazy lady following me. Did you know she tried to have Tear Drop deactivated? Really? This is what I have to put up with? And it's not just me ... I heard one of the soldiers joking that they were going to show her how an airlock works. Anyway, I love you, Dad. Hope you're on your way back here." There was a fleeting smile and the message ended.

Jason clicked on the message from Nan. She was smiling but he could see the strain in her eyes. Wearing a pastel yellow blouse and gold earrings with matching necklace, she looked as beautiful as ever. She was wearing her auburn hair a little different—parted more on the side, which gave her a somewhat younger, more playful look.

"Hi, Jason, I hope you're doing well. We're all counting on you—not to heap on the pressure too much. Things are different on Earth. Everyone pretty much knows what's going on. I guess I'm doing what I'm supposed to in that regard. Did you know they're making play toys of *The Lilly*? And, of course, there's action figures of Captain Jason Reynolds, Billy, and even Traveler ... heavy hammer and all." Nan casually brushed her hair back with her fingers and looked into the camera for several beats before speaking again. "I didn't want to handle this via a vid-message," she said with an awkward smile. "Jason, there's something I've been meaning to talk to you about. I'm not sure how you will react to the news and, again, I'm sorry how I'm having to convey this ... Jason, I'm pregnant." Nan stared for several seconds and then smiled, shaking her head. "If your first question is, *is it mine?* Rest assured, *it is*. Must have been that night we were together at the old scrapyard house about eight weeks ago. I've known for a while. Wasn't real sure how to talk to you about it." Nan hesitated, biting her lip the way she did when feeling insecure.

"Look, I know you have something going with Dira. Or, at least you had something going the last time I saw you. I know she cares about you. I don't want you to think I'm planning on getting in the way of any of that. That's not what this is about. But I did feel you had a right to know. Just understand, you can be involved as much or as little as you want. But you also have to know I'm keeping the baby, and I'm finding myself more and more excited about it every day." Nan was smiling again, "Guess I should stop calling *him* an *it* ... Jason, you're going to have a son."

Jason sat there, looking at the blank screen in the silence of his ready room. His thoughts turned to Dira. She loved him and he loved her, that wasn't even a question. The truth was, he loved Nan as well. He'd always loved her—it wasn't his choice for her to leave him, to seek a divorce. So what was Nan asking of him now? Or was she even asking for anything? Did she want him back in her life, or was she simply telling him there was a baby on the way—that he was going to be a father again? One thing was definitively certain ... Jason had no idea how to proceed.

Jason started clicking on the other messages waiting in his inbox. They were, for the most part, emails from Allied fleet personnel. Many were from other warship officers. One by one, Jason scanned their texts and soon felt the heavy burden of the perilous days ahead return. The Alliance was breaking down—a bad situation had turned dire. There were three separate requests to have the admiral relieved of duty and for Jason to assume that post. Jason felt his anger rise. What the commanders didn't seem to realize was that without Admiral Reynolds there wouldn't be an Alliance—no one would be holding his assigned position to even voice a complaint. He decided to write a bulk email, one that would not be cc'ed to his father. He kept it short and sweet:

To: Allied Fleet Commanders
From: Captain Jason Reynolds

In response to multiple queries and out-and-out requests for the removal of Admiral Perry Reynolds from the post of Allied Forces Commander, I remind you that none of you have shown any interest in taking on this thankless position. For sixteen years Admiral Reynolds has dedicated his life, at the cost of giving up his home and family on Earth, to fighting the relentless advances of the Craing. Where one after another of the star systems within this sector have either been destroyed, or their populaces fallen into total subjugation to the Craing, the Alliance has, for the most part, held strong. Know that I have neither the desire, the inclination, nor the ability to effectively lead the Allied forces. There is only one person among us who can effectively do that, and that's Admiral Perry Reynolds. It is time you stopped complaining and second-guessing the admiral. I, for one, am thankful we have someone with his dedication, heart, and capability standing at the helm.

My fellow commanders, I will not sugarcoat this. We have entered our darkest hour. We are up against what seems to be an unbeatable opponent. An enemy that has turned its full might on destroying the very things we are fighting to sustain: our freedom; our Allied survival; Hell, life itself.

But I have not given up. The admiral has not given up. Let us join together, as we have done so many times in the past, and defeat the Craing Empire, once and for all.

— — —

Jason reread the email message and hit *send*. One way or another, he'd let them know his thoughts on the matter. It would be up to them, individually or as a whole, to continue following his father's lead into battle, or not.

Chapter 33

Jason entered the *Minian*'s Engineering department to find Ricket, Chief Horris, Granger, and Bristol three stories up on a catwalk, standing in front of the dual drive systems. As Jason made his way across the catwalk to join the huddled up group, he expected to hear more bickering. As it turned out, repairing any one of the still inoperable systems was best accomplished as a team. Horris and Granger were wrestling with what looked to be a problematic four-inch-thick cable. With a grunt and the chief putting his substantial girth behind it, he and Granger secured the cable's connector into a bulkhead mounted receptacle.

"Well, I didn't expect to find you all here. What's going on?"

Chief Horris was the first to speak: "We have propulsion. Both drives are up and running and seem to be operating, albeit not at full efficiency."

"That's wonderful news," Jason said. "Why do I get the feeling there's a *but* to that statement?"

"Not so much a *but* as an *and*," Ricket said. "Weapons are back online. The phase-synthesizer is reconnected to internal systems."

"So we can get the hell out of here, you're saying?"

Ricket was the first to answer, "Not if you want to call up a wormhole. Comms are still out here, and I need to see what's going on with *The Lilly*. Why there's no access to the interchange."

"Sounds like that should be the next order of business. Put your collective minds together and solve the problem," Jason said.

Bristol's face scrunched into a dissatisfied grimace, as if

something obvious was being missed.

"Speak up, Bristol," Jason said.

"As usual, Granger's been holding back on us."

Granger's eyes bored into the skinny young genius with contempt. "What Bristol's referring to are the capabilities of the *Minian*'s weaponry systems. All I said was that they were far more advanced, and with that, far more destructive than any of them are aware."

Bristol shook his head. "Bullshit. You said the *Minian*'s fully capable of taking out each of the seven Craing worlds."

Jason looked at Granger, who wasn't denying Bristol's statement. "Seems we need more discussion. I want all of you in my ready room in ten minutes." Jason turned and walked away. His mind was reeling with the implications of what Granger had said.

* * *

Twelve minutes later, there were ten seated around the conference table. In addition to those he'd talked to in Engineering, he'd invited the XO, Brian and Gaddy, as well as Orion and Billy.

Jason looked around the table and spoke to the group as a whole. "We are not the Craing. We do not arbitrarily destroy planets." Jason turned his attention to Gaddy. "You've lived on both Halimar and Terplin?"

"Yes, Captain."

"Talk to us about the general population's sentiment about Earth."

Gaddy shrugged. "The general sentiment?"

"Yes. How do the Craing people regard humans and Earth as a whole?"

She was nodding even before Jason finished the question. "I can only speak for the youth; you know, kids in college ... I guess what people on Earth don't realize is that we are tuned into their music, the media ... TV, the movies ... We devour anything pertaining to Earth's culture. We dress like kids on Earth. Our companies produce millions of products identical to those found on Earth."

"So the Craing as a whole don't see Earth as the enemy, per se?"

"You have to see things from the Craing perspective. We don't look at Earth being our enemy any more than we do any other planet. But the Craing Empire's ruling body is all about control. Control of its own people, as well as controlled power of every known world across the universe. It's why so many of us became dissidents and why so many within the Craing worlds are rebelling."

"Gaddy, billions of lives have been lost due to the empire's two hundred-plus years of ruthless expansion. As of late, they are very close to destroying all the Allied worlds—including Earth."

Jason stopped to let that sink in. Gaddy's eyes welled up with tears and she looked down at the table.

"I didn't say that to hurt you. But we're at a point where we need to very carefully consider every option. I want everyone seated around this table to understand the difference between the Craing people, and what past and present Craing emperors are trying to achieve."

"You can't destroy the Craing worlds. Please ... We are not all bad. We are not all like my uncle," Gaddy pleaded.

Jason put a reassuring hand on Gaddy's arm and smiled. "Thank you for sharing, Gaddy. We have some tough strategic decisions to make. I want you to go with Dira now, and let the rest of us talk some more."

Dira had been standing nearby and she gently coaxed Gaddy up from her seat. Gaddy looked at Jason, tears streaming down her cheeks. "Please don't destroy my home." She stopped and looked at each participant, her gaze finally coming to rest on Ricket. He nodded silent reassurance to her as she was escorted out.

Jason put the question to the group: "Thoughts? Now's your time to tell me what you think."

Billy spoke up first. "We perhaps have the means to completely destroy the Craing Empire ... by doing so, we can end their plundering, once and for all. I say we think long and hard about doing just that."

"But that's suggesting the total annihilation of a civilization," Orion blurted out, looking disgusted at Billy.

"I think you made your point, Captain," Granger said. "Yes, a knee-jerk reaction would be to take advantage of this rare opportunity we've been given. We can destroy the enemy. Do it now, while we are so close to them, and since we have the means."

Ricket stayed quiet while the debate bounced around the table. Inquiringly, Jason turned to him. "Well?"

"If we do decide to attack the Craing worlds, we'll need to move away from here quickly. Even the *Minian* could not withstand a prolonged attack from hundreds of dreadnaughts. Once we fire our volley of missiles, expect the Craing forces to unload everything they have on us. That alone could seal our fate."

Eventually the side talking in the room went still. Jason had heard and evaluated the opinions of his most trusted advisors. "No, we will not destroy the seven Craing worlds. But we will go after all their military and their strategic assets. We will also target Emperor Lom himself, as well as their council of high priests. If that seals our fate, as Ricket so eloquently stated, so be it. But it just may cease their endless warring."

No one spoke for several moments. Jason clapped his hands once and said, "Cheer up, people. We're not dead. Ricket, do everything you can to reestablish connection to the interchange. That alone would save our bacon. Aside from that, maybe we can execute a series of well-planned phase-shifts. Granger, I realize that even the *Minian* has limitations on how many phase-shifts she can initiate before needing to recharge. We need to know what that number is."

"The maximum distance the ship can phase-shift to is twenty thousand miles per phase-shift. She'll need to recharge if you utilize that full distance over a duration of fifteen minutes."

"And what's the distance necessary to clear that field of dreadnaughts?"

This time it was Brian who spoke up. "Having first-hand knowledge of moving through that maze recently, I guess it would be in the neighborhood of one hundred thousand miles ... give or take. That would give us a little breathing room on the other end."

"That would be five phase-shifts with a combined recharge time of one hour. But that's only if we're standing still while recharging. That won't be the case." Jason turned to Chief Horris. "I understand we won't have light-speed capabilities. So you'll need to ensure that our sub-light speeds are as high as you can manage. If we can cut the distance down to four, or even three, phase-shifts, so much the better."

The chief made an exasperated expression, but didn't say anything.

"Cap, I'll need to take a look at the *Minian*'s available munitions," Orion said. "Last I checked I wasn't able to access that information from the AI."

Jason didn't need to say anything, as Granger spoke up, "I'll provide you with the necessary access protocols."

Perkins brought up a 3D holo-display that showed local space and the seven Craing worlds. "I should have a list of strategic targets within the next ten minutes, sir."

Chapter 34

The Craing's full attack started two minutes after the meeting broke up. Jason and Perkins were still calculating targeting solutions when Orion announced from the bridge that four dreadnaughts were moving in close. Already at General Quarters, Orion's standing orders were to fully engage the enemy if any of the dreadnaughts entered the fight.

Jason rushed from the ready room, ordering the XO over his shoulder to go ahead and upload the targeting information to tactical.

By the time Jason was seated in the command chair there were two hundred, and counting, incoming missiles headed for the *Minian*.

"Captain, incoming are maximum yield, fusion-tipped warheads. Looks like they've given up trying to salvage the Ion Station."

"Understood. It's time. Why don't you show me what this ship can do, Gunny?"

"Deploying rail cannons ..."

A new overhead segment came alive, showing the virtual battle logistics of Craing space. Jason took in the virtual, massive blanket of red icons ... dreadnaughts, light and heavy cruisers and other, smaller, Craing warships. A small green icon on the right signified the *Minian's* present position, idling next to the Ion Station. Hundreds of yellow icons were making rapid progress across open space—heading in their direction.

Jason felt a familiar vibration coming up through the deck

plates; all four of the *Minian*'s powerful rail cannons were firing simultaneously at the incoming missiles. One by one the yellow icons blinked out.

"Good job, Gunny," Jason said, and held her stare for several more seconds before giving her a slight nod.

The overhead display changed perspective, providing a view of the seven Craing worlds. They were beautiful ... each completely different from one neighboring world to another. Granger, Brian, Perkins and Billy stood a half step behind the command chair. Jason was aware of their presence. Even now, there were doubts racing through his mind. Perhaps he should try to contact the admiral—let him make the ultimate decision that could cost thousands, if not millions, of lives. Only when he felt the pressure of a hand on his shoulder did his second-guessing of himself come to a halt.

"You didn't start this war, buddy. But it is up to you to do everything you can to end it," Billy said. "Now pull the trigger so we can get the hell out of here."

Jason concentrated on the display. The seven planets now pulsed with multiple red target icons.

"Craing's land-based defenses number in the thousands," Orion said. "There are also shipyard and armaments manufacturing, military bases, and academies."

"Approximate loss of life?"

Orion hesitated, looking down at one of her console displays. "I don't know for sure, Captain."

"An approximation is fine, Gunny."

"Three million lives lost."

The bridge went quiet. No one there wanted to give the order; no one wanted to trade places with Jason at that particular moment. "Too many."

Orion shrugged, looking exasperated. "How ...? What targets

should I take off the table?"

"Manufacturing facilities, military academies. Don't target those."

"And the Emperor's Palace?"

"Yes, destroy it. Go ahead ... Do it."

Without knowing the specifics, Jason was aware Gunny and Granger had recently spent time reviewing the *Minian*'s remarkable offensive weaponry. Like The Lilly, missile warheads were manufactured on the fly, via the phase-synthesizer. But the Minian's JIT munitions were far more advanced and even more customizable, which made them unique. Targeting could be specific—an added level of detail that would ensure collateral loss of life, of non-strategic areas, was kept to a minimum. But even removing manufacturing sites and military academies as targets, Jason knew millions of Craing lives would be lost.

The *Minian* let loose a barrage of missiles that lasted close to a minute. All eyes were on the overhead display. Bundled together at first, the missiles soon separated into smaller clusters and then broke into individual missiles, each one following its own targeting vector.

"Incoming!"

Virtually all space blazed with the crisscrossing vectors of plasma fire. Any enemy ship with a clear shot was firing plasma cannons and deploying missiles.

"We're taking substantial plasma fire from just about every ship in the vicinity. Shields are already down to eighty percent, Captain," Gunny reported.

He wanted to turn away. To give the order to phase-shift to the first set of coordinates, twenty thousand miles from where they currently sat. But Jason continued to watch the Craing worlds and the *Minian*'s missiles as they closed on their respective targets. He owed any innocent Craing people that much. When the destruction came, it was nearly simultaneous. Multiple segments on the display changed to close-up video feeds, showing their missiles honing in, and vaporizing, intended targets. With a heavy heart, Jason watched the centermost display feed. The Emperor's Palace, standing tall and imposing ... in a flash, it was gone. Angry now, Jason continued to stare at the ravaged landscape. Barely audible, Jason clenched his fists and said, "Fuck you, Lom. May you burn in hell for making me do this ..."

"Shields down to thirty percent and falling fast, Captain!"

The Ion Station, taking multiple missile strikes, erupted into a magnificent fireball. The outward effects of the blast moved the *Minian* nearer to the closing dreadnaughts.

"Helm, phase-shift us to the first set of coordinates," Jason commanded.

McBride must have had his finger poised over the button because the bridge immediately flashed white. Reappearing twenty thousand miles away, the *Minian* was enmeshed on top of a dreadnaught, lying at a perpendicular angle, toward the bow of the Craing warship.

Those standing on the bridge were thrown to the deck. Grating sounds of metal shredding metal continued until the *Minian* slowly stabilized and came to rest.

"Status?" Jason barked.

"Shields are completely down, Captain," Orion reported. "Looks like they saved us from substantial damage but now they're gone."

This wasn't the first time Jason had phase-shifted into another vessel. In fact, he'd made an ongoing practice of doing so. But losing their shields couldn't be good.

"Captain, we're ... stuck," Perkins said, standing at the console directly to Gunny's left. "Looks like a support beam from the dreadnaught is wedged into the *Minian*'s starboard flight deck."

"I can confirm that, Captain," McBride said. "We've got propulsion. We're just not able to break free from the clutches of that dreadnaught."

Jason leaned back and rubbed the stubble on his chin. It was then he noticed the approaching ships.

"There are six dreadnaughts nearing. They've changed course toward the *Minian*," Orion said, sounding almost apologetic.

"Okay, here's what I want to happen. Gunny, keep those other ships away from us. Fire at your discretion. Brian, how about you organize a team, perhaps the same team that broke us free from the Ion Station scaffolding."

"We've got incoming ... nukes this time. Two thousand warheads headed our way. And that's just the first wave." Orion turned in her chair, shouting, "That's it. I'm sorry, Captain, but there's no way we're fending off four, or six, or ten thousand nukes with no shields. Also, don't forget all the dreadnaughts out there looking for revenge on what we just did to their home worlds."

Orion was the last person Jason expected to lose it—to give up. She'd obviously reached her breaking point. "We're far from over, Gunny. Pull yourself together and man the guns. This isn't about winning this battle, we can't. It's about giving us enough time to get out of here. So first thing's first: take out that first wave."

Orion didn't move for several beats, then turned back around, "Aye, sir."

"Looks like we're going to be here a while," Jason said, looking around to find Billy standing at the rear bulkhead. "What do you say we dramatically improve our odds?"

"I'm up for that. What are we waiting for?" Billy answered with a wry grin.

"XO, you have the bridge. Billy and I are taking *The Lilly* out for a spin."

* * *

With the exception of Toby Jackson, still tasked with guarding Granger, twenty-four Delta Force combatants were assigned to the *Minian*. Putting up a defense position within the Minian's breached starboard flight deck, their presence would allow Brian's repair crew to work on getting the two ships dislodged.

Back on *The Lilly*, Jason confirmed Ricket was still on board and then hailed his fighter squadron leader, Lieutenant Craig Wilson.

"Go for Wilson."

"Lieutenant, need you to get your butt up to the bridge ASAP. You'll be at the helm. Tell Grimes and the others to be ready to launch their fighters into open space within two minutes. We've got incoming."

"Aye, Captain, I'm on it."

Chapter 35

The bridge crew included Ricket as XO, one of the Gordon brothers on comms, Bristol at tactical, and Lieutenant Craig Wilson at the helm post. Jason gave the order to phase-shift *The Lilly* from the relative safety of the *Minian*'s large hold into open space.

Since the *Minian* was undergoing attack from all sides, Wilson had prior needed to coordinate with Orion a safe haven location that would be clear from any friendly fire.

"Incoming from ... shit, everywhere," Bristol yelled.

"Watch your language," Jason said with an irritated glare toward tactical.

The Lilly's large arsenal of plasma and rail cannons came to life as the latest wave of Craing warheads headed toward them.

Jason answered an incoming hail: "Go for Captain."

"We're phase-shifting fighters in thirty seconds," Lieutenant Grimes said.

"Copy that," Jason responded, then hailed Orion on the *Minian*: "What's going on with the drones?" He recalled the row upon row of idle drones from the first time he'd been on the *Minian*'s flight deck. Those advanced little killers could make a big difference over the next few minutes.

"Both sides of the *Minian*'s flight deck are still obstructed by the top portion of the dreadnaught. I needed Granger's help figuring out how to phase-shift them as a unit into open space.

They should be deployed within the next minute."

Jason shifted his eyes to the logistical display segment and felt his heart sink in his chest. It was clear—every ship in Craing space was quickly making its way to their location. He was reminded of his recent words to Orion—we don't need to win the battle, just to hold on long enough to escape. To do that he'd need help. Jason looked at the nearby dreadnaught, and I know just where I'll get it.

Expecting to see *The Lilly*'s six red fighters, Jason was surprised to see twenty-five bright blue *Minian* fighters suddenly appear around *The Lilly*. *Of course*, Jason thought. Grimes and her expanded squad of twenty-four Top Gun pilots opted for the significantly more-advanced fighters stationed on the *Minian*'s flight deck. Now moving across space at incredible speeds, the squad wasted no time attempting to repel the constant barrage of incoming ordnances. But even their resounding defense wasn't going to be enough. With the *Minian*'s shields down, as well as the shields on the dreadnaught, the two goliath-sized ships were sitting ducks for what seemed to be an endless onslaught of plasma fire, and wave after wave of incoming missiles.

"Orion ... we need those drones—"

Jason cut his command short on seeing several hundred small drones suddenly appear. Blue, similar looking to the fighters, they quickly spread out and went to work countering the ever- increasing volley of missiles. He watched as two Craing missiles made it through their defenses, exploding into the top of the dreadnaught—far too close to the *Minian* for comfort. Four nearby drones were instantly vaporized and the *Minian*, abruptly jerked, shifted within the still tight grasp of the Craing warship's outer hull.

Jason hailed Orion but got no response. A moment later he was hailed by Perkins. "Go ahead, XO."

"Orion took a knock to her head. She'll be all right—actually, she's coming around now. We can't take another hit like that, Captain," the XO said, his voice unsteady.

"When does Granger expect to have the *Minian*'s shields back up?"

"About fifteen minutes was the best I can get from him."

Jason continued to watch the display—the Minian remained locked tight within the dreadnaught's grasp. "Maybe there's something else we can do in the meantime. Ricket, you're with me."

Leaving Wilson in command of *The Lilly*, Jason spent the next ninety seconds on comms rounding up an assault team, then moved toward the largest of the shuttles, the Magnum.

The last time Jason attempted to pilot this type of shuttle, one of the newer shuttles from the *Minian*, he'd had mixed results. Even with all the HyperLearning he'd gone through in a MediPod, actual real-time behind the stick was still essential.

"You're flying?" Billy asked, climbing into the copilot seat.

Jason didn't dignify the question with an answer. He turned and verified his teammates were on board: Ricket, Rizzo, Chief Petty Officer Woodrow, and Traveler. "How's the foot?" he asked the latter.

Traveler stamped his left foot down several times on the deck. "Good as new."

"What's the plan, Cap?" Billy asked.

Ricket reached into the cockpit and configured the shuttle's phase-shift coordinates.

"The plan is to help convince the dreadnaught bridge crew to defend themselves. That simple." In a flash, they phase-shifted into the dreadnaught's primary corridor.

"Feels like old times," Billy mumbled around a fat, unlit stogy hanging from the corner of his mouth.

The corridor was undifferent from other dreadnaught main corridors they'd been in over the past year, with one exception: this one bustled with activity. Multiple repair droids had been activated and were whizzing about in different directions, presumably to attend to the ever-increasing outer hull damage. No less than ten, slower moving, open-air crew carriers hovered as the shuttle passed by them. The closest was mere feet below them and Jason saw some startled faces looking upward as he powered the shuttle over their heads. Within ten seconds they'd reached the end of the corridor and the section of the ship containing the bridge. He reset the *Magnum*'s controls to maintain their current hovering position.

Jason and Billy stood at the same time and both activated their segmented helmets to close.

"We have zero time to waste. Ricket, you need to get this dreadnaught to defend herself. We also need to see if getting her shields working is a possibility."

The team phase-shifted as a unit and appeared by the raised officer section on the bridge.

"Who's in charge here?" Jason yelled, his multi-gun raised and pointing toward four Craing officers who sat with their mouths agape before him. Truth was, he already knew. He repositioned his weapon to point at the officer wearing a gold medal around his neck. The Craing captain raised his hands even higher than they already were. "What's your name?"

"I am Captain ... I am Sto-Pip."

Jason was glad Billy didn't make a snide comment about his name. "It's time you defended your vessel. Other dreadnaughts out there are firing on you."

"I cannot ..."

Jason shot the captain with a high-level stun pulse. "Ricket ... go to work. Let me know if you need help from these other officers."

As many as forty Craing crewmembers nervously stared up at Jason and the assault team; he expected to see hatred in their eyes but saw none of that. *Why?* Jason wondered.

Ricket quickly found an open console and within seconds looked up at Jason. "As of now, this vessel is fully engaging the surrounding Craing warships. Nuclear and fusion-tipped warheads, as well as plasma cannons, are targeting the nearby ships." He turned his attention back to the console. "I believe if I section off the damaged area, where the *Minian* is located, I may be able to reinitialize the shields—or at least some of them."

He had a random discouraging thought. Were there prisoners here, being held on board? He'd certainly observed countless jail-like cages lining the main corridor, but he hadn't noticed if they were occupied.

"Ricket, is there a way for you to check if the prisoner cages are occupied?" Jason asked.

Ricket looked confused by the question. "Why would you—" He cut himself short and moved from one console to another three posts away. He gestured for the Craing crewmember to vacate his seat. Ricket, fingers flying across the input device, suddenly stopped and looked up at Jason, and then to Traveler. "Captain, there are eight hundred prisoners on board this vessel. One hundred and thirty of them are rhino-warriors."

That statement got Traveler's full attention. His deep voice boomed across the bridge. "We will rescue the rhino-warriors."

Jason looked blankly at Traveler for several beats, not sure what to say. There was absolutely no time for a rescue operation. Hell, they'd be lucky to get out alive as it was ... Why on earth had he mentioned the prisoner cages? He hailed the *Minian*.

"Go for XO."

"Status?"

"Better now, Captain. The dreadnaught you're on is emitting

an excellent amount of firepower. Enemy ships in the area have backed off ... at least, somewhat. There's still a lot of incoming fire, but it's manageable. Looks like Ricket has the shields up as well—that should help."

Jason figured Ricket had gotten the shields up in the last few seconds. "And the flight deck crew?"

"Brian's crew is still trying to extricate the ship. Cutting through the crossbeam has been problematic. They'll need more time before we'll be able to phase-shift."

"Understand, XO. Let me know when anything changes."

Chapter 36

Chief Commander Ot-Mul was fast asleep in his quarters when he was awakened by his second-in-command. He didn't want his sleep disturbed and had made that quite clear. Unless there was a dire emergency, he was not to be bothered by trivial or inconsequential news. He quickly discovered the disturbance this time was anything but inconsequential.

By the time he made it onto the bridge he only knew the bare basics of what had happened; the Craing worlds had been attacked and the status of acting-Emperor Lom was yet unknown.

Ot-Mul took his seat on the raised officer's platform and faced the other four officers. "Tell me what happened."

Ot-Mul's second-in-command, Ry-Jon, looked distraught, almost as if he'd been crying. Ot-Mul disliked Ry-Jon and had already put in the necessary work order to have him transferred off his vessel. But now, having to endure his emotional dolefulness was quickly getting old and under his skin.

"Chief Commander, it is with great distress I inform you that acting-Emperor Lom ..."

Ry-Jon stopped mid-sentence to look down at the floor and steady himself. Ot-Mul watched the whimpering fool with astonishment, having to restrain himself from backhanding him across the face. "What? Acting-Emperor Lom is what?" Ot-Mul demanded. Here, his destiny lying in the balance, and this doddering idiot couldn't manage one simple sentence.

"Acting-Emperor Lom is gravely injured. I am so sorry to tell you this news, Chief Commander."

"You told me the palace was destroyed. How does Lom still live?"

Ry-Jon looked at his commander with an appalled expression. It was no secret Ot-Mul had high ambitions, wanting to advance to emperorship himself one day, but his disrespectful usage of the acting emperor's name ...

"Tell me, you cowering windbag, or you'll be sharing a cage with an Algarian flesh-eater!"

Ry-Jon stammered on: "The acting emperor, as well as the panel of high priest overlords, sought refuge in the royal bunker below ground. But the palace was hit with multiple high-yield nuclear weapons. I don't have all the facts, only that the royal bunker was nearly crushed. The high priests, I'm sorry to report, have all been killed. Acting-Emperor Lom is alive, but barely. He is not expected to survive his injuries."

Ot-Mul sat back in his seat, doing his best not to look pleased with the news.

"Sire, there is more. By the provisions set forth by the new acting overlords, you are the acting-ruling magnate ... you are now, officially, acting emperor of the Craing worlds."

Ot-Mul stared back at the Craing officer in disbelief. *How had such an amazing turn of events happened so quickly? So perfectly?*

The other four officers stood, waiting silently as the rest of the bridge crew followed. Sounds of a religious mantra began broadcasting into the bridge and, quite assuredly, throughout the ship. Then, simultaneously, Craing crewmembers knelt down onto the deck. Quietly, at first, the bridge crew soon droned in harmony with the aired mantra, which got louder as time went on. Ot-Mul watched and listened as they droned reverence to him, their new leader. He waited for the familiar sounds of the snapping of bones. The sounds echoed and stirred him to his very core. The crew suddenly turned in unison and faced in another direction—bowing several times in rapid succession. When the snapping sounds came again, as one the crew turned forty-five degrees and bowed again. Four times they completed the traditional ritual—bowing north, south, east, and west. When the repeating mantra finally ended, Ot-Mul continued to look upon his crew, making eye contact with each one. He bowed and gestured for them to rise and continue with their duties.

Ot-Mul sat down, still somewhat in a euphoric haze. Someone was speaking to him. He turned his attention to Ry-Jon. "I'm sorry, please repeat that."

"What are your orders, my lord?"

"Talk to me about the attack. What's the disposition of our assets in Craing space? It certainly must have been a formidable adversary ... a fleet of incomprehensible—"

"Not at all, sire. This was not a brazen fleet of enemy warships, my lord. More a clandestine act of subterfuge. Very few details are known yet, but the latest information speaks of a cloaked Alliance vessel that made its way to the Ion Station. Once there, a small team invaded the station and absconded with a most important Caldurian piece of equipment. Another team, equally small, captured the Caldurian vessel, the *Minian*."

Ry-Jon paused to settle himself. He licked his lips several times and swallowed, then continued: "They somehow restored power to the Caldurian vessel. Not long afterward, the emperor's security force was defeated. We believe that a guest of the emperor, a Caldurian named Granger, was actually an accomplice and assisted the enemy. It was he who gained them access to the *Minian*'s formidable, highly advanced, weaponry. When the missile attack came, Craing planetary defenses could do little while hundreds of missiles destroyed Craing military targets on all seven worlds. In the end, the Emperor's Palace was also destroyed."

Ot-Mul listened intently. None of this seemed remotely possible. Either the emperor's security force was unimaginably inept, or the attackers were truly cunning. He suspected it was the latter, or maybe a combination of both.

"While attempting their escape aboard the *Minian*, they soon came face-to-face with far too many of our awakening dreadnaughts. As things stand now, we believe it is only a matter of time before we defeat these Allied bandits and retake the *Minian*. My lord ... can I announce our hasty return to Craing space?"

"No, Ry-Jon. You cannot. Our original destination remains the same: Earth."

Ot-Mul was suddenly struck by the precariousness of his new position. For far too long the Craing Empire had underestimated the resilient, and obviously ingenious, capabilities of the Alliance. Even now, with many of the Allied fleets decimated and their star systems facing imminent annihilation, they were still attacking with unbridled cunning. Ot-Mul was well aware where the root of their assault originated—primarily with the Earth-born fleet commander, Admiral Perry Reynolds. And now, a possibly more dangerous threat to them was Captain Jason Reynolds, his son. How one man's exploits, within the span of one year's time, could be allowed was incomprehensible. Craing fleets, thousands of the empire's most powerful warships, had been repeatedly bested. What's worse, the Craing populace, especially the youth, held some kind of admiration for Earth's barbaric, backward, society. Like a festering, growing disease ... it was time to put an end to the Alliance and that would commence with planet Earth. Ot-Mul contemplated on how he would make them suffer. One thing was certain: it wouldn't be quick and it wouldn't be painless.

Ot-Mul turned to his junior officers. "In four days or less our joint fleets will have journeyed from distant space to assemble both there, in the Craing worlds, and also at the arm of Orion. Although he was struck down before it could be realized, acting-Emperor Lom's dream, what we have come to know as the *Great Space*, will become a reality. The Vanguard fleet will now commence this historical, cleansing endeavor, and it will start with the Sol planetary system. It will start with Earth."

Chapter 37

Jason answered an incoming hail from his brother. "Go for Captain."

"All done. It was hard, but we've got the *Minian* extracted from the Craing dreadnaught."

"Damage to the *Minian*?"

"The starboard flight deck hatch needed to be welded shut. Port side's fine."

"Excellent. Hey, you know how to fly a shuttle, right?"

"Um, yeah, of course. Why?"

"We'll have a few additional passengers. Take the *Perilous* shuttle and it's best if you leave the hopper behind on the *Minian*."

"I can do that," Brian replied, sounding unsure about what was going on.

"As soon as you're situated on board, you'll see I've forwarded you the phase-shift coordinates."

That left both the *Epcot* and *Oracle* shuttles still available. Jason hailed Lieutenant Grimes.

"Go for Grimes," she answered, sounding distracted.

"Lieutenant, can you spare two pilots?"

There was a brief hesitation before she replied. "We've lost three fighters, sir. Lieutenants Boyle, Rodrigues, and Masters were just dusted by the Craing."

Jason let that sink in ... "I'm so sorry, Lieutenant Grimes ... Nancy. Forget I asked; we'll make do."

* * *

Jason left Chief Petty Officer Woodrow keeping guard over the dreadnaught's rounded-up bridge crew, with explicit orders that no one was to touch anything.

He was surprised to see that two of Lieutenant Grimes' fellow fighter pilots were now available. Although the onslaught from the surrounding Craing dreadnaughts was still total mayhem ... relentless, and certainly not a battle that could be won, their incoming missiles were being taken out and, for the most part, the *Minian*'s bridge crew were holding the Craing at bay.

Even with the four shuttles transporting hastily released rhino-warrior prisoners into a hold on board the *Minian*, it was taking too long. As with every dreadnaught Jason had come into contact with, here, too, Serapin Terplins roamed the catwalks—a most effective and proven security measure for the Craing.

Jason, piloting the *Magnum*, was cruising back and forth along multiple decks of prisoner cages. The onboard database Ricket had turned up was inaccurate regarding which species occupied which cage. Turned out, it was better to personally check each one. Traveler helped make the process somewhat easier. With the rear of the shuttle open, he was leaning out, his arm extended, and calling out to Jason when he spotted a fellow rhino.

"Stop here, Captain. Two more," Traveler bellowed.

Jason brought the shuttle to a standstill, moving the hull closer in to the catwalk. He turned and nodded to two already freed rhino-warriors, who stood in the shuttle's hold. They looked somewhat confused, though happy to be gaining their freedom. Traveler climbed over a four-foot railing and approached two side-by-side cages. After some words were spoken, Jason saw the two captives move further back. Three solid strikes from his heavy hammer were all it took to break apart the latches on both cage doors.

From the other side of the main corridor, Jason saw the *Epcot* loading three other rhino-warriors. In similar fashion, Few Words was hammering on a latch to break open a cage. He looked over at Jason with a startled expression.

In the few seconds Jason's attention was diverted, three equally large Serapins attacked. Jason quickly stood and headed for the shuttle's rear opening, but by then Traveler and another rhino were desperately fighting for their lives.

Traveler's hammer caved in the skull of one of the now prone Serapins, but two others were upon him ... one with its widespread jaws clenched tight around his right thigh while the other's jaws were closed on his opposite upper arm. Wearing his hardened battle suit, Traveler looked to be fine   only concerned with freeing himself. Jason, who hadn't had time to grab his multi-gun, shot from his dual, wrist-mounted, integrated weapons. The first plasma strikes did little but infuriate the beasts. Ratcheting up the power level to maximum, Jason fired again and bore two through-and-through holes into first one's abdomen, and then the second's.

Clattering came from behind them. As Jason turned he saw another just-freed rhino-warrior being dragged by his leg down the catwalk in the opposite direction. As Jason raised his arm to fire, Traveler brushed by him with his heavy hammer held high. Seeing Traveler's rapid approach, the Serapin released its quarry and quickly back-stepped down the catwalk. Now running, Traveler swung his outstretched arm in a complete circle, releasing his hammer at the perfect moment. The fleeing Serapin, having no time to react, took the brute force of the heavy metal object in the throat. Both clawed arms came up as the Serapin frantically struggled to breathe. But with the amount of damage inflicted on its windpipe, the beast staggered and fell to the catwalk, dying.

After retrieving his heavy hammer, Traveler helped the bloodied, but seemingly okay rhino back to his feet. Jason escorted him into the back of the shuttle while Traveler went to work on the remaining cage door.

Jason answered a frantic-sounding hail from Perkins.

"Go for Capt—"

"We can no longer hold them off, Captain. We've lost two more fighters and eleven drones. The dreadnaught's shields are down to twenty percent. We're out of time; we need to phase-shift out of here!"

"Understand. Recall everyone back to the *Minian*. Have Ricket go ahead and phase-shift The Lilly back as well."

Overriding Traveler's objections, Jason secured the *Magnum*'s rear hatch and immediately phase-shifted them directly onto the Minian's flight deck.

* * *

Jason made it back to the bridge just in time to witness the next phase-shift. In the blink of an eye they'd traveled another twenty thousand miles. Same as before, combined fleets of Craing warships surrounded them ... they were everywhere. Jason sat in the command chair and watched the overhead display.

"No collisions this time, Captain," McBride said from the helm. They were progressing at sub-light speed, apparently catching the nearby warships, mostly light and heavy cruiser and various destroyers and smaller gunships, off guard. Jason watched and thought, again, about the Craing's reasoning for this colossal convergence of ships. He realized they'd assembled here to commence the *Great Space* assault: a systematic annihilation of all non-Craing life within the sector ... "Gunny, over the next quarter hour, prior to phase-shifting, target and destroy as many Craing warships as possible."

"Aye, Captain."

Within thirty seconds, the *Minian* began targeting, and ultimately disabling or destroying, hundreds of Craing vessels. As Jason watched the logistical display and the swath of destruction the *Minian* was capable of causing, it became crystal clear to him why the Craing were so hell-bent on not only obtaining this Caldurian vessel, but also duplicating her. If Earth, the Alliance, was to have any hope to survive, or perhaps prevail over the Craing, that was exactly what they, the Alliance forces, needed to do. Having a fleet of Minian-type ships could be the answer to ending the war against the Craing Empire once and for all.

"Incoming," Orion said, sounding surprisingly calm. "Dreadnaughts directly ahead. Took them a while to coordinate an attack, but now that they've plotted our course, we'll be lucky to fend off the incoming barrage."

Jason chided himself for the unbelievably stupid mistake he'd just made. It would have been far better at this point to proceed with short phase-shift jumps to maintain the element of surprise. The Craing's slow reaction time had offered them an opportunity to hopscotch across their space relatively unscathed. Now, they'd have to wait another quarter hour before they could phase-shift again. Jason made eye contact with his XO, and then with Orion. The three nodded their heads in unison, each coming to the same, obvious, realization at the same time.

Jason stood and stepped closer to the display. "Is that a meganaught?"

"Aye, cap. Well, actually we'll be passing three meganaughts, one after another."

"Terrific. What's that dark patch there?" Jason asked,

pointing to a section of space closest to the nearest meganaught.

"That would be a drone swarm, Captain. You're looking at thousands of drones; collectively ... that's going to be a problem," Orion replied.

Jason continued to focus on the ominous, widening patch of blackness, and the ever-growing number of incoming missile icons. "Options?"

"We could turn back into the Craing fleet—perhaps ..." Orion dropped that idea as she quickly realized it wouldn't work.

"Let's get Ricket and Granger up here. Quickly as possible."

Ten seconds later Ricket and Granger, along with Toby Jackson, phase-shifted onto the bridge. Jason quickly brought them up to speed on the situation.

"We have less than two minutes before that first wave of missiles hits. With substantially diminished shields those drones will cut us to pieces."

Granger stood with his hands on his hips, concentrating on the display. "Get me to the Zip Farm," he said, looking at Toby, who'd accompanied him to the bridge.

Toby looked to Jason. "What's a Zip Farm?"

Ricket moved fast and took Granger by the arm. A half-second later they both disappeared in a flash of white light.

* * *

They phase-shifted into one of five Zip Farm compartments, where multiple rows of   equipment, similar-looking to large ten-foot-high by thirty-foot-long generators or turbines, were located. Virtually every inch of the compartment was occupied. Ricket was familiar with this area of the ship and had, in his spare time, been researching the capabilities of the Alurian technology, from a distant planet in the Corian Nez constellation system.

Granger took off at a full run down the narrow row of Zip accelerators. Close on his heels, Ricket followed. "What are you thinking? Using these Zip accelerators somehow?"

"This technology is how the Caldurians crossed over to other planes of the multiverse."

"I know that. Are they operational?"

Granger made a quick right turn down another row and increased his speed. Ricket, having much shorter legs, was having difficulty keeping up.

"Perfectly operational," Granger said over his shoulder. "The Craing hadn't yet begun dismantling this section of the ship." Granger finally came to a stop at a bulkhead at the end of the row. Here sat a console and, like the Zip accelerators, everything looked black and greasy. Ricket figured this was the Zip Farm interface, and though at first it looked like older technology, it was somehow different.

Granger went right to work, tapping commands into a mechanical input device. The display, which was a strange combination of virtual holo 3D and actual hovering, materialized items, updated as Granger continued to input information. Granger suddenly stopped and looked down at Ricket with a frustrated expression.

"I'd forgotten. We're not using the *Minian*'s power base, are we?"

"No," Ricket replied. "Well, not completely. *The Lilly*'s power-coupled ... supplying a substantial portion of the *Minian*'s drive propulsion ... as well as supplying power to other systems."

Granger finished inputting. "Get us back to the bridge!"

Chapter 38

"Shields are holding at sixty percent," Gunny said. "But Captain, *The Lilly*'s power reserves are being depleted at an accelerated rate. Carrying the extra load of the *Minian* is simply too much for her. There's not enough power to phase-shift—at least not anytime soon."

Jason saw that the first wave of incoming missiles were taken out by the *Minian*'s plasma and rail fire, but now more and more missiles were getting through. Jason considered shifting *The Lilly* again, out into open space, but that could have adverse effects ... most notably, leaving the Minian without power to defend herself.

Ricket and Granger flashed back to the same bridge location from which they'd earlier left. Immediately, Granger moved to the left side of the bridge and tapped at a never-used open console. Jason and Ricket joined him there and watched as the upper portion of the console lowered and slid away, only to be replaced by a black, more mechanical-looking interface. As it rose up and clicked into place, Granger brought up another quasi-3D display, again with actual hovering materialized items.

Ricket said, "You're looking at Alurian technology. This is the bridge's interface to the *Minian*'s Zip Farm, which we found down on a lower deck."

Jason returned a blank expression. "Okay ..."

"The means by which the *Minian* crosses over to the multiverse," Ricket clarified. "The problem is raw power. As is, *The Lilly* is barely providing what's needed for the *Minian*'s sub-light propulsion and phase-shift capabilities. Not to mention her weapon systems."

"Explain how this Zip Farm—the multiverse—helps us out of our current predicament?"

"Captain, the drones are now twenty seconds out," Gunny interjected. "And ... as I mentioned, we have no power reserves to phase-shift."

Granger looked at Jason with mild annoyance. "We move this ship onto an alternate plane of the multiverse, perhaps a plane where there are no Craing warships in close proximity. It's basically another form of phase-shifting, with several very important differences. You have access to alternate planes of existence, versus just your own, and you'll have the option of staying there long enough to survive a bad situation. See what I mean? All our immediate problems disappear. It'll give us enough time to clear this area of space."

"So what's the problem? Why not just do it?" Jason asked.

"I told you. Power. The way things stand—it would have to be a one-way trip."

Jason let that sink in. *Yes, we could save our own hides, but that would still leave Earth and the Alliance to deal with the impending Craing attacks.*

"Think of another alternative," Jason said.

Granger stared back at Jason for several long beats.

Suddenly Ricket's head jerked toward the display, his attention focused on one of the nearest Craing vessels. "Craing dreadnaughts have modular power bales. Fairly transportable, they're stored in sub-zero containment lockers. The power bales provide for replacement of antimatter, as needed, for the ship's multiple drives."

"Can the *Minian* be adapted to utilize those, what did you call them ... power bales?" Jason asked.

Granger nodded and looked at Ricket appreciatively. "He's

right ... it's nothing that could be used long term but yes, you could adapt them to the *Minian* fairly easily."

Ricket broke in. "Give me two minutes and I'll have an interface manufactured by the phase-synthesizer."

Jason asked, "So how do we get ahold of them?"

"They're modular," Ricket replied. "Eight-inch cubes. Their sub-zero temperatures and high levels of radiation will make transporting them somewhat problematic. I suppose if you're quick enough your battle suits will provide adequate shielding."

"Two questions: how many of these things will we need, and where, exactly, will I find them?"

Granger chewed on that for several moments. "You'll need no less than ten of them to accommodate a round trip."

"As for finding them, that's the easy part. The containment lockers are positioned directly beneath the dreadnaught's Engineering sections," Ricket added.

As if on cue, Perkins provided an enlarged schematic of a dreadnaught into a new display segment above them.

"You'll have to get close enough in to phase-shift inside that compartment there," Ricket said, pointing to a now-enlarged section of the dreadnaught.

"So we get in, grab up the power bales, and get out," Jason mused.

Granger shrugged, as if it were as easy as buying a quart of milk at the corner supermarket.

"Go ahead ... get cracking on manufacturing the interface, Ricket."

* * *

Jason was rapidly going through his pre-flight checklist—readying the *Pacesetter* for the trip into space and also eyeing the closest Craing warship—an imposing-looking meganaught. Suddenly, *The Lilly*'s flight deck began to shake and he knew the *Minian*'s shields had just gone down. A moment later, everything resettled. *The Lilly*'s own shields were now extended out to fully encompass the *Minian*, but further depleting *The Lilly*'s own diminishing power reserves, which meant there would be no power remaining for either propulsion or weapons ... So now both ships were sitting ducks, with mere minutes to survive the ongoing Craing onslaught.

"Don't even think about lighting that thing," Jason warned.

"Wouldn't dream of it," Billy replied from the adjoining cockpit seat, directly behind him.

Jason double-checked the series of three phase-shifts that would be necessary to enter into the Engineering section of the last of the four—rearmost—dreadnaughts.

"Ready?"

"All set," Billy replied.

Jason initiated their first phase-shift into open space. By mere chance they reappeared at the precise coordinates of an incoming Craing missile. The *Pacesetter*'s mass superseded that of the missile, causing the remaining sections of the missile to spin off in separate trajectories into space.

"Nice," Billy said, "bet you couldn't do that again if you tried."

Jason ignored the comment and within several seconds the second phase-shift was initiated, bringing them closer to the five-mile-long Craing meganaught.

"One more. Ready or not, here we go."

The third and final phase-shift brought them into an area of total, pitch black darkness.

Jason brought the *Pacesetter*'s exterior lights up, including its big, forward spotlight.

"Looks like this dreadnaught's unoccupied—deserted," Billy

commented.

"Yeah. This one showed the least life signs and output power signals. We lucked out."

Jason took in the virtual icons on the ship's 3D holo-display, with schematic-like outlines depicting the surrounding features of the still too-dark-to-see-clearly area. Jason took a moment to orient the position of the *Pacesetter* relative to the rest of the Engineering section. Ricket had provided excellent phase-shift coordinates—they were close to the containment lockers.

Jason set the *Pacesetter* down onto the Engineering deck. Once the *Pacesetter*'s canopy was open, Jason and Billy climbed down. Each wore an empty rucksack slung over a shoulder and carried a multi-gun. The cavernous space seemed to swallow up all light—their helmet lights enabled them to see no more than two or three feet distance away.

Battle suit proximity sensors, interfaced to their HUDs, allowed them to navigate around obstructions, such as large pieces of equipment and bulkheads. Jason, hurrying and quick as possible, was suddenly stopped in his tracks as he walked into something at head level, which he discovered was a low-hanging crossbeam of some kind.

"You okay?" Billy asked.

"Fine. But I'd duck down a bit lower here for the next few feet."

Jason moved as fast as he dared, knowing both the *Minian* and *The Lilly* would be without shields in a matter of moments— maybe less. They'd reached an opening in the deck that was surrounded by a two-foot-high metal railing. At an open section a stairway led down into another, totally dark area of Engineering. If Ricket was correct, this area was where the containment lockers were situated. Jason moved down the stairs first. It was a fairly long stairway, and Jason noticed his HUD external temperature readings were quickly dropping to near zero.

They reached the bottom of the stairs into a narrow hallway with banks of equipment lining both walls. Jason could easily extend his arms and touch both sides. As they continued forward there was an ever-increasing icy fog encircling the air about them.

Thirty yards further down the corridor, according to Jason's HUD, the area opened up a bit. They entered into a larger, circular compartment where the fog was so thick their helmet lights could hardly penetrate.

"We're in the right place," Jason said, slowly turning on his heels, taking in the compartment. "Take your pick; we have floor-to-ceiling storage lockers all around us."

"Cap, we have company. Something just brushed against my leg."

Chapter 39

"You're imagining things. As far as I can tell, HUD's not picking up any additional life forms in this vicinity," Jason said, moving over to the curved wall. Seeing the rows of the vertical, rectangular compartments, he was reminded of what looked like old, high school-type lockers.

Each locker had a security latching mechanism. Billy joined Jason and together they looked at the locker in front of them at eye level. "Ricket didn't mention any security latches," Billy said.

"No, he didn't." Jason hailed Ricket.

"Go for Ricket."

"Take a look at my helmet cam feed. The lockers have security latches."

"There won't be time to figure that out, Captain. We're in trouble over here. I'd suggest you blast the latch. Be careful not to actually hit any of the power bales, although antimatter containers such as those are usually stable ... I have no idea what a direct plasma blast might trigger."

"How am I supposed to destroy the latch and not hit anything behind it?"

"I don't know, Captain, but please hurry."

Jason took a step back. "Okay, Billy. We're going to have to blast them and hope for the best." Billy took several steps backward.

Ricket's nervous voice echoed in Jason's head: *We're in trouble over here ...*

Jason made a best-guess plasma power level selection from his HUD, aimed ... and fired. The locker directly in front of him disappeared in a thundering blaze of fire and black smoke.

"Maybe that was a bit of an overkill setting, Cap. Let me try ... use a somewhat lower setting." Billy aimed and fired. The locker, two over from the demolished one, now had a clean circular blast hole where the security latch had been just seconds before.

Jason rushed forward and opened the freed locker door. Stacked two high and four deep were eight power bale cubes. Blue and pulsating, each looked like a large glowing ice cube. As Jason reached for the top left one, he was stopped by a piercing alarm sound emanating into his helmet. He saw a coinciding, flashing, red warning message:

ULTRA HIGH RADIATION – DEATH IS IMMINENT

Jason hesitated and looked over to Billy.

"I guess we'll need to move fast," Billy said.

They removed their rucksacks from around their shoulders, opened them up at the top, and prepared to grab. It was then Jason felt something smack into his inside right calf. He ignored whatever had hit his leg, as well as the ever-present alarms and warnings. In seconds, they each collected four bales and their rucksacks were filled.

"Time to get the hell out of here," Jason said, turning back in the direction they'd entered. They nearly made it out of the containment locker compartment when first Billy went down, and then Jason, a second later.

Jason felt as if his ankles were tied together. Although it was difficult to see through the fog, darkness, and the continuing warning light messages on his HUD, he could see that *something* had indeed wrapped itself around both legs. Jason heard Billy cursing and also trying to free himself.

"Snakes! Fucking, fucking snakes!" Billy yelled.

Jason first got one gloved hand, and then his second, around the tube-like creature that had bound his legs together. Flailing and squirming, the translucent snakelike creature was actually more like a long centipede—a centipede with hundreds of barbed legs and a gaping, tooth-filled mouth—now trying to bite through his battle suit.

Jason squeezed with all his strength. Immediately, he felt the battle suit's powerful, strength-enhancing micro-servos engage. The creature, whatever it was, began to release its hold—uncoiling from around his legs. He continued to squeeze until he felt a definitive breaking, a snapping, of its internal bone structure. He'd no sooner dealt with that one, when another centipede-like creature wrapped itself around his neck and upper torso. *Damn thing must be six feet long*, Jason thought to himself.

Getting to his feet, he saw Billy already standing and dealing with a centipede coiled around his waist.

Jason continued down the narrow corridor. "Deal with it later ... we need to get back to the *Minian*."

They ran, entangled in tightly gripping creatures, into the fog and darkness. Jason cursed the Craing's bizarre means of security, as he'd done many times in the past. Hell ... if it wasn't Serapin Terplins, it was acid-spewing pill bugs, and now these frozen, radiation immune, centipede things.

They no sooner made it halfway up the stairway to the Engineering level when the centipede slowly released its hold from around Jason's neck. Not slowing, he watched as the two centipedes fully uncoiled and quickly slithered away, back down the steps behind them to the frigid containment lockers.

Out of breath and feeling the mounting, nauseating effect of radiation poisoning, Jason was the first to reach the *Pacesetter*. He staggered and nearly fell backward. Billy helped steady him from behind. Taking in a deep breath, Jason swung himself onto the ship's inset stepladder. One ridiculously slow step at a time, he inched upward. Somehow all his strength had dwindled away. And now ... for the first time, he wondered how they could ever make it back in time. So tired. *I'm so very, very tired.* Jason had to stop. Rest for just one more second. Halfway up the ladder, he looked down at Billy. Two steps behind him, Billy looked like death warmed over. *God, do I look that bad?*

The thought of pulling himself up even one more step ... let alone managing to get into the cockpit, was too daunting. Maybe it was time to just stop ... time to give up. He'd given it a good fight, but there was always a winner, as well as a loser, in war. The Craing had won. He'd lost. Jason felt his grip on the rung loosen ... Confused, he thought he heard voices in his head. Was that Ricket? *I don't want to speak to Ricket right now.* Everything was spinning... *need to let go.*

"Are you coming back to me, Jason?" Dira said, concern in her voice.

Jason let his fingers somewhat tighten on the ladder rung. *What a delightful voice.* He'd always loved that accent ... he heard it again.

"Jason. I want you to come back to me. I love you. You need to keep going ... come on ... climb. One hand at a time, you can do it."

Jason looked down and saw Billy gazing up at him. It was subtle, but he'd nodded. He'd give it a try, if Jason would. They climbed. Rung by rung. Near the top of the ladder the *Pacesetter*'s storage compartment side-panel was already open. As if moving through thick, viscous syrup, Jason first transferred his multi-gun and then his rucksack into the locker. A step and then another and he was lifting his left leg over the top cowling of the cockpit. *Everything's spinning ... stop the spinning.*

Billy was next, trying to get his leg over and into the cockpit.

If their situation wasn't so dire, it would have been humorous. But this was far from funny. Behind Billy's amber visor, Jason could see glistening tracks of tears on his friend's cheeks. He simply had nothing left ... his reserves were totally spent.

"Ready to lead, ready to follow, never quit," Jason told him. The SEAL motto was barely audible, but his Cuban friend heard it. Billy's eyes locked on Jason's.

"I'm sorry buddy. I don't think I can—"

Jason cut him off. "Ready to lead, ready to follow, never quit. Come on. Say it with me, Billy ... ready to lead, ready to follow, never quit."

Billy mumbled the words in unison. Jason repeated them louder. Billy also spoke them a bit louder. Then both voiced the motto still louder, until both were yelling the SEAL motto, *ready to lead, ready to follow, never quit*, at the top of their lungs. Billy finally got his leg up and over into the cockpit and tumbled inside.

The last thing Jason remembered before blacking out was the sound of the vacuum *thump* as the cockpit closed securely around them.

Chapter 40

Ot-Mul's orders were explicit. He was to be kept up to date on all activities concerning the Caldurian vessel, which was apparently now powerless as well as defenseless, and sitting marooned amidst thousands of surrounding Craing warships. Destruction of that ship was no longer an option. The technology was so advanced—its destructive prowess so amazing, Ot-Mul realized the ship was essential to the future success of the Craing Empire. He shook his head as he reread the most recent detailed accounting of the battle currently going on in Craing space. Only now had he come to realize, and appreciate, Lom's over-preoccupation with the Caldurian vessel. How a single ship had fended off thousands—full fleets of Craing warships—was beyond amazing.

Looking up to the display before him, Ot-Mul's amazement quickly turned to anger. The video feed, emanating from seventy-five light-years away, showed the *Minian* back in Craing space. But scorched and battered—nearly unrecognizable, she looked more like space trash than the technological wonder she truly was.

He'd already given the order for the fleet to back off—to stop any further destruction of the vessel. They were to recover the *Minian* and take her back to Terplin. Yes, soon … he would have that ship for his own.

"My Lord, we are nearing Carz-mau space."

"I've already made my orders perfectly clear. We'll continue on to Earth without delay."

"Yes, my Lord," his second-in-command replied. "We have new information. What remains of the Mau fleet, more than four hundred warships, has been detected by a small Craing outpost. According to them, they are less than one day out from Carz-mau. It is apparent they are returning to protect their home world."

Ot-Mul continued to stare at his second. He was right—this did change things. He didn't like the Mau. The truth was, they unnerved him. Their gaping, open-mouthed faces were hideous. They were an abomination. Carz-mau and all other planetary systems in the sector were slated for destruction as part of the *Great Space* initiative. Letting the Mau fleet of powerful warships return home could come back to bite him in the ass later.

"Change course for Carz-mau space. Thank you, Ry-Jon, for bringing this to my attention."

* * *

It took nearly four hours for the Craing fleet, along with his six Vanguard dreadnaughts, to reach the outskirts of Carz-mau space. As far as Ot-Mul was concerned, seeing the distant planet now coming into view, it was just one more drab-looking, dirt-colored planet, amongst thousands—millions—of other dirt-colored planets in this part of the sector that needed to be expunged ... turned to dust.

Ot-Mul ordered his Vanguards to break formation and take up their proper upper-orbit positions around Carz-mau.

"Sire, we have incoming ordnances from the planet surface. Also, five Mau warships are headed inbound from their closest moon."

"Go to battle stations. Order the fleet to deal with the

warships first. They can use the practice."

"We are tracking thirty-two inbound fusion-tipped warheads, sire. Six of them are locked onto our vessel," Ry-Jon reported.

Six missiles against the might of a dreadnaught? A Vanguard dreadnaught, no less. Ot-Mul smiled and gave the order: "Take them out."

He stifled a yawn and let his mind wander a bit. He thought about his mate, Molis. He missed her and mentally vowed he would return to her soon—to their home on the most distant, the seventh, Craing world. He wondered if she was proud of his recent accomplishments and if she was looking forward to relocating to Terplin. Of course ... a new Emperor's Palace would have to be built. All that would take time.

His undisguised disinterest in events now taking place in Carz-mau space, and the six approaching missiles, changed to something resembling mild curiosity. Thus far the missiles had avoided Craing defenses with relative ease.

"Is there a problem?" Ot-Mul asked, now sitting up straighter in his seat.

"There does seem to be a temporary issue ... we have not been able to get a lock on the missiles just yet," Ry-Jon said, not sounding in the least confident.

Both Ot-Mul and Ry-Jon got to their feet and stared at the largest of the bridge displays. Ry-Jon turned and smiled. "Four of the incoming missiles have been destroyed ..." His words were interrupted by a distant rumble then followed by multiple violent tremors. Ot-Mul reached for something to hold on to and grabbed the armrest of his chair. He knew exactly which part of his ship was struck; they'd just lost one of their primary drives. The ship shook again, this time far more violently. Apparently, the second Mau missile had also evaded their defenses.

Ot-Mul watched the display in disbelief. As surprising as it was, his own highly-advanced Vanguard warship was damaged; numerous damage reports were also coming in from other Vanguard ships. None had gone unscathed.

Ot-Mul ordered, "Destroy that planet. Do it now!" He continued to watch the display, waiting to see plasma pulses from his ship and the other Craing ships pound the planet below. But the plasma pulses weren't coming. "What's the problem, my second?"

"It's the Mau ships, sire. They are evading any of our attempts to lock on and track them."

Ot-Mul stifled the anger building within his solar plexus. "Give the order one more time. Their first priority is to destroy that planet. Any of my captains who disobey me again will find themselves butchered, thrown into hot caldrons, and feasted on for tonight's ritual."

Ry-Jon conveyed the orders, as well as Ot-Mul's specific threats, across the Vanguard fleet. Within moments Ot-Mul watched as his Vanguard dreadnaughts began their relentless, thundering plasma fire assault onto the planet below. With a relatively low water content, Carz-mau was soon a dark red, glowing, orb. Certainly by now, he figured, every living thing on the planet was dead, and that was some consolation for the damage inflicted on his fleet.

Ot-Mul's eyes moved from the scorched planet and leveled on the Mau warships still in space. The smile returned to his thin lips. He wondered what the crews of those vessels must be experiencing at this moment: the anguish ... the horrific realization that their repugnant species was so near extinction. "That should take a bit of the fight out of them, don't you think?" Ot-Mul questioned to no one in particular. He returned to his seat and continued to watch the skirmish with the Mau warships.

In a distant fireball, one of the Mau warships exploded.

"One down, four to go," Ot-Mul said, with surprising levity in his voice. The display zoomed closer in on a dreadnaught and the remaining four Mau vessels, which were rolling and darting about in a vee formation that was so tight, so in unison, it was hard to distinguish the wings of one vessel from the next. The Mau ships increased their already spectacular speed and moved further away from the closest dreadnaught.

Ot-Mul sneered, "Go ahead and flee. You have nowhere to go ... you have no home to return to." But his words sounded hollow in light of what followed next. In a sweeping, almost majestic-looking arc, the small fleet of Mau warships came out of their final tight maneuver only to increase their speed once again. Like the tip of an arrow, the tightly bunched Mau ships drove their combined momentous force of exotic metals, antimatter propellant, and biological substances into the dreadnaught's most vulnerable, most combustible location. Not one, but two horrendous explosions occurred simultaneously, as both the dreadnaught and the planet Carz-Mau ceased to further exist.

With a gaping, open mouthed expression, not too dissimilar to that of a Mau, Ot-Mul continued to stare at the empty space beyond. The silence on the acting emperor's command ship bridge was absolute. No one dared speak for several long minutes.

"My Lord, what are your orders?"

Ot-Mul turned his gaze to his second-in-command. "First, we alter course for the closest loop wormhole coordinates. Next, you will ensure a replacement dreadnaught has been delivered there and is waiting for us by the time we arrive. We will then proceed, with all haste, to our original destination. We will have no more diversions or distractions ... by this time tomorrow, we will be sitting in Earth's high orbit."

Chapter 41

Jason awoke in a MediPod. Other than feeling thirsty and somewhat tired, he felt pretty good. He saw movement through the small observation window and then saw Dira's face looking back at him. As the clamshell lid began to open, she stood back and waited—her arms crossed beneath her breasts. She smiled, but there was obvious strain showing in her eyes. Jason sat up and she helped him out and to stand up. With a quick glance into the next MediPod, he saw it occupied by Billy.

"He'll be fine. He was in a bit worse shape than you. He'll need another few minutes in there," she said. Jason felt her arms encircle him and her head on his chest. Her muffled voice said, "I thought you were dead. I thought I'd lost you." She raised her head and he could see she'd been crying.

"That was a close one. I have to admit, I didn't think we'd make it back."

She stood on her tiptoes and pulled his head down for a kiss. When they pulled apart she continued to hold his face in her hands. "Don't scare me like that again, okay?"

"I'll do my best. What's going on with the power bales? Was Ricket able to get them interfaced to the *Minian*?"

The strain returned to her face. She shook her head and stepped back. "Jason, it was horrible. Once the shields went down, the *Minian* was defenseless. The pounding was intense—impossible to withstand ... the missile strikes kept coming and coming. It was so awful. We were pretty much resolved we were all going to die."

Jason pulled her close again while listening for sounds around them. "So what happened? I don't hear anything ..."

"Well, that was the strangest thing. One second the *Minian* was being hammered, the hull breached in multiple locations and venting air out into space, and then they just stopped. They no longer fired on us."

"That's because someone high up the Craing food chain ordered them to stop. Destruction of the *Minian*, as well as *The Lilly*, would be counter-productive to their long-term plans to dominate the known universe. I'm guessing they want this ship's Caldurian technology more than ever. Now that we're apparently no longer a threat, they can wait us out for as long as it takes."

Dira said, "That's what Ricket and Granger figured as well. Anyway, everyone's back here, on *The Lilly*, except Ricket, Granger, and several others, who are all trying to get those power bales connected to the *Minian*."

Jason thought about what she said. Truth was, he knew the Craing would only wait so long before they'd attempt to take back the *Minian* by force. And they wouldn't attack alone. That wasn't their style. Hell, they had ample supplies of Serapins or pill bugs or centipedes, or whatever else, in their arsenal. No, soon they'd be coming, to breach their hull, sending in as many of their alien killing-machines as it took.

* * *

Jason made a stop in his quarters where he showered and quickly looked at his messages. The admiral needed to talk to him. There were also separate video messages from Nan and

Mollie, as well as one from Boomer, on the *Cutlass*. He'd watch them later. Right now he needed to get up to speed on Ricket's status with the power bales, and getting the *Minian* safely out of Craing space.

Jason hailed Ricket.

"Go for Ricket."

"Where are you at?"

"*Minian*'s Engineering section. Environment systems are down. You'll need a battle suit, Captain."

"I understand." Jason triggered the small SuitPac device attached to the front of his belt and waited for his battle suit to expand in segments around him. He configured the appropriate phase-shift coordinates on his HUD and, in a flash, stood in the middle of the *Minian*'s Engineering department.

Jason immediately noticed the *Minian*'s gravity generators had been adversely affected—half of what they should be. He was finding he needed to watch his movements, his steps; it was too easy to drift upward for prolonged moments, before slowly drifting back down again. He followed the life-icon locations, displayed at the bottom of his HUD, and moved down several wide corridors and around a corner to a smaller compartment, where he found Ricket, Granger, and Bristol kneeling in front of a towering rack of equipment. They were huddled around something lower to the deck. Ricket had plugged something together and Jason saw that the eight power bales were contained within a clear housing of some sort, with multiple cables attached that connected the power bales to equipment connectors on the *Minian*.

They all turned to acknowledge Jason's arrival. Ricket said, "Captain, it's good to see you up and around."

"It's good to *be* up and around. I'm guessing it was you who remotely phase-shifted the *Pacesetter* back here? Saved our lives."

Ricket shrugged, "It was not difficult."

Granger was adjusting something on the bottommost device on the equipment rack. He was tracing each of the cables, one at a time, to ensure their proper connections. Seeming satisfied, he stood and looked at Jason. "We'll only have one shot at this, Captain. Eight power bales would power a dreadnaught for six months. It will power the *Minian* for mere minutes."

"What we really need is time to repair the *Minian*'s own propulsion systems," Bristol added.

"How long would that take?"

"Hell if I know … Several days, probably."

"We don't have several days. I'm sure you are all aware what's coming next. How the Craing will take back control of this vessel," Jason said flatly.

Ricket and Granger both nodded while Bristol didn't seem to know.

"Tell me what to expect … the whole multiverse aspect?" Jason asked. He was highly aware their options for fleeing Craing space were now limited. The *Minian*'s capability to travel into the multiverse had always intrigued him, but had made him nervous at the same time. What if they got marooned there? How far could he trust Granger that this wouldn't be some kind of hoax for him to gain his freedom?

"It's really quite simple," Granger said. "We'll initialize the Zip Farm interface and, if everything is operating correctly, we'll find ourselves at the way station. You've seen it before, Captain."

Indeed, Jason did remember. He'd been there, in the caverns beneath the Chihuahuan Desert outpost, close to a year earlier. On first impression, it had reminded him of Grand Central Station, in New York City, but on a much grander scale. Massive portal windows, hundreds of them, filled the walls: across, below, to their sides, and even above them. Space vessels, some massive in size, slowly moved from portal to portal. He remembered there was an eerie soundlessness to everything. He let his mind return to that past conversation ...

Jason spoke first. "These ships. They're moving throughout the universe?"

It was Ricket who answered. "Not the universe, Captain. The multiverse."

Granger smiled down at Ricket and nodded. "Continue, Ricket."

"We've discussed this before, Captain. But seeing it manifested like this is something else entirely ... There are infinite layers or membranes of separate universes that exist and coexist in time and space simultaneously."

Granger added, "Where we are standing is actually located in a multiverse membrane that depicts events in six dimensions, versus your three dimensions. What you're looking at is a multiverse way station."

"So, you're saying this isn't actually the sixth dimension?"

Granger answered, "No, this is only a three-dimensional representation of the sixth dimension. The sixth dimension takes place strictly in the realm of math, not physicality."

Ricket nodded approvingly. "I take it those ships are Caldurian vessels moving between multiverse layers?"

"That is correct."

Jason returned his focus to the here and now. "All we need to do is travel beyond Craing space, back to the Orange Corridor, where we can reunite with our convoy and head back to Earth. Will this setup," Jason gestured toward the power bales, "give us enough time to move from here to there?"

Bristol was incensed with Jason's question. "Well, let me lay out your options for you, Captain ... *The Lilly*'s lost her ability to connect to the interchange ... something that is beyond bizarre

... The *Minian*'s communications equipment has been ripped out by the Craing so she also can't call up the interchange ... that means no accessing an interchange wormhole. Added to that, the *Minian*'s drives were completely torn apart by the Craing and she'll be powerless for God knows how long ... and finally, *The Lilly*'s power reserves were so completely exhausted battling that colossal fuckwad amount of Craing warships, she's just barely on life support."

Jason looked to see if Ricket or Granger had anything to add to that, but from their compliant expressions, they looked to be pretty much in agreement. Jason returned his gaze to Bristol. "Talk to me like that again and you'll be spending several weeks in the brig, you understand?"

"Yes, sir. Sorry. Guess I get a bit overexcited," Bristol answered sheepishly.

Chapter 42

Twenty minutes. That's how long Granger said he'd need before the *Minian* as well as *The Lilly*, which was still secured within her largest hold, could attempt to enter the multiverse. But it was something Bristol earlier mentioned that was nagging at Jason. Why had the interchange ceased communicating with *The Lilly* ... with him? He'd been meaning to speak with the interchange—to work through any problems or issues—to reestablish their relationship. A relationship he felt was strong. The truth was, Jason hadn't had a spare second to meet with him.

He used the DeckPort to access Deck 2 and entered *The Lilly's* Zoo. He crossed directly over to the Drapple's habitat. Jason was reminded how the window portal for the Drapple was among the most dramatic and beautiful of all the habitats. There was blue sky above an aquatic, ocean-like expanse, which spanned before him into the distance. Below the waterline was a crystal-clear aqua sea, which was void of any movement—which was typical. Jason tapped on the portal in hopes of attracting the Drapple's attention.

In less than a minute he saw him coming. From far out on the horizon, like a dolphin, the Drapple was moving fast: a combination of high-in-the-air jumps, followed by quick dives, melded into fluid swimming motions below the surface of the water. The six-foot-long worm-like Drapple arrived with a flourish: a dramatic backwards flip sent him soaring ten feet into the air, followed by a perfect dive back into the water. Now, swaying and buoyant in the aqua sea, the Drapple waited.

"Thank you for coming," Jason said.

The Drapple turned to face him. His features were calm and he had what looked to be a smile across his small lips. The portal window began to vibrate and, as it had in the past, there were sounds similar to how a radio frequency signal is tuned in— full of static at first and then, over time, becoming stronger and clearer. A strong voice emanated into the Zoo; the interchange was speaking:

"It is good to see you, Jason."

"Thank you for coming. I've needed to speak with you for some time now," Jason said.

"Yes. I've been waiting to hear from you. I have been watching ... you are in a most tenuous situation," the Drapple said, now becoming serious. "I believe I know why you are here and what you have to ask me."

"Then perhaps you can tell me why the interchange no longer communicates with my ship? Have we—have I—done something to offend you?"

"These are dark times for your kind, Jason. For many in this small corner of the universe, on this particular plane of existence, it seems an inevitable end is close at hand. I am sorry. I have pondered this situation much in recent times ... but my direct involvement, to help you, typically would go against my purview ... one which dictates I let nature take its natural course."

"So you've turned your back on us? On a whole sector of living beings?"

"On the contrary, I have already gone well beyond my purview. Yes, your ship has lost its ability to contact the interchange. But it is only temporary, only for as long as you remain close to the Craing worlds. It is my decision whom to allow the gift of uninhibited travel across the universe. I will not assist the Craing on their quest to annihilate billions. This area of space, what you call Craing space, does not, and will not, allow for any interchange wormhole travel. This denial has been done *for* you, and for others. Find your way out of this dismal place, Jason ... if you can. I hope you do, so that once again you can regain the gift of the interchange with unrestricted wormhole travel."

* * *

By the time Jason returned to the *Minian*'s bridge, Granger was ready to bring the Craing power bales online and attempt initialization of the ship's Zip Farm. Only Jason, Granger, Ricket, and Bristol remained on board; everyone else was moved back into *The Lilly*. Not only were multiple damaged sections of the *Minian* open to space, the ship was unstable. With the onboard gravity generators barely working, moving about any more than necessary was dangerous.

Jason was watching the primary display, which was continuously losing sync, flickering on and off. He answered an incoming hail. "Go for Captain. What's up, XO?"

"Captain, we have a bit of good news. *The Lilly*'s power reserves are coming back online. It'll still be hours before we have access to any more than basic ship functions, but at least things are improving in that regard. But not all the news is good."

"I already see them, XO. The bridge here is still functioning, though minimally; we see their heavy cruiser approaching from our stern. We'll need what power we get from the power bales to engage the Zip Farm. Have Billy assemble dedicated teams at each of the breached hull locations."

"Aye, Captain."

Granger turned away from the Zip Farm's interface console on the bridge and nodded toward Jason.

"What happens once you flip the switch? What do we do?" Jason asked.

"I've preconfigured our entry into the way station. Best if I simply show you. Time is a factor," Granger answered, looking up at the now-jumbled display. It was difficult to see, but it appeared the Craing cruiser had come alongside the aft section of the Minian.

"We're in your hands, Granger. Let's get to it."

Ricket, already seated at the helm, inputted something on the console and Jason immediately felt the familiar vibration of the ship's power plant coming back online. Dormant consoles and holo-displays were repowered around the bridge, and the overhead display came back on—its flickering and sync issues apparently resolved. Granger was again busy at the Zip Farm interface console, while Jason's attention was back on the Craing cruiser, parked by one of the larger, gaping holes in the hull.

The Zip Farm interface began making mechanical clicking and ratcheting noises. Since Granger was nodding his head appreciatively and smiling, Jason assumed things were working, at least so far, correctly. Something had just happened. Unlike phase-shifting, there was no bright flash nor feelings of momentary disorientation. But two things were evident: the Minian was indeed moving forward, and they were no longer surrounded by thousands of Craing warships. They were approaching an asteroid. Cold and desolate-looking, it was much larger than Jason had originally estimated.

Granger stepped back several paces to stand at Jason's side. Both of them watched the overhead display.

"You do realize that what you're seeing isn't actually real, don't you? That it's simply a visual representation, offered up by this plane of existence?"

Jason didn't answer. The Minian was quickly approaching the asteroid at a far greater speed than, under normal conditions, he knew to be prudent. He watched as other ships, clearly advanced, probably Caldurian, were also inbound and headed for a single opening—like an entrance to a cave on a spectacular scale. No less than ten other vessels entered the asteroid's open entrance at the same time, with plenty of room for twice that many. As they entered the cavernous space within the asteroid, Jason realized he'd seen the place before—only from a completely different perspective. This was the way station! Jason glanced to his side and saw Granger smiling again, obviously enjoying Jason's astonishment.

"We have entered a multiverse membrane that depicts events that occur on a six dimensional landscape, versus your customary three dimensions. We have entered a construct, a representation of a multiverse way station."

"I remember. You explained this before ... everything here on this plane takes place strictly in the realm of math, so in reality, none of this is really here ... something like that?"

"Something like that," Granger replied.

The Minian was making her way across the open void within the asteroid. Hundreds, if not thousands, of distant portal openings filled the distant, curved cavern walls. "How is it determined where we will go? Which portal to enter?"

"That's a difficult question to answer. Your frame of reference is not sufficient to understand many abstract concepts ... such as multiverse membranes that exist purely as potentialities—still to be conceived in one realm while already existing in another. The closest examples I can give you are DeckPorts. How does a DeckPort know which level to transport you to? Actually, you've made this same DeckPort transport an infinite number of times so this reality already exists. The DeckPort knows which level of the ship you want to go to even before you do ... or at least before you realize you do. The Zip Farm can be thought of as a means to match potentialities. Where our own reality of Craing space shows thousands of warships all around us, the Zip Farm uses our intention, which is different than want, to call up the closest mathematical match—one having the intended properties and characteristics: a Craing space that is identical in all other ways but is clear of enemy ships. That's what's really taking place right now, Jason. All this visual imaging of a way station is really a means for the Zip Farm to capture our intention."

Jason continued to stare at Granger, not sure if he understood half of what he was saying. "Whose intention, though? Suppose there are multiple people, and each person intends something different?"

"Good question. The answer is twofold. Reality is not limited. One, two, or even a million different, combined, intentions have a certain outcome possibility. You're forgetting what infinity really means." Granger pointed to the console on their left. "This strange device, one we have replicated onto thousands of Caldurian vessels, yet, truthfully, we hardly understand ourselves, cannot be programed, or have coordinates inputted like you do at the helm here or on the The Lilly. It just doesn't work that way."

Apparently the appropriate intention had been realized, because they were moving toward one particular portal.

"Let me add one thing, Captain. Perhaps more of a warning. Traveling the multiverse can be compelling. For my own people, the progressive Caldurians, they chose to leave their own plane, your plane of existence, for a completely different one."

"Why?"

"They thought they had found the perfect realm, where there was immortality, lack of pain, no war ... no suffering."

"And did they find that place?"

"They thought so at the time. Now, I'm not so sure. Pay attention, Jason. You'll notice that things here on this plane are quite similar but not identical ..."

They made it through the portal and were, presumably, back within Craing space and now traveling within a different plane of existence from their own. Just as Granger promised, there were no other vessels—no heavy or light cruisers, no dreadnaughts anywhere to be seen. If it weren't for his distant view of the seven Craing worlds, Jason would question where they were.

"Captain!" Ricket said. "Full power has been restored to the Minian. We also have phase-shift capabilities and everything else is back online and working perfectly."

Jason answered an incoming hail. "Captain, The Lilly's power reserves are at one hundred percent," Orion announced, sounding more than a little confounded.

Jason turned to Granger. "I really didn't expect ..."

"Then it's a good thing that I did, isn't it? Remember. Traveling into the multiverse is not the same as phase-shifting. Why would you limit this particular plane to the same conditions as the other? Here, the Craing are a peaceful race of people. There is no war here. There was never a reason for the interchange to restrict wormhole travel."

"So we can simply phase-shift back to the Orange Corridor? Simple as that?"

Granger looked bemused by the question and nodded. Jason sat down in the command chair and stared at the overhead display. Something was different about this place ... this realm. Perhaps it was nothing more than his realization that it was not his home.

"Ricket, shift us to the Orange Corridor."

The usual phase-shift experience, one typically involving a

bright white flash followed by an unpleasant bit of disorientation, didn't occur this time.

Chapter 43

The phase-shift flash was a warm yellow and, all in all, a far more pleasant experience. Jason's first reaction was one of concern. They must have inputted the wrong coordinates. He was viewing a spectacular-looking planet, with bright violet oceans, continents with lush green plains, and ridges of mountains so dramatic they made the ones back on Earth look like molehills. In the few seconds since they arrived, several space vessels moved out of the planet's orbit into space.

"Incoming hail from the planet, Captain," Ricket said. "The Allarian space command welcomes us and wants to know if we will be entering orbit."

Jason continued to look at the magnificent planet below and felt deep sadness within him rising—full realization of what he was truly seeing. This was what could have been ... what should have been, before the Craing embarked on their reign of misery and destruction.

"Our convoy, the seven U.S. vessels we left here, in Allarian space. They're not here, are they?"

Granger replied, "No, Captain. There was no need to send them here ... at least, not in this reality's dimension."

"I understand. Fire up that contraption of yours, Granger. Time we got back to our own reality."

* * *

They returned to the asteroid, crossed through the open void, and entered the portal to their own plane of existence. The *Minian* arrived at the exact spatial coordinates in Allarian space that they'd left mere minutes before, only now a horrific space battle was in progress all around them. The U.S. convoy, all seven of the white, heavy and light cruisers, along with as many Allarian vessels, were going up against a Craing dreadnaught.

Jason looked over to Granger. "A part of me sees why your people left."

"Incoming!" Ricket said, his voice somewhat elevated.

Jason felt his anger rise up, like a volcano ready to erupt. They'd come so far, beaten insurmountable odds to get to this point. Was it all to be for nothing? Jason slammed a fist down onto a nearby console, resulting in a fist-shaped impression being left behind. "Damn them ...Damn the Craing to hell!" He steadied himself and forced himself to breathe. "What do we have for weapons?"

Ricket stared flatly back at him. "*Minian*'s back to her previous condition. Still not enough power to charge weapons. *The Lilly* has recharged some, but not enough—"

Ricket's words were cut short by a spectacular explosion in space. Jason realized the quickly dissipating fireball was one of the U.S. convoy ships. His heart stopped in his chest. "Which ship was that?" He held his breath and said a silent prayer that it wasn't the *Cutlass* ... that he hadn't just lost his daughter.

"The *Bastille*, Captain."

Jason was hailed by Orion. "Captain, we've been boarded."

"How the hell ... There's no one around us ... boarded from where?"

"It must be that cruiser back in Craing space. They entered through the *Minian*'s breached hull," Orion said.

"Who? What are they?"

"From what I can tell there are about fifty Serapins and twenty of something else. Sloth-like things. All furry ... with tusks. I guess a cross between a polar bear and a walrus."

"I take it Billy is dispatching teams?"

"We're all suited up, Cap. I'm leaving the bridge now."

"Keep me up to date."

Jason took one more glance at the mile-long Craing dreadnaught, firing continuous barrages of missiles and plasma fire. "They're not taking another ship. Not if I can help it," he said aloud. "Ricket, hail each of our fighter pilots and tell them to be ready to kick ass in two minutes." Jason activated his battle suit and phase-shifted into the *Minian*'s flight deck.

A massive space, the *Minian*'s flight deck was hundreds of yards across. Fifteen blue space fighters, their engines revving up, occupied the center of the deck.

Grimes, dressed in a battle suit, met him halfway as he approached. "I've got a fighter, this one here, winding up for you, Captain. What's the plan?"

"We're going inside that fucking lunchbox-looking colossus and wreaking havoc." Jason didn't smile and didn't slow down. He climbed the inset ladder and seated himself in the cockpit within seconds. "Grimes, keep us all on an open channel."

"The channel's open, Captain," Grimes acknowledged several moments later.

"Listen up, everyone. I'm about ready for some serious payback. I hope you are too. If you're ready, follow my lead." With that, Jason phase-shifted his fighter into open space. Within five seconds the other fourteen fighters appeared in a closed vee formation behind him. Jason estimated the dreadnaught to be less than two thousand miles in front of them. He rechecked his next set of coordinates and phase-shifted away.

Jason's fighter arrived within the dreadnaught main corridor, still traveling at a good clip. It felt good to be at the controls again and he liked the feel of this more advanced ship. It took him several moments to acquaint himself with the controls, and how the HUD and the fighter interfaced to each other.

"Orders, Cap?" came Grimes' voice. Jason saw on his holo-display that all fourteen fighters were now speeding down the massive inner corridor in his wake.

"I'm not going to micro-manage any of you ... with that said, this would be a good time to unleash some of your own internal frustrations. I know I will. All I ask is that you avoid firing into the cages ..." Jason was the first to commence firing into the enormous ship's inner bowels. He selected the rail-cannon and kicked the setting up to what he guessed meant pure firing mayhem. It didn't disappoint him. He let loose a barrage of fire that turned everything in its path to exploding fragments. Within seconds, he found the familiar crisscrossing catwalks that were located just outside the bridge bulkhead. Three more fighters joined him, and together the four of them hovered there. Jason squeezed the trigger and watched as the catwalks disintegrated. Then, with the combined rail munitions fire the four fighters let loose, the bulkhead was next to go. An ever-expanding opening appeared, as the first bulkhead was shredded. A second bulkhead, the one enclosing the bridge, soon went too, disappearing in a devastating hail. As the bridge came into view, Jason directed his fire in the direction he estimated the Craing officers were sitting, up on their raised platform. The hell storm that ravaged the bridge was beyond devastating—it was all consuming. What Jason didn't expect was that multiple bulkheads, on the other side of the bridge, would also disappear, leaving a twenty-foot-wide gap now open to space beyond. What wasn't secured or battened down was sucked out into the void of space ... Jason continued to stare and thought he saw the glimmer of gold, what looked to be the upper torso of a Craing officer, being sucked out through the gaping hole. In that brief span of time, no more than a minute or so, although it felt quite a bit longer, Jason was conscious of all the pain and devastation the Craing had inflicted on so many, mostly innocent, people. He wanted his moment of primal retribution to count for something. Sitting in his fighter, watching as the last particles of the dreadnaught bridge were swept out and away into space, he had to admit ... he did feel better. Perhaps he needed to feel a sense of retaliatory pride in order to face whatever was coming next. Jason knew right then and there that this was just the beginning of their retribution. He was reminded of a particular Shakespearian quote from *Julius Caesar* he'd read back in high school. He said the words aloud:

"Cry 'Havoc' and let slip the dogs of War."

Chapter 44

The other fourteen fighter pilots opted to stay on the dreadnaught—there were still plenty of things to shoot at and this was the most fun any of them had experienced in a long time.

Jason phase-shifted back onto the *Minian*'s flight deck and hailed the XO for an update on the intruder situation.

"Captain, we've had to bring reinforcements over from the other ships. As bad as the Serapins are, and definitely they're bad, it's the sloths. Something to do with their furry coats. Plasma fire has relatively little effect on them. We've found projectiles work the best, but the resulting damage to the ship is too much of a negative consequence. Did I mention they're big? Ten feet tall and as wide as a small car."

"Where are they? How far into the *Minian*'s hull are we talking about?"

"They're all over the place, Captain. Billy reports he's already lost ten SEALs."

Jason cut the connection to the XO and hailed Ricket.

"Go for Ricket."

"What happened to the security drones we had roaming around the *Minian* a while ago? Any chance we can get them into the fight, help take out the intruders?"

"I'd already thought of that, Captain, and yes, they are still around. Currently, they have been deployed where there are the heaviest concentration of ... um ... the beasts."

Jason found Billy's *Minian* location via his life-icon on his

HUD. At first, finding it hard to find an adequate landing space on the ship, Jason eventually went forward and phase-shifted further away than he'd planned. He landed in an area of the *Minian* he was unfamiliar with, which wasn't surprising since the ship was as big as a dreadnaught, and he'd had limited time to explore her many corridors and compartments. The particular corridor he'd phase-shifted into was wide—close to twenty feet across. Up ahead, he saw a small group of SEALs, including Billy and Rizzo, and also his brother Brian, all firing toward a white wall.

Jason realized it wasn't a wall at all, but one of the giant sloth creatures. The XO hadn't exaggerated: it was easily ten feet tall and took up nearly half the corridor. Jason had to do a double take on his HUD. The amount of plasma fire coming from the team's multi-guns spiked the temperature—now climbing to over three hundred degrees. The sloth, enduring ongoing hits, probably some well before Jason arrived, was faltering. It roared like a lion, exposing thick yellow teeth between two-foot-long tusks.

The beast took two steps backward and stumbled over the corpses of two fallen SEALs. Billy and his team moved forward, continuing their onslaught. The beast's end came quickly. It wavered one last time before crashing to the deck, which felt like an earthquake.

It was then Billy noticed Jason's presence. "Oh, thanks for all the help. Enjoy the show?"

"You seemed to have everything in hand." Jason brushed by everyone to get closer to the sloth. He knelt down next to it, muttering, "These things are badass."

Brian replied, "They're worse than that. Earlier, I saw one kill a Serapin, simply because it stood in its path."

"So nobody's come up with a way to stop them? At least

265

more effectively than what you've been doing?"

Billy, Brian, and Rizzo together gestured toward the corridor, previously blocked by the sloth. Brian said, "The hopper. He's killed about five of the things."

"Seriously?"

They all nodded again. "Hopper's the real badass. Gets those sharp claws of his up and jams them forward like a pile driver right into their chests. Then he eats them."

"Eats the sloths?"

"No ... the hearts. He likes their hearts," Brian said.

"What about the Serapins? Does the hopper do the same thing with them?" Jason asked.

Brian said, "Actually the hopper has stayed away from the Serapins."

"Although the Serapins are half the size," Rizzo added. "We supposed the hopper didn't much like the taste of Serapin meat or maybe was afraid of them."

A thumping noise, coming from down the corridor, was getting louder. "Something's coming." Jason picked up a dead SEAL's multi-gun from off the deck and, after checking its settings, he pointed it in the direction of the approaching sound.

"Don't shoot," Brian barked. "I know that sound. Hopper has a peculiar gait."

Sure enough, it was the hopper. Bloodied from head to foot, it slowed when it saw the group and came to rest behind Brian.

Jason looked at his HUD and saw no more sloths ... nor Serapins, either, for that matter.

Jason hailed Orion, "Status?"

"Looks like the area of the ship you're located in has the least amount of sloths and Serapins now, Captain," Orion said. "There's two sloths approaching a DeckPort on Level 1. They've been squeezing into them from the start. Tight fit, but it shows they're fairly smart. The Serapins are on the same two decks they were on when they originally entered the ship. Okay, here's an update: the two sloths are now on Deck 5 ... you know, where the ship's bridge is located."

"We're on it, Gunny," Jason said, and pointed toward the closest DeckPort. "We need to get up to Deck 5. Sloths are headed for the bridge." Brian took off first, followed by the hopper, and the others close behind him.

When Jason arrived on Deck 5 from the DeckPort, two sloths were about halfway down the corridor to the bridge. Moving fairly quickly, with one behind the other, they ignored the crew's presence and kept going their own way. Billy and Rizzo, both kneeling on one knee, fired multiple pulses into the sloth's broad back. That caught its attention and it reared around, roaring angrily. Both clawed hands, which were each about the size of a baseball mitt, came up as if clawing at the air. Billy and Rizzo stopped firing and, as if sensing the right timing of things, the hopper darted forward. As he approached the sloth he slowed, obviously wanting to avoid those big claws. Then Jason noticed the other sloth continuing on toward the bridge.

Scrolling through his various HUD menu settings, Jason found a micro-missile ordnance that looked like it might do the trick. He raised his gun to fire, but now the hopper was weaving back and forth down the hall, snakelike, and Jason didn't have a clear shot. He looked at his HUD and saw that Bristol and Granger were both in the bridge.

Jason hailed Bristol.

"Yeah?"

Jason wanted to reprimand him for his poor comms etiquette, but let it go. "Do you have a multi-gun anywhere around you?"

"No."

"You wearing your battle suit?" Jason asked.

"Um ... yeah. Well, partially ... My helmet's retracted."

"Well, put it up. In about five seconds a sloth is coming through the door. You can use the suit's integrated plasma guns. You'll need to hold it off until we get there."

"A sloth is comi—"

Jason watched as the lead sloth moved closer to entering the bridge. The hopper was now only feet from the closest sloth. Jason caught Billy's eye and mouthed the words, *"How long does this take?"*

Billy exhaled and shook his head, whispering back, "He dances around awhile before he strikes."

Jason saw Bristol peering out from the bridge entrance up ahead and quickly disappear back as the sloth approached. Jason was tempted to let Bristol deal with the beast on his own for a while, but was more afraid of the damage that might occur inside the bridge.

Jason phase-shifted from the corridor into the bridge. Bristol was firing from his two wrist-mounted plasma guns, while Granger hid behind a console, not far from where Jason appeared.

"Bristol, take two steps backwards," Jason ordered.

Bristol did as he was told and Jason brought up his multi-gun. The sloth's fur had proven to be nearly impregnable, so when he fired, he aimed for its head. The timing of the micro-missile couldn't have been more perfect. As the sloth opened his jaws to let out another roar, the missile entered its gaping, wide open mouth and, a nanosecond later, exploded. The result was the smattering of bone, various chunks of muscles and tissue, along with a surprisingly large amount of gray matter, all splattering out into every direction. Bristol, standing two steps away from the beast, took much of the gory mess in his face. He'd neglected to raise his helmet as Jason had ordered.

Chapter 45

Nan Reynolds was on her knees, her mouth poised over the lip of a toilet. Now only dry heaves, she waited to see if this was a longer respite or if she was going to be sick again. She'd suffered morning sickness with Mollie, too, but she didn't remember it being anywhere near this bad. She thought about Jason and how she would do physical harm to him right now if he were anywhere near her vicinity.

She reeled off several toilet paper sheets, ripped them from the roll, and dabbed the corners of her mouth.

"You okay in there, Mom?" a voice asked from the other side of the door.

"I'm fine."

"You sound like you barfed up a Volkswagen."

"Pretty close to what if felt like. Why don't you watch TV, Mollie? I'll be down in a few minutes."

"You have a phone call. It's from the White House. They say it's urgent."

"I'll be right out."

* * *

Nan, with Mollie in tow, was picked up in front of their Georgetown brownstone and quickly couriered to the front steps of the White House. This wasn't Nan's first White House meeting over the past few days, but it was her first impromptu one. Mollie was free from school for the weekend, and they'd planned to spend the day together. Mollie had mentioned something about wanting to visit the Smithsonian, but no museums today. She'd have to settle for seeing the inside of the White House instead.

Nan was by no means the president's only visitor. Pulling into the sweeping driveway, she spotted on the north lawn a U.S., formerly Craing, light cruiser. Along with the limo she and Mollie were passengers in there were ten others, also waiting to drop someone off at the White House steps.

Nan looked over to Mollie, who had moved from seat to seat in the spacious limousine and was currently sitting across from her, trying to open the liquor cabinet.

"There's nothing for you in there. Why don't you come sit next to me? We're almost there."

"What do you think the president wants to talk to you about?" Mollie asked, joining her mother on the long leather seat.

"I think there's new developments in space."

"Do you think Dad's okay?" Mollie asked, her voice sounding tight and controlled.

"Yes, I'm sure he's fine. Let's just wait and see. Here we go, we're here."

The limo's rear door was opened by someone in a uniform. First Mollie, then Nan, stepped out of the car and were ushered into the front entrance of the stately building. As they passed into the expansive front foyer, Nan saw people scurrying here and there with a marked sense of urgency. Several glanced in their direction, first staring at Nan and then Mollie. *It's a Saturday, I have a daughter, so deal with it*, Nan thought.

A young woman in her mid-twenties approached them and smiled. "Hi, Nan, my name is Kalinda White. I'm an aide here, in the White House. And you must be Mollie," she said, smiling down at the impetuous nine-year-old.

"That's me."

Kalinda's smile began fading fast as she put a leading hand on Nan's arm and firmly urged her to follow. "We need to move fast, Nan. President Ross is in a meeting with the Joint Chiefs, and your father-in-law, or I guess ex-father-in-law."

"Grandpa's here?" Mollie asked, perking up.

Kalinda nodded and picked up her pace as they moved deeper into the West Wing. They passed through an empty room with two secretary desks; a plate holding two open-faced bagels topped with cream cheese caught Nan's eye and her stomach churned. She brought up a hand to her mouth and gave a silent prayer she wouldn't throw up on the president of the United States.

Kalinda opened another door and held it open for Nan to pass through. "I can watch Mollie for you, if you wish."

Nan realized she was standing at the threshold to the Oval Office. "That would be great." She looked down at Mollie and winked at her. "I'll come find you as soon as I'm done here." She watched as Mollie was escorted away and already asking Kalinda questions about something or other.

Nan entered the Oval Office and saw only two people in the room: the president and Admiral Reynolds. She had a most terrible realization. Jason must have been killed on his mission to the Craing worlds. The admiral, as well as the president, wanted to convey this dire information themselves. *Oh God, how do I tell Mollie?*

They both looked up and stood as she came into the room. "Mr. President, Admiral Reynolds."

They must have seen the stricken look on her face because the admiral quickly shook his head. "Jason's fine, Nan ... at least as far as I know."

Nan let out a breath of relief and shook the president's

outstretched hand and gave the admiral a hug.

The president wasted no time getting to the point. "Nan, I need to bring you up to speed on the latest events in space."

"You are referring to the Allied mission sent to the Craing worlds?"

"No, Nan. I'm referring to the six Craing dreadnaughts that just entered our solar system."

The room went quiet while Nan processed that bit of information. "Are these the same—"

"We believe so," the admiral said.

As secretary of inter-stellar relations, Nan was well aware of the current state of affairs in space. She spoke to Admiral Reynolds at least once a day. As of late, the Craing had amassed thousands of warships at two key points: one within the star system at Orion's belt, and the other, in Craing space. Recent destruction of certain Allied worlds included Lapoine, Coral-19, Halperon, Vori, Lear-Escott, and, partially, Jhardon. And, more recently, Carz-Mau. The vast devastation signaled the Craing had indeed begun what they referred to as the *Great Space*. The only good news to date, and that hadn't been confirmed yet, was the tactical bombing of the Craing worlds by Jason's space team. Now hearing six dreadnaughts had entered their own solar system was the worst news possible. Beyond doubt, they were the same six black dreadnaughts, the Vanguard fleet, the planet killers, she'd heard about from the admiral.

The admiral said, "Nan, it's more than the oncoming dreadnaught fleet. We estimate there are close to fifteen hundred Craing warships following close behind."

"What of our own fleet? How soon can they be here to protect us?"

"What's left of our fleet can be here in minutes. We're holding steady at about four hundred fifty warships. If prior actions speak for themselves, the Vanguard fleet will enter Earth's orbit within the next few hours. The other Craing warships will engage any ship that tries to assist our planet."

"We need to get people below ground ... try to save as many as possible."

President Ross said, "From what the admiral's informed me, their Vanguard fleet atomizes planets. Going below ground would be an act of futility."

Nan's thoughts went to Mollie and Boomer and her unborn child, and then to Jason. "Where's Jason's convoy right now? Where's the *Minian*?"

Chapter 46

One sloth and three Serapins to go. Lack of sleep was taking its toll on Jason. He'd spent the last four hours hunting the remaining sloths and Serapins. One by one they were going down, but at a cost. Fifteen SEALs and three Delta Force men were lying in the *Minian*'s morgue, in Medical.

Billy and Rizzo had switched over to the same micro-missile setting Jason introduced them to, and had fairly good results. The trick was catching a sloth with its mouth open—amid a roar was good.

Brian's hopper had slowed down as well, only attacking a sloth when it became perilously close to Brian. Another thing Jason noticed was the hopper, at least until this point, hadn't directly engaged a Serapin. According to Jason's HUD, the four beasts still living were on their same level and not moving, near the bottom section of Engineering.

It was just the five of them—Jason, Brian, Billy, Rizzo, and the hopper. The plan was to enter Engineering from two entrances and catch the beasts in a cross fire. Their primary concern was to avoid damage to equipment and the *Minian*'s drives.

Jason, Brian and the hopper took position at the starboard entrance and waited for Billy and Rizzo to get in position at the port entrance. There was another entrance mid-ship, but it was completely blocked off by two dead sloths, lying atop one another.

"We're in position, Cap." Billy's voice came over their open channel into Jason's NanoCom.

"Careful what you shoot at, everyone. Let's go." Jason and Brian entered the large equipment-filled compartment, side by side. Located there were the fronts of the *Minian*'s massive two drive systems. Each drive protruded into Engineering. Looking like fronts of Goodyear blimps, they filled the rear bulkhead, reaching high above, into multiple decks. But what stood in front of the drives had Jason most concerned: it was the last remaining sloth, standing tall. Three Serapins moved around it, as if on patrol.

"They're guarding him," Brian commented.

Before Jason could respond, the Serapins charged. Maybe it was fatigue, too many hours without sleep, or overconfidence by Jason and his team, but they were caught totally off guard.

Two of the Serapins sprang toward Jason and Brian and before Jason could react, his multi-gun was knocked from his hands and came to rest twenty feet away. One second he was standing and the next he lay pinned to the deck. The Serapin's jaw snapped: whipping strings of saliva flew into the air—some splashing across Jason's visor. Visibility would have been a problem, but when the Serapin's jaws completely engulfed the front of his helmet that became the least of his concerns. As Jason looked into the beast's throat, he thanked his lucky stars he was wearing one of the new battle suits. The Serapin began flailing its head back and forth like a puppy with a new toy, attempting to rip his head from his shoulders. He'd witnessed the power of the suit's micro-servos in the past, but they were useless if the human was inactive. His two arms were completely immobile, bearing the weight of the beast's legs, and a thousand pounds of mass straddled across his chest.

Jason was exhausted, his reserves spent. All he could do was watch the numerous virtual HUD readouts hover before his eyes. A new flashing warning message appeared:

Helmet Seal Breach – Imminent!

Jason realized the Serapin might just get his way and tear his head off after all. The Serapin moved on top of him, as if trying to get better leverage with the whole head-ripping-off action thing. But it was enough. Jason slipped one arm forward and up against his own ribcage. The suit's integrated plasma weapon, along the inside of his wrist, was still facing his own body, but it was also close to the Serapin's abdomen. Jason gave it one more try—forcing his arm to move. It budged an inch ... and then another. He fired, and kept on firing until the Serapin released his helmet from its jaws and screeched out in agony. Then Jason's other arm became free and he was able to fire that wrist's integrated plasma weapon as well. The Serapin was trying to get away, but the plasma fire must have damaged its spine—paralyzing it below the waist. It died suddenly, its own weight pulling it backwards onto the deck.

Freed from the beast's oppressive weight, Jason rose into a sitting position. He looked down and saw he was covered in the Serapin's blood and shit and God knows what else.

"Jason! Do you mind? A little help here!"

He turned to see Brian lying beneath another Serapin. Both arms were pinned beneath its weight, as Jason's had been moments before. On the other side of Brian was the hopper. He was alive, but barely, his tail severed clean off. The third Serapin lay dead, eight feet away, its chest an open gory mess.

From across the Engineering department, Jason saw the last sloth lying prone on the deck plates. Billy and Rizzo began walking in his direction.

Billy said, "Looks like you guys had all the fun with the Serapins."

Jason didn't answer, only motioned for his friend to give Brian a hand getting out from under the Serapin. Too exhausted to get up, Jason scooted back and leaned against a bulkhead.

Once extricated, Brian joined him, followed soon by Billy and then Rizzo.

"You got an extra one of those?" Jason asked, gesturing toward the stogy hanging from Billy's lips.

"Just so happens I do." Billy retrieved three more of his Gurkha-brand cigars from somewhere in his battle suit and passed them out. One by one he leaned in and lit them.

Rizzo leaned forward and eyed Jason, "Hey Cap?"

"Yeah, Rizzo."

"Are we going to win this thing?"

Jason took a long draw of his cigar and blew out three consecutive smoke rings. "You know Rizzo, I think we just might."

Jason watched Brian, sitting directly next to the curled up hopper, giving him several pats on his head. "He going to be all right?"

"Yeah, it'll grow back."

* * *

The *Minian*'s bridge had a skeleton crew that included Jason, Ricket, Bristol, Granger, and the latter's around the clock guard, Sergeant Toby Jackson. Since *The Lilly* was still parked within the *Minian*'s hold, and the bulk of his bridge crew was now down on her bridge, Jason had the communications officer, Seaman Gordon, keep a channel open, allowing him to maintain command of both vessels.

Within several minutes, *The Lilly*'s depleted propulsion system had recharged sufficiently to begin the maneuvering of the *Minian* to open space. Jason grabbed a catnap, once Allarian space was determined to be clear of Craing, and the crew had ensured there were no more beasts lurking in the corridors. Earlier, Jason spent several minutes speaking with the Allarian captain, the one they called Chromite, and offered him a MediPod device from the *Minian*. It was the least he could do for their assistance—assistance that had, most probably, saved their lives. Transport of a MediPod onto one of the Allarian vessels took over an hour. Ricket spent another hour explaining the process they'd need to use in reverting other Allarian bodiless brains back into fully-restored, functioning bodies, such as they'd done for Chromite and Silicate. It would take a while, perhaps even years, but eventually they could rebuild their civilization and regain some form of normalcy in their lives.

"XO, status of the other convoy ships?"

"The remaining six cruisers are waiting for your command, Captain."

"Seaman Gordon, request a wormhole from the interchange. XO, prepare to leave the Orange Corridor."

There was a collective sigh of relief when the now-familiar space anomaly distortion occurred two thousand miles off the Minian's bow. Once the wormhole had expanded to its full size and stabilized, Jason gave the order to procced forward at sub-light speed.

The *Minian* was first to enter the wormhole, followed by the rest of the small convoy. A fraction of a second later, they exited from the wormhole's other mouth and entered the Sol system.

"Captain we're receiving multiple hails. The admiral is waiting to speak with you."

"Put him on screen, Seaman Gordon."

Jason was surprised to see his father wasn't alone. Nan was at his side and, like his father, looked frazzled.

Nan spoke first. "Oh, thank goodness you're alive! Jason, the Craing are here."

"Earth?"

"Not yet, but they've entered the solar system. They're holding up near Saturn. Is that right, Admiral?"

"Yes," the admiral replied. "Look, I'm not sure what they are doing or why they're waiting there, but we need you back in Earth's orbit right away. What's the condition of the *Minian*?"

"She's better than she was when moored at the Ion Station, now being operational. But she took a terrible beating leaving Craing space."

"Can she defend Earth? We need those big guns of hers if we're going to have any chance at all of holding off the Craing fleet."

"Hell, she needs several months in dry-dock. That's what she needs. Hold on ... Ricket, is there anything you can do short term to bring her back to life?"

Ricket replied, "I'd need a day, preferably two."

"You heard that?" Jason asked.

"I heard. We may not have that long ... but who knows?"

"*The Lilly* is another thing; she'll be there within the hour. But I don't think I should bring the *Minian* anywhere near Earth, including the moon station. We'll need to keep her hidden until she can do us some good." Jason thought for several beats. "I'll take her to last year's battle wreckage site, left from the Craing fleet. It's actually not far from where we currently are. Truth is, she should blend in perfectly with the other wrecks in that area. I'll leave a heavy cruiser there, too, and Ricket, Granger ... and the kid, Bristol."

"Tell them the fate of the world lies in their hands," the admiral said.

Jason nodded and brought his attention back to Nan. "We'll be back soon. Boomer will be ecstatic to see you. You and I can talk then, okay?"

Nan nodded. "Oh, you can count on it," she said with a warm smile.

Their faces disappeared from the overhead display. Jason stood and looked at Ricket. "It doesn't have to be perfect, Ricket. Weapons, shields, the ability to phase-shift would be very nice ... those are your priorities for the *Minian*."

Ricket said, "We'll get as much done as we can, although I would suggest you have realistic expectations, Captain. The ship has been badly damaged ... and, let's not forget, all the key components pilfered from her recently, by the Craing."

"Sergeant, your duty, watching over Granger, is more important than ever. Don't let him out of your sight."

"Yes, sir. You can count on me."

Before leaving the *Minian*'s bridge, Jason spoke through the open channel: "Ensign McBride, set a course for the battle debris at the edge of the solar system. XO, with the exception of the *Determined*, have the convoy immediately depart for Earth. We'll join them soon on *The Lilly,* once we've dropped off the *Minian*. Inform the *Determined* she'll be staying behind, with the *Minian*."

"Aye, Captain. The *Cutlass* is making repairs; minor damage from their skirmish with the dreadnaught. They've asked permission to rejoin the convoy in Earth's orbit within the hour."

"That will be fine," Jason replied, taking one more glance around the *Minian*'s bridge as he was leaving.

Chapter 47

At a distance of about three thousand miles, he knew the sudden appearance of a wormhole meant only one thing. Incoming ships. Captain Stalls ordered all three of his refurbished Craing cruisers to shut down and bring their power signatures as close to zero as possible. He wondered if that would be enough, if they would still be detected. It was a fluke. He'd arrived at the precise time the spatial anomaly occurred.

After leaving the battlefield wreckage behind hours earlier, Stalls had moved his small fleet into an area of open space and was preparing for the long trip back to his home planet. Once there, he'd find the *Rangoon* and fellow pirate, Crank Bonilla. With the addition of these Craing warships he'd be able to rebuild a truly formidable fleet. Only then would he return, to once again face Captain Reynolds, and take back the most beautiful, the most perfect, woman he'd ever encountered. Nan would be his. He'd already resolved himself to the simple fact he'd need to be patient. That it all would take time.

The first of the warships to arrive was a gargantuan Caldurian ship. It looked battle-worn, with some areas of the hull scorched, and other sections completely open to space. Less than a minute later, six white Craing cruisers followed and were now parked in a loose formation, in relatively nearby space.

"Captain, we're picking up inter-ship communications between the Allied ships," Rup-Lor said.

Stalls looked over at Rup-Lor, and a small, skinny Craing crewmember sitting at the comms panel. "You can do that?"

The skinny Craing nodded and smiled, showing a mouthful of gray, crooked teeth. He said, "Someone named Dad on the Caldurian vessel is talking to a Boomer on one of the smaller cruisers."

Stalls' heart rate increased twofold. *Honestly, could his luck be this good*? "Let me hear it! Hurry up!"

Sure enough, it was Captain Reynolds's daughter's voice:

"Why's everyone ... all the soldiers ... leaving the ship?"

"They're transferring to another cruiser."

"So we're stuck here alone, on this old smelly barge?"

"Temporarily. Come on, it will only be another hour or so, Boomer. I think you can wait that long."

"Why can't I come back with you?"

"Just be patient. Petty Officer Miller isn't keen on your being on board The Lilly. Look, they'll have the repairs done to the Cutlass *in no time and you'll be headed home. Mom is waiting for you. She can't wait to see you."*

"Okay, okay."

Stalls stood up and began to pace the width of the bridge. His mind was reeling ... *this changes everything ...*

"Captain, the ships are departing."

Stalls watched the display as the large Caldurian ship, along with one of the Craing cruisers, headed off in one direction, while three other cruisers headed off in another direction. That left, singly, the light cruiser *Cutlass* sitting alone in space.

"Wake up our ships! Battle stations! Charge weapons and target that ship's drives."

Captain Stalls stood with his hands on his hips in deep thought. "Rup-Lor, help me round up a boarding party ..."

Stalls continued to watch the lone vessel. *I warned you, Reynolds. Soon I'll have your daughter and you'll give me what I want.*

To be continued ...

Thank you for reading Craing Dominion. If you enjoyed this book and would like to see the series continue, please leave a review on Amazon.com – it really helps! To be notified of the soon-to-be released next Scrapyard Ship book, **The Great Space**, *contact* <u>markwaynemcginnis@gmail.com</u>, *Subject Line:* **The Great Space List.**

Other books by Mark Wayne McGinnis:

Scrapyard Ship

(Scrapyard Ship series, Book 1)

HAB 12

(Scrapyard Ship series, Book 2)

Space Vengeance

(Scrapyard Ship series, Book 3)

Realms of Time

(Scrapyard Ship series, Book 4)

Craing Dominion

(Scrapyard Ship series, Book 5)

Mad Powers

(Tapped In series, Book 1)

Edited by:
Lura Lee Genz
Mia Manns

Avenstar Productions

ISBN 13: 978-0-9903314-7-6

ISBN 10: 0990-331474

www.markwaynemcginnis.com